THE WEDDING THAT ALMOST WASN'T

Sienna Waters

Find out more at www.siennawaters.com. And stay up to date with the latest news from Sienna Waters by signing up for my newsletter!

To N.–

Happily ever after,
xxx

CHAPTER ONE

Emily turned the page in the battered paperback and a chunk of pages promptly fell into her lap.

"Let me guess," Sara drawled from the sand next to her. "That's where the dirty part starts?"

Emily hurriedly stuffed the pages back into place with a sheepish grin. She had no intention of admitting that the crack in the book's spine was not at all where the sexy stuff started. It was the characters' first kiss under a snowy tree and sparkling stars, a scene that made her heart leap every time she read it.

"You know, a) there are other books in the world, and b) Kindles exist, right?" Sara said, closing her eyes against the bright sun.

"I'm well aware of that," said Emily. "And don't think that my Kindle isn't chock full of all the books my little heart could desire."

"But *The Christmas Bride* is the book that you have to read at the beach," sighed Sara. "I know, I know. Little weirdo that you are."

"It's tradition," said Emily primly, adjusting her beach umbrella slightly to ensure that she was firmly in the shade. "As for weirdo, you're the one literally cooking your skin lying on the sand like that."

Sara grunted but didn't respond.

"Exactly," Sabrina said from the other side of the picnic

blanket. "And you'd better not be sunburned for the wedding."

"And you'd better not give me shit or I'll paint myself red for the wedding," Sara snapped back.

Sabrina sighed and rolled her eyes. "I'm going for a swim."

"Don't drown," Sara called after her sister.

"You guys never stop sniping," said Emily.

"It's love," Sara grinned. "Savannah would back me up if she were here."

"Where is she exactly?" asked Emily, trying not to sound too interested.

Sara shrugged. "Who knows? Lying in bed with a waiter she just met? Leading the rest of the bridesmaids in a conga around a Chinese restaurant? Buying a top of the line racing bike? With Sav it's anyone's guess."

Fair point. Out of the three sisters, Savannah was the oldest and most unpredictable. Sabrina was the middle child and coolly logical and kind. Sara was the youngest and Emily's best friend. Not that she didn't love all the Laretto family because, well, because they were like family. A family that had somehow adopted the lonely only child next door and let her grow up as part of a rambunctious and occasionally bitchy but lovable clan.

"We're glad you're here," Sara said, like she knew just what Emily was thinking. "It wouldn't be the same without you."

"I wouldn't dream of missing it," Emily said, even though as delighted as she was to go to a wedding, this whole last minute bachelorette party thing wasn't exactly her thing.

"Bullshit. You'd rather be curled up on your window seat reading a romance, we've got your number Emily Jackson, don't think that we don't know who we're dealing with."

"If it's any consolation, I'm very much looking forward to the actual wedding."

"Who wouldn't be?" snorted Sara. "A week-long event in the Scottish highlands, it doesn't get much fancier than that. Trust Sabrina. When it comes to my turn I'll be getting hitched right here in Atlantic City, just you wait and see."

"To be fair, Sabrina is marrying a rich English banker and

not a high school drop out with a burgeoning alcohol problem," Emily said, lowering her sunglasses down her nose so that she could see Sara better.

"Joel was an artist and had no need for formal education," Sara scowled.

"He had a frequent need for beer at six in the morning though, and you're better off without him."

Sara sighed. "You'll get no argument from me on that score. Although going stag to a wedding is kind of a bummer."

"I'm sure you'll find yourself a lovely little lordling or a count to play with."

Sara snorted again. "You read too many of those damn romance novels. Fill your head with that stuff and reality will never live up to it."

"Oh, you mean like it did for Sabrina?" Emily asked, sliding her sunglasses back up her nose. Romance was real, no matter how much people like Sara might want to pretend that it wasn't. She was damn sure of one thing in her life, and that was that one day, she would have her moment. Her kiss under the snowy tree, her sparkling dance in front of her friends and family, her whirlwind weekend romance that would steal her heart away.

"Yeah," Sara said, closing her eyes and settling back down on the sand. "I suppose that kind of did work out for her, didn't it?"

"Work out for her? Four months ago she was an intern at a New York bank and now she's marrying an English lord."

"He's not a lord."

"With a name like Gabriel Hamilton?"

"He's not. He's just rich. And getting hitched is the easiest way to get Sab into the country. He has to go back to London to work and without the wedding they'd be in visa hell. It's all about practicality."

Emily grunted but said nothing. She knew damn well that there was more than logistics involved in this. She could tell by the way Sabrina looked at Gabe. They were in love and it was beautiful.

"Even if you do want your romance, you're going to have to do more than go to work and sit at home reading books to find it, you know?"

"You'd be surprised how many butch lesbians with labradors come into the surgery," Emily said.

"Then for God's sake, date one of them."

"How do you know I'm not already?"

"Because we've already bought the plane tickets and we didn't get a plus one for you," said Sara.

Which made Emily laugh because Sara really was all about the practicalities. "Fine. But maybe I'll meet one on the plane."

"Not many labradors get to ride planes nowadays."

"Oh, be quiet. Stop bursting my bubble," Emily said, re-opening her book. "And it's very hard to pretend that Cate Blanchett is lying next to me when you keep opening your mouth."

"Ugh, the love is palpable," groaned Sara, but she was laughing as she said it and Emily settled back down to her book with a grin on her face.

THE WAY SAVANNAH'S body gyrated made Emily's stomach hurt and her cheeks flush. She couldn't tear her eyes away. Watching other people dance was just about as much clubbing as Emily could stand, though she didn't particularly mind watching over bags and wraps whilst everyone else did their thing.

Especially not for the Larettos.

She owed them and she knew it. Not that they'd ever say or imply anything of the sort. Sure, they'd taken her in and given her peanut butter sandwiches at lunch and let her play in their yard and included her on beach trips and amusement park tours.

It was more than that though. More than Emily ever knew how to repay.

She'd been fifteen when her parents went out one night and didn't come home again. A drunk driver three blocks from their house. They'd never seen it coming. Emily had never seen it coming. One minute she was writing English class essays and asking her dad how to spell 'succinct' and the next the house was empty and aching with tears.

It had been the Larettos that had saved her, of course. Mr and Mrs Laretto becoming official guardians. Sara and Sabrina and Savannah running in and out of the empty house until it wasn't empty anymore and Emily could smile again. They'd all saved her and she'd never be able to repay them in any way, shape or form.

The body on the stage shimmered under the lights, the curve of a hip, the swell of a breast making Emily's mouth dry right up.

"Drink this." Sara banged a shot down on the table in front of her.

"No," said Emily.

"Fine, sip at it and look like you're having fun." Sara slipped into the booth beside her.

"I am having fun."

"You're not, but it's fine, we all have to do things that we don't like sometimes," said Sara, clinking her glass against Emily's. "And you're pining again."

"Am not," said Emily, taking a reluctant sip of whatever atrocity Sara had presented her with. She pulled a face. "Jesus, this tastes like you strained it through your socks. I forgot that there's a reason I don't drink alcohol."

"My socks are beautifully clean. And you are. Pining that is."

"Am not."

Pointedly, Sara looked toward the body still gyrating on the stage. Emily sighed. There was no hiding things from Sara's eagle eye.

"Fine, I'm trying not to pine."

"When does this stop?" asked Sara. "It's been over a decade, Em. We've all told you not to get involved."

"The heart wants what the heart wants," Emily said, long past the point now that her crush could embarrass her. At least with Sara.

"In this case, what the heart wants is a solid talking to and possibly a spanking." Sara downed her drink. "As much as I love my sister and as much as I love you, Em, if there's one thing that the two of you should not be it's together."

For a second a flash of an image came into Emily's mind. Savannah, her long dark hair pouring down her back, her cheeks flushed with the cold, her lips swollen for the want of kisses, standing under a snowy tree.

"Em, she's no good for you. I'm not sure Sav is good for anyone other than herself, to be honest."

"That's not a nice thing to say about your own sister."

"Maybe not, but it's a true thing. Sav is... she's Sav. You know that. I'm not sure she's ever going to settle down. Look at her right now, just look at her."

Savannah was still dancing on the stage like she owned it and Emily could see people being attracted to her, could see her pulling them to her like a magnet so that she became the center of attention.

"She'll grow out of it," Emily said.

Sara rolled her eyes. "Not anytime soon. You need to focus on finding your Cate Blanchett complete with labrador or whatever it is. Forget about Sav, she'll use you like she uses everyone else that's crazy about her."

"Again, not a nice thing to say about your sister."

"Fine," pouted Sara. "I'm off to dance. I'll come check on you in a half hour or so, okay?"

She was gone before Emily could answer. Not that that was a bad thing, because Emily's eyes were firmly back on Savannah dancing on the stage.

Yes, she was happy to be with her adopted family. Yes, she was happy that Sabrina had found love. Yes, she was happy to be going to Scotland for a week-long wedding.

But most of all she was happy about the opportunity. Because a week-long wedding in an isolated Scottish hotel meant a week stuck in the same place as Savannah. A place that Savannah couldn't run from or hide in. She had a week to finally tell Savannah how she felt.

CHAPTER TWO

"**G**ood girl," Harry said, tying Elsie's lead to the hook outside the small tea shop. "I won't be long, don't you worry."

Elsie looked at her with big, brown eyes and Harry sighed before getting a treat out of her pocket.

"You know, you're definitely putting on weight. Golden Retrievers aren't known for their svelte figures. You could stand losing a pound or two."

Elsie cocked her head to one side and Harry relented, handing over the treat.

"I really won't be long," she promised. She checked up and down the street. No sign of anyone that looked like a dog robber. And the road was quiet enough for London. The sun was out, Elsie had shade, there was a bowl of water and a sign that said 'Doggy Parking,' so she shouldn't feel too guilty.

Which didn't stop her tossing Elsie another treat before she pushed her way into the tea shop.

Inside, it was fussy and fancy and there were enough frills that Harry felt her allergies start acting up. She sneezed and then realized that the flowers she was standing next to were real. Hurriedly, she took a step away and scanned the room.

No sign of him.

Typical Gabe, she thought, as she made her way to a small table as far away as possible from the flowers by the entrance. A year and two months gone by and he's still going to be late.

She settled herself down, pulling the menu over and going through it. Also typical Gabe going for the priciest place he thought he could get away with. Mind you, he'd be paying the bill, he always did. Another thing that was typical Gabe. It was hard to be cross with him when he was an absolute gentleman.

She ran her eyes over the menu again. A pot of tea would do nicely. The slice of Bakewell tart looked tempting, but Gabe would definitely pick up the tab and she wasn't going to order extras. That wasn't fair.

"What can I get you today?"

Harry hadn't noticed the shadow fall over the table. Now she looked up, ready to make her order, and practically fell into big blue eyes. The waitress smiled a little and had a dimple and her hair curled on her forehead from the heat and Harry had to say that she thought this might just be the prettiest woman she'd seen all day.

She opened her mouth and nothing came out.

"Madame?" asked the waitress, perfect brow furrowing.

"Oh, I'll, um, well…" Harry fumbled with the menu, unable to look away from the disaster that was rapidly unfolding and that she was taking part in. "Um, I, uh…"

"She'll take a pot of tea and a slice of Bakewell tart," said a voice from behind the waitress. "In fact, make that two."

"Gabe," Harry sighed in relief.

"Harry!"

The waitress hurried off and there he was, tall and broad-shouldered, with his twinkling blue eyes and his immaculately ruffled dark hair and Harry practically threw herself into his arms.

"Steady on there, Harry, I'm not back from the dead."

"You do know that this is the longest we've ever gone without seeing each other?" she demanded, releasing him and letting him sit down.

"Well, except for the first eighteen years when we didn't know each other at all," he pointed out.

"Doesn't count."

"So you divide life into before Gabe and after Gabe do you?" he asked in amusement. "And you don't have to worry, I'm back for good now. Secondment over, back to dreary old London. Which, to be fair, is looking quite chipper today."

"I'm glad," she said because she was. Not that she'd died of loneliness or anything, not that she didn't know anyone else. But Gabe was her other half, her best friend, the one who knew her better than anyone. And life without him was just a little bit smaller and sadder.

"Psh, I'm sure you were living it up while I was gone," he grinned.

"Tea," said the waitress, setting a pot of tea on the table between them.

"Oh, uh, thanks, I think, yes, thanks..." stumbled Harry.

"Thank you," Gabe said with a charming smile at the waitress. Then he turned his eyes back to Harry. "So, nothing's changed then? Still can't eke out a sentence in front of anyone remotely attractive?"

Harry poured some tea. "Don't tease me. You've been away forever." She could feel herself blushing, could feel the heat rising in her cheeks. "And," she added almost accusing, "you're coming back with a woman."

Gabe laughed. "Darling, you had your chance, you can't be jealous now."

Which was true. Sixteen years ago, when they'd been in university and Harry had harbored some confused thought that she might not be quite gay, or that maybe she was missing out on something, she and Gabe had dated for a thoroughly embarrassing and yet sweetly gentle two weeks.

He remained to this day the only man she had ever kissed. The only person she'd ever kissed really, if you didn't count wrinkled aunts and grandmothers, which she didn't.

"I'm not jealous," she said. "How could I be? I'm curious though." She looked around as though Gabe's mysterious girlfriend might have appeared out of thin air. "Where is she?"

"Probably still packing," Gabe laughed.

A plate of cake was put in front of him and Harry braced herself as the waitress slid one in front of her. "Um, thanks," she managed to say, but only because she didn't actually look at the waitress.

"Honestly, Harry, hasn't this got any better?" Gabe said as the waitress left and he picked up his fork. "I thought you said you were going to work on this, get yourself on lesbian Tinder or whatever."

"Mmm," Harry said, filling her mouth with cake so that she didn't have to answer.

It wasn't that she didn't want to date, she desperately did. It was just that any time she found herself in front of anyone the tiniest bit attractive her brain sort of misfired and turned her into some kind of drooling ninny. Not an attractive look. Or one that most women responded to.

"You need a date, Harry," Gabe said, cutting into his tart. "You need to find someone to settle down with, you need to make an effort, put yourself out there. You've got a lot to offer, you're sweet, funny, pretty, the whole package. Any girl would be lucky to have you."

Harry said nothing because she'd heard all this before, and frankly, the argument wasn't improving with age.

"Seriously, Harry. Maybe you should see a shrink about this?"

She had actually seen a psychologist. A doctor who'd turned out to be a tall blonde with eyes so green and piercing that Harry hadn't even managed to admit why she was there.

"Mmm," she said again, mouth still full.

"Harry, come on."

She swallowed. "Maybe," she said and she saw his face start to change, his mouth start to open to protest and instead of leaving the word hanging she repeated it. "Maybe I'm seeing someone," she said.

The stunned look on his face was enough to make her smile. It only faded when he shook his head. "No, you're not."

"Maybe I am," she said, trying to be mysterious. "Maybe a few things have changed since you've been gone."

She adored him, truly did. He was fun and gentle and smart and the kindest person she knew. She'd missed him. She hadn't missed the nagging though. Gabe was one of those people that thought everyone should be as happy as him, and if they weren't, well, they weren't trying hard enough. His only real fault, and one that she could easily forgive most of the time.

"Really?" he asked suspiciously.

She shrugged, keeping up the mysterious part as long as she could before filling her mouth with cake again.

"I'm not here to nag you," Gabe said, pulling a small blue folder out of his inside jacket pocket. "I'm actually here to give you this."

"What's that?" Harry asked, quickly swallowing.

"Look, I haven't been quite honest."

Harry raised her eyebrows.

"Don't look at me like that, it's just that I wanted to tell you in person, not over Zoom," said Gabe.

"Go on then," she said. "Spit it out."

"Well, um, okay, it's like this. Sabrina and I are getting married."

Her eyebrows raised so far that she thought they might shoot off her head. "Married? When?"

"Um, next week?" he offered.

Harry choked and had to gulp down some tea. Married? Next week?

"Don't be offended," Gabe said. "It's all been a bit of a rush getting everything planned. Sab needs a visa and this looked like the easiest way of doing it. I mean, obviously, we were planning to do it in the long run anyway, but things got pushed forward and, well, we're getting married."

"You've known each other for six months!"

"Less," grinned Gabe. "But when you know, you know." He held out the blue folder.

"What's this?" Harry asked.

"Well, the wedding is this whole week-long thing. What with

Sab's family coming from the States and all, we couldn't ask them to come for just an afternoon. So we decided to rent out a hotel up in Scotland. That way we can all spend some time together. This is your train tickets and your hotel reservation."

"Gabe," Harry said, looking down at the papers. The train ticket was first class, obviously. "You didn't have to do this."

"I very much did," said Gabe. "And not just because you're always dead broke."

"Am not."

"Are so," Gabe said. "Freelance writing pays terribly and I know it. One day your genius will be recognized and you'll be rolling in the big bucks. Today is not that day. So I did actually have to buy your tickets and everything."

"Gabe..."

"No, no, I don't want to hear it. This was very much in my own self-interest. I can't have a wedding without a best man. Well, best woman in your case, I suppose."

And Harry's mouth dropped open.

"Sorry, let's do this right," said Gabe. "Harry, will you be my best... person?"

CHAPTER THREE

Sabrina and Savannah squealed, practically climbing over each other to see out of the plane window. Sara rolled her eyes at Emily. "It's at times like these that I see why mom and dad upgraded to first class."

"They got upgraded, not the same thing," Emily said. Her insides were bouncing up and down with excitement, not that she was planning on showing it. As casually as she could, she leaned over to peer out of her own window.

Beneath them, a huge, gray city spread out, a glimmering of gray-blue water cutting through it. She suppressed her own squeal of excitement.

"I think it's just the joy of seeing the ground," Sara said, nodding at her over-excited sisters. "Honestly, seven hours on a plane is way too long."

"Stop being grumpy," said Emily. "You're just cranky because you didn't sleep and you didn't like the breakfast. We'll get you something once we get off the plane."

"We have a train to catch once we get off the plane," Sara reminded her. "Another six and a bit hours of sitting down in an uncomfortable seat."

"Stop complaining," said Sabrina, turning around in her seat. "You're here for a good reason, you get a free trip, so quit your bitching and get on the good mood train."

Sara flashed her a fake grin that was so wide that after a

second they were both giggling at it. Then the fasten seat belt sign came on and Emily was too busy watching the ground approach to pay attention to anything else.

It was her first time out of the country, not that she was proud of that. In fact, she'd longed to travel as a kid. It was just that for a while there, any form of travel was off the table. The thought of getting in a car made her feel sick and anxious, a feeling that began to spread to all other kinds of transport, and then to leaving the house altogether.

Predictably, it had been the Larettos that had pulled her out of it. Ma Laretto finding her a therapist, and Savannah of all people sitting in the waiting room with her.

"It's like the Kardashians," Savannah had said while they waited. "I mean, I've never been to a real shrink's before."

And Emily had had to laugh which had turned into tears which had led to Savannah taking her hand and squeezing it tight.

With Savannah's support, she'd overcome what needed overcoming. But then she'd had school and vet school and then interning and her first job, and all of that stuff meant that she'd stayed firmly on American soil for her entire life.

Until now.

The plane bumped on touch down and her stomach shook, then they came to a screeching, shuddering halt. Emily carefully pulled her Kindle from the seat pocket and put it in her backpack.

This could be her chance. After all, didn't a whole bunch of romance novels and romantic movies start by putting people in unfamiliar countries? There was always the chance that she and Savannah would have to share a room and that the room would have only one bed and...

"Come on, you can't stay on the plane all week," Sara said, jostling her to unfasten her seat belt. "England awaits."

"Scotland, actually," said Sabrina, already getting her bag from the overhead compartment. "Completely different countries."

"Yeah, well, we landed in England, didn't we?" said Sara.

Emily blocked out the familiar sound of comforting voices arguing. She had to decide what to say to Savannah, she had to decide how this was going to happen. It had to be a moment, a real moment, like something out of a book.

"Come on, pea-brain, get off the damn plane," Savannah sniped at Sara.

"Pea-brain yourself," snapped Sara back. "Just because you got a flight attendant's number doesn't make you queen of the world, you know."

"Like you could get anyone's number," Savannah said back.

Emily picked up her backpack and followed the sisters down the aisle of the plane.

THE STATION WAS packed.

"Look!" Sabrina said. "A real train."

"You've seen trains about a million times," said their mother, a short lady with gray hair and a tired smile.

"Not English ones," Sabrina countered.

Her mother shook her head. "Alright, we're leaving from platform six in twenty eight minutes. You've got your tickets, be on time. In the meanwhile, get snacks or whatever you need."

Emily bounded into the closest bookshop and was busy perusing the shelves for something she hadn't read when she caught sight of Savannah sitting on a bench outside the window.

Savannah alone.

She glanced down at the book in her hand, one she certainly hadn't read and could really use for the train journey, sighed, and put the book back on the shelf. She had to take every opportunity, she reminded herself. Every opportunity.

The thing was, she couldn't actually imagine her life with anyone other than Savannah.

As weird as it seemed, it was just the way things were. From the moment she was able to understand what her feelings were, it had been Savannah's face in her dreams and only hers. That dark hair had sprayed across her pillow a thousand times, those eyes had watched her across crowded rooms. Whether she was dreaming of Cinderella or Carol, it had been Savannah's face.

Her best friend's older sister, what could be more perfect? After all, they'd grown up together. And with one perfectly formed sentence, one beautiful proposal, she really could be part of the Laretto family.

Savannah was pouting, that much was obvious. Emily sat down on the bench next to her.

"What's wrong?"

"Nothing."

Emily bit her lip and looked at the ground. If Sav didn't want to talk, maybe she should leave? No, she needed to give it one more try.

"Come on, you're mad or sad or both. I could tell on the plane. Why don't you tell me what's going on?"

Sav huffed. "Fine. But if you tell Sab I'll break your neck."

Emily's hand went up to her throat. "Message received. It'll be between me and you."

Sav's dark eyes closed. "It's just... well, I'm the oldest."

"Okay," Emily said slowly. Then it dawned on her what Savannah was saying. "You're the oldest and Sabrina is getting married before you."

Sav nodded and Emily almost laughed but didn't quite. "But you know that this is sort of a rushed thing. Not that they don't love each other, but, well, Sab needs the visa."

"I know," Savannah said. She tossed her hair over her shoulder.

"Besides," grinned Emily. "Do you really want to get married right now?"

Savannah eyed her, then grinned back. "Nope."

"That's what I thought," laughed Emily. "So I don't think I'd worry about it too much if I were you."

Savannah sighed and nodded. "You're right." Then she turned so fast that Emily barely knew what was happening and enveloped Emily in a hug. "You always know the right thing to say, Em. Thanks."

"You're welcome," Emily mumbled, face buried in the fragrant softness of Savannah's shirt.

"Right, there's a train to catch." Savannah abruptly let go and stood up. Then she slumped slightly again. "God, I'm soooo tired."

Emily shot a glance back at the bookshop then at the cafe that was right beside it.

"Get me a coffee will you, Em?" Savannah said, grabbing the handle of her case. "I'll see you at the platform. I just need to find somewhere to have a sit down before we have to get on the train."

"Sure," Emily said. "Coming right up."

Coming right up. For real? Who even said that? She took a precious second to treasure the memory of Savannah's perfume, the memory of her touch, then shook herself off. Right, Savannah wanted coffee.

The line was coming all the way out the door, but Emily steeled herself and got to waiting.

IN A GOOD story she might put something in the coffee, she thought, as the cup burned her fingers. Obviously, she'd put in the one brown sugar and one sweetener that Savannah preferred, plus a dash of cinnamon, which was what she liked.

But in a nice paranormal romance or fae story, she'd add in a dash of love potion and all her problems would be solved.

She danced around the crowds, avoiding spilling the coffee by a mere millimeter.

She wasn't stupid. She knew that Savannah was spoiled and bratty. But she also knew that Sav could be kind and gentle and understanding. She just needed to grow up a bit.

Okay, so she'd been saying that since Sav was sixteen and now, going on thirty five, the growing up was taking longer than Emily had thought it would, but we all move on different timelines. She knew that Sav could be a good person. She just needed another good person to show her how life could be.

"Ow!"

Hot coffee splashed on her fingers and Emily swore. She paused to grab a tissue from her purse and wipe her hand and then realized that she'd forgotten which platform Ma Laretto had told her and spent another minute or two looking it up on her phone.

Then she tugged at her suitcase again, carefully balancing the coffee as she looked for a sign.

Finally, thankfully, she found what she needed and started to jog, case bumping behind her, until the coffee almost spilled again and she had to slow down and walk.

All of this added together meant that she reached platform six just in time to see the Scotland train pulling out of the station.

Her mouth dropped open as she watched, coffee hot in her hand. But there was nothing she could do. The train was gone.

CHAPTER FOUR

H arry rounded the corner, saw the shop and immediately crossed to the other side of the street. Elsie sat down and whined.

"Come on," hissed Harry.

Elsie whined again and Harry tugged at the lead.

"I just need one more go around the block."

Elsie's big brown eyes looked up at her and Harry let the lead go looser again. Finally, Elsie got up and started to walk slowly, very slowly, her head turning to watch the pet bakery on the other side of the street disappear.

"Just one more time," Harry promised her, feeling awful.

Surely it wasn't supposed to feel this bad? She should be nervous, certainly, but not almost physically sick.

"This is your fault," she told Elsie as they went around the corner. An elderly woman with a shopping bag on wheels hurried past her as though she was insane. Elsie ignored her and kept walking.

"If you hadn't been such a glutton, I'd never have found the bakery," persisted Harry. Elsie whined at the word bakery. "Fine, fine."

Harry put her head down and started to walk a little faster.

The problem was that she was all out of options. If her goal was to get a date, and it sort of was, then she didn't quite know what she was supposed to do. Online dating was fine, but she couldn't possibly judge someone by a few pictures. And as soon as she had to meet anyone attractive in person, well...

Her last hope was the pet bakery lady.

Tall and slim, with a half shaved head and an array of colorful tattoos, the woman was smiley and bright and friendly. Attractive enough that the two times she'd been to the bakery, Harry had been forced to dawdle around the shelves until the owner, a round, jolly man, had taken over the cash desk.

But today was going to be the day.

The thing was, Gabe was right. If she never spoke to anyone, how was she ever going to find anyone? And she had promised to try harder. Before he'd left she'd said that she would and then she hadn't fulfilled her promise, which made her feel like a shitty best friend. Then along came Gabe asking her to be his Best Person and she felt even worse that she hadn't done what she'd told him she would.

They once again rounded the corner and the bakery came into sight. Elsie pulled on the lead, walking ahead.

"Okay, okay," grumbled Harry.

She stopped in front of the shop next to the bakery, checking herself in the window. Scruffy dark hair, short on the sides and too long and curly on top, check. Freckles sprayed liberally across her nose and cheeks, check. Eyes wide enough that she permanently looked like a surprised rabbit, check.

She took a deep breath. Alright, she could do this.

Elsie practically dragged her into the shop.

Tattoo woman was behind the counter and called out a cheery hello, but was busy serving another customer, so Harry disappeared into the shelves, delighted to have a few more seconds of not making an idiot out of herself.

What was she supposed to say? Just small talk, she'd practiced this. Just be yourself, that was what Gabe always said. Except Gabe was an actual charming and sensible human being who didn't mumble or stammer or knock things over all the time.

Just be normal, she thought to herself. Be Gabe, that was it. Pretend to be Gabe and she'd be fine. She drew herself up taller, breathing in through her nose and out through her mouth.

"I'm sorry, are you alright?"

Harry whipped around, scattering the display of organic dog food cans that she'd been standing in front of, to see tattoo lady looking at her with a worried look.

"Yes, I, uh, you see, um…"

Cans clattered to the floor and Elsie barked, making Harry step back into a spinning display of chew toys that promptly rolled away down the aisle.

"Sorry," Harry said. "So sorry."

"It's quite alright," said tattoo lady. "Happens all the time. Here, let me." She took the two cans of food that Harry had caught. "Can I ring these up for you?"

Harry's face felt like it was on fire, her stomach felt like it was water, and her feet felt like they were stuck to the earth. Elsie barked again and pulled on the leash.

"Um, no, I'd better, I mean, I have to, I…" She nodded down at Elsie who was nervous now and pulling toward the door. Tattoo lady smiled and started to say something and Harry let Elsie pull her around and then made her escape.

"IT WAS AWFUL," she groaned.

"It was just nerves," her father said, patting her knee. "You'll get over it."

"When?" she asked. Elsie was lying on the mat in front of the TV chewing on a bone she'd had to buy from the butcher on the corner. "I'm in my thirties, dad, it's not like I'm sixteen any more."

He laughed and patted her knee again, his face wrinkling up into a smile. "Your mum was just the same."

"Was she?" asked Harry.

She had very few memories of her mother. She remembered a perfume that she couldn't name, but sometimes she smelled it on the street and it always stopped her short, made her pulse quicken. She remembered freckles like her own, and a smile that had a gap in the front.

She'd been six when her mum died. An asthma attack. She supposed she'd been lucky, at six she wasn't old enough to remember a lot of things. Unlike her older brother and sister, who'd seemed to grieve much more deeply.

"She was," said her dad now. "She couldn't talk to an attractive man without dropping her handbag or accidentally spitting on him or something of the like. I always used to say that she was lucky I was ugly enough not to trigger her nerves."

Harry laughed. Her father wasn't ugly. He was a perfectly normal looking man. "So what happened then? Did she empty a dinner plate down your front? Stand on your toes? How did she end up speaking to you?"

Her father shrugged. "Natural as anything, she asked me for some change in front of a parking meter and then I asked her out for a meal."

"But she wasn't... well, a disaster?"

He shook his head. "Never was, not around me. She said that it must be fate, that when the right one came along she had no nerves at all." He sniffed and picked up his cup of tea. "Still say it's 'cos I'm ugly as sin though."

Harry sighed and sat back on the couch. "So I'm just supposed to wait around until someone doesn't make me into a blithering idiot?"

"Maybe you just need to want it less."

"Dad, are you calling me desperate?"

"No, no," he said hurriedly. "Not at all. Just, well, it's not the only thing in life, is it, having a girlfriend?"

Harry looked at him, he was really trying, she knew that. One of the things that she loved about her dad so much was just how much he tried. Like when she'd told him that she was gay and he'd immediately gone out and got a rainbow flag sticker for the front window of his flat.

"I want you to be happy, Harry. Just like your brother and sister. Whatever happiness looks like to you. You've got Elsie, you've got friends, you've got a job that you love."

"Even though it pays peanuts."

"You've got me," he said, slurping his tea. "And you're going to a fancy wedding for a week in Scotland. Can't say fairer than that, can you? Sounds like you'll be living in the lap of luxury for a week, eh?"

"It does sound like it'll be a nice break."

"Need me to keep Elsie here?" he asked hopefully.

Harry shook her head. Her dad and her dog got along well. Too well. Elsie always came back weighing more than when she left. "Gabe says she's welcome at the hotel and he wouldn't have a wedding without her."

"You could have done worse than Gabe."

"Well, other than the penis thing," said Harry.

Her father barked with laughter. "You never know, kiddo. This might be your lucky trip. Meet a girl at a wedding, decide to get wedded, happens all the time."

"As long as she's not attractive enough to turn me into an idiot, according to you."

"Or the perfect match, according to your mother."

"Yeah, well, don't hold your breath. I'm starting to think that I'm doomed to die a spinster and then have my face eaten off by cats."

"You don't have any cats," said her father. "And Elsie would never eat your face off, would you Els?"

The dog opened one eye, glared at him for disturbing her nap, then closed it again.

"Yeah, that was a definite maybe," laughed Harry.

"It's really bothering you all this, isn't it?" asked her dad.

"A bit," she admitted, turning the remote control over and over in her hand. "And then I've got Gabe telling me to try harder and you telling me to try less hard, it's not exactly ideal."

Her father nodded. "I can back off with the advice for a bit."

"No, no. No need. You know I appreciate your help," she said, taking his hand and threading her long fingers through his thick, stubby ones. "And maybe you're right, maybe this is my chance to meet a millionaire and have a fairy tale wedding."

"Wouldn't mind a million or two meself," said her father. "Could do with a new telly."

"This one's just fine," Harry said, flicking it on with the remote. "Now, are we watching Eastenders or not?"

"Watching," he said, grabbing a plate of biscuits from the coffee table.

Harry changed to the right channel and put the remote down, accepting a chocolate digestive with her other hand.

She hoped her dad was right, she hoped that something would happen at the wedding, but the truth of the matter was that she knew it wouldn't. She'd been filled with hope before, and didn't need to be disappointed again.

She should just get used to the fact that she was going to be forever alone, right?

CHAPTER FIVE

"You alright, love?"

Emily opened her mouth but nothing came out. She couldn't believe she'd done this. The wedding of the century and she'd missed the damn train.

"Love?"

She finally tore her eyes away from where she'd last seen the train to see a middle aged man with a mustache and a uniform standing in front of her. Savannah's coffee was burning her fingers and without thinking she thrust it toward the man.

"Oh, um, thank you, but I'm afraid I can't accept any form of gift from the public," he began.

"I'm not trying to bribe you," said Emily quickly. The last thing she needed was to not only miss the train but then to be sent to English prison. Not that English prison would be any better or worse than American prison. Just all in all she'd rather not get sent to prison at all.

When she snapped back to attention, the man was looking at her with kindly eyes. "Why don't we put this down here," he said, putting the coffee down on top of a trash can. "And get you sitting down here next to it." He gently took her elbow and guided her to the bench. "There, that's better."

"Thanks," mumbled Emily, eyes still darting to where the train had disappeared.

"Now, why don't you tell me what's up? You don't need to

worry. I've heard all sorts working here. Husband didn't turn up, fancy man's wife followed him down, you wouldn't believe the scandals I've heard."

"Oh," said Emily, suddenly smiling a little. "Oh, it's nothing like that. It's just…" She stared longingly after the train. The train that was currently carrying Savannah as far away as it was possible to be. "Well, I've missed my train."

The man laughed. "Is that all?"

She glared at him. "It was rather an important train. I'm going to a wedding, you know."

"Today?"

"No," she said, slightly regretting being sharp. "At the end of the week."

He chuckled again. "Then we'll get you there in no time. Come on, I'll take you to the ticket office and you can get a ticket for the next train. Heading up to Scotland?"

She showed him the now invalid ticket.

"Psh, there's another train leaving in an hour and a half, you'll barely notice the delay. Come on, just you follow me."

The English, it seemed, were very friendly. Or at least this one was. As Emily followed him, she wondered if they were all like this. What a wonderful place. A little island all crammed with perfectly lovely and polite people.

"Oi, the fuck you doin'?"

"Oh dear," said the man in uniform. "There's going to be a fight, I fear. Listen, the ticket office is over there, just show them your old ticket and they'll help you get a new one. I must go."

He hurried off towards where an otherwise ordinary looking man in a suit was swearing and cursing at a much younger man wearing running pants. Not the island haven of politeness that she'd been imagining then. She grinned to herself as she pushed into the ticket office.

A mere half an hour wait and she was leaving the office with a new ticket in one hand and her phone in the other.

"I'll be there before you know it," she was saying to Sara.

"Just how the fuck did you manage to miss the damn train?"

Sara was still complaining.

Emily guiltily thought of Savannah's coffee that she'd abandoned on the top of a trash can somewhere and cleared her throat. "Just lost track of time," she said. "At the bookstore," she added, knowing it would make her story more believable.

"Seriously, Em?" groaned Sara. "And now you've left me to fend for myself on a train filled with my sisters?"

"Not everyone on the train is your sister. I'll be there as soon as I can, I swear." She was already thinking about the book at the bookstore that she now definitely had time to buy.

"Fine, just don't go into the bookstore again," Sara said.

"Mmm." Which was answer enough because Emily had no intention of promising something she wasn't going to deliver.

* * *

The station bookshop was crowded and Harry had a hard time squeezing through to the magazine rack to choose something for the trip. She never read magazines unless she was on a train, and then she chose the most scandal-laden and atrocious ones she could get her hands on.

She soon found one that sported the headline 'My Baby Was Eaten By Alien Bacteria' with the salacious additional promise of a story that would 'Change the Way You Think of Toilet Paper Forever,' and took it to the cashier.

The woman eyed her suspiciously. "This for you?" she asked.

Harry shrugged. "Can't get enough of alien bacteria," she said. "Plus, you know, aren't you a bit worried about the toilet paper thing?"

The cashier's face turned a shade paler. "Important is it?" she asked. "I'm only asking 'cos my mum told me to pick up some Andrex on the way home and now I'm wondering if I should get a different sort."

Harry shrugged. "Haven't read it yet." The girl paled further and Harry took pity on her. "Still, I should think that a big brand name like Andrex should be alright, don't you think?"

"Yeah," said the girl, quickly ringing her up. "Yeah, I should think so."

Harry smiled at her and left to go and reclaim Elsie from her spot in front of the shop door.

Now why couldn't every interaction be like that? Light, friendly, teasing, fun. If she could just talk like that to any attractive woman between the ages of say twenty five and fifty, she should be set. Given that the cashier had been all of sixteen, there'd been no nerves, no anxiety, Harry had felt perfectly comfortable.

She sighed. "Maybe dad's right," she confided to Elsie. "Maybe I just want it too much. Maybe I am desperate."

Elise whined and looked up at her with big brown eyes.

"Ah, yes, you'll be wanting a wee before we get on the train, won't you," said Harry. She glanced at her watch, there was just enough time to walk Elsie around the block before they needed to get on the train.

* * *

Emily settled herself into a seat. She'd never actually been on a real train before. Obviously, she'd been on the subway, but this was nothing like that.

Her seat was upholstered in something scratchy and hard-wearing, and the colors made it look slightly like someone had vomited over it. But it was comfortable enough once she was sitting. There was a table in front of her, and another pair of seats facing her. Her suitcase was safely stowed by the carriage door, and her purse was on the window seat next to her.

It was a pretty nice set up. She couldn't help but feel a little guilty. Here she was in perfect peace and quiet, with hours to read her new book and no one to bother her. Meanwhile, Sara would be in the center of the small tornado that formed whenever the Larettos went anywhere.

Not that she minded traveling with them, she really didn't. Together they'd gone on road trips and vacations, Emily always included without question, something she was truly grateful for.

But one thing that Emily had that the others seemingly didn't was a need at times to be alone. Just for five minutes of peace and quiet. Or, she supposed, six and a bit hours in this case.

It was rather nice to have some time to herself, undisturbed, with no one to talk to her or distract her.

With a smile to herself, she pulled her book out of her back. And as the train began to roll away from the station, she cracked open the spine and began.

❉ ❉ ❉

What, with taking Elsie on a toilet walk and rushing to the platform, there'd been no time for refreshments. So the first stop was obviously going to be the dining car. Though, Harry thought, dining car was a pretty fancy name for a shelf of sandwiches and a coffee machine.

Still though, she left Elsie outside and helped herself to a cup of tea. She smiled at the, thankfully male, cashier as she paid, and then made her way back out to reclaim Elsie.

The train wasn't packed, but it was full enough. That and she wanted a seat where Elsie could rest easy at her feet and not get in anyone's way. So she skipped the carriage next to the dining car, all forward facing seats with little leg-room.

Through the noisy carriage-connector they went, Elsie trailing along the way, and into a nicer, brighter, more spacious carriage. This one had tables, so Harry was hopeful they could get a comfortable spot.

But as she was battling her way up the aisle, hot tea in hand balanced against the swaying of the train, someone else was walking down.

She was tall and blonde and had the kind of figure that made

Harry wonder honestly why all women weren't gay. She could feel her heart start to throb in her chest already, could feel blood pounding into her cheeks. Shit.

Her eyes darted from side to side, trying desperately to find a seat, but they were all full. She slowed as much as she could, but there was nothing she could do. The woman was approaching fast and Harry turned, flattening herself against the side of a table, looking firmly at the ground.

The train jolted and Harry's head jerked up just in time to look into dark blue eyes.

"I'm so sorry," the blonde said. "Excuse me."

She began to sidle past and Harry moved more so that they wouldn't have to touch, but the eyes had made her feel dizzy and her mouth was dry and as she turned she caught the woman's coat with her elbow.

Her arm twisted, the woman tripped, and Harry...

Harry emptied her entire cup of tea over the table next to her and the poor woman sitting at it.

CHAPTER SIX

Emily yanked her book back so that it wouldn't get wet.

"Oh god, I'm so sorry. Sorry, sorry," said the woman. She deposited the now nearly empty cup on the table and pulled a wad of napkins out of her pocket.

"At least you came prepared," Emily grinned.

"What?"

The woman turned to her and Emily saw twinkling dark eyes, freckles, a button nose, and a very worried look. "I mean, at least you have napkins."

"Oh, these?" The woman began dabbing at the tea on the table. "I mean, I'm a clumsy so and so, the least I can do is clean up after myself, right?"

"I guess," laughed Emily. She reached into her bag and pulled out some moist towelettes. "These might help."

"Wet tissues," the woman said almost in awe. "Wow, and I'm the one that's prepared."

"Getting on a long haul flight without these babies would be a mistake," Emily said, tearing the package open.

"God, did I get any on you?"

"Just a bit, but it's not too hot and cotton pants dry fast, don't you worry."

"And all over the floor too," wailed the woman.

Emily looked down. "Um, I think your dog's taking care of that," she said.

"Elsie, stop that," the woman said, then paused. "Although actually, no don't stop, at least people won't slip on it if you lap it up." She looked up at Emily again. "She loves tea, I don't normally let her have it, but she'll take it at the slightest opportunity."

"As long as it's not every day," Emily said. Then she grinned again. "I'm a veterinarian, I'd probably have to report you if you let your dog subsist on tea."

"I'm English," grinned the woman back. "I'd probably have to report myself if Elsie didn't have at least a mouthful of tea a month."

Emily laughed. "Why don't you sit down? The table will dry off and there's plenty of room underneath for Elsie."

The woman stared off down the corridor for a second, to where the blonde woman who'd caused all this fuss had disappeared to. Then she turned back and smiled. "Are you sure you don't mind? I mean, I did just dump a cup of tea on you." She laughed a little and a dimple appeared in her cheek. "Welcome to the UK, by the way."

"Is that a traditional welcoming ceremony? The tea thing?"

"We do try to baptize foreign visitors as soon as possible," dead-panned the woman, tugging at the dog's lead so that she slinked under the table, and taking the seat opposite Emily. "I'm Harry, by the way."

"Emily," said Emily, holding out her hand.

Harry took the hand and narrowed her eyes. "You're not going to a wedding, by any chance, are you?"

"Headed in the same direction?" asked Emily, feeling Harry's hand soft and warm in her own.

"Big hotel in Scotland? Gabe and, um…"

"Sabrina," filled in Emily. "That's the one."

Harry grinned and the dimple flashed again. "Thank god, I thought that Gabe might be the only person I knew in the whole place."

"No, no, you've also baptized the bride's youngest sister's best friend, so you've got connections."

Harry's eyes twinkled again and Emily felt a rush of liking for her. "Tell me about the bride, I'm so curious. Oh, I'm the best man, by the way. Well, best person. Gabe's my best friend."

Emily slid her book into her bag. "I've only met him a couple of times, but Gabe seems really nice. He truly cares about her. And Sab is smart, she's funny, and out of the three sisters she's definitely the logical one. She's got her head screwed on tight. She's kind and, well, I'd hardly tell you if she had three dead husbands under her bed already, I suppose."

"Three seems prolific," nodded Harry. She grinned. "I trust Gabe's judgment though. If he thinks Sabrina's reformed her ways and he's not going to end up a statistic, then I believe in him."

Emily glanced out of the window. The English countryside was whooshing by so fast she wasn't even getting a chance to see it.

"Things have moved a bit fast though," Harry was saying.

She turned back. "But it's so romantic! Don't you believe in love at first sight?"

"I've never experienced it," Harry said doubtfully. Her hair was short on the sides but long enough on top that it could flop over her eyes.

"Two halves of the same coin, separated only by an ocean, until fate brings them together..." She trailed off for a second, looking speculatively at Harry. It couldn't be, could it?

Spilling drinks on a crowded train. Meeting up before the wedding even started. This wasn't fate dipping her hand into circumstances?

She dismissed the thought immediately. Obviously not. What fate had done was put her in a hotel with Savannah for a week. That was celestial interference alright. Now all Emily had to do was figure out what to say to make things right and she'd get her happy ever after.

"Ah, big believer in romance, are you?" Harry asked, with a pointed look toward the garish romance novel that was still peeking from her bag.

Emily shrugged. "What's life without love?" she asked.

"Romance is... it's the seasoning, I suppose. It's what makes life taste good."

Harry snorted. "I'll have to take your word for that."

"Hmm, hardcore single, huh?" Emily teased. "Well, we'll have to do something about that. Weddings are very romantic places, you know."

"I wouldn't count on anything happening," Harry said. "You've just seen what happens any time I see a woman even remotely attractive."

"You... you spill tea?" ventured Emily.

"Or I trip, or I spit, or I say something stupid," filled in Harry. "As long as it's something terribly embarrassing, it doesn't seem to matter."

"Huh." Emily sat back in her seat. "I'll have to think about a solution to that one, I'm afraid. But I'm sure it's just a matter of exposure. I mean, like being afraid of spiders. You just sort of expose yourself to them."

Harry frowned. "Are you suggesting that I expose myself to women that I find attractive? I don't know about the States, but here you'd get arrested for that."

"Not what I meant," Emily said, but from the grin on Harry's face she guessed that she knew that. "I just mean that, well, at first you go see spiders at the zoo in glass cases. Then you're in the same room as one. And before you know it, a tarantula's climbing over your hand and you're loving it."

Harry pulled a face. "I'll keep that in mind."

"Tell me more about Gabe," Emily said, hastily changing the subject.

And for most of the next six hours they chatted about anything and everything. The time flew by.

"JESUS CHRIST," EMILY said as she stepped out of the cab. "This is some kind of palace or something."

The hotel stretched out on both sides, long wings of windows surrounding a huge front door with steps and a canopy.

"It probably used to be a private house," Harry said as she pulled suitcases from the trunk of the taxi. Elsie was becoming intimately familiar with a bush at the side of the driveway.

"For a king?" asked Emily, handing the cab driver a wad of notes.

"Probably for an important family," said Harry. "A lot of these old houses get turned into hotels or conference centers or whatever. The upkeep costs are just too much for most families these days. The costs of heating alone are astronomical."

"You seem to know a lot about it," Emily said, squinting at Harry's merry face in the afternoon sun. "Sure you're not a lordess or countess or whatever?"

"London born and bred and not an aristocratic bone in my body," Harry said cheerfully. "But I did write a biography of a big stately home in Kent for the National Trust."

"You did?" Emily asked because it sounded like such a strange thing to do.

Harry nodded. "I'm a freelance writer. And that's just the sort of thing that American tourists snap up in gift shops."

"I see." Emily pulled at her case. "Shall we go in then?"

Harry whistled to Elsie, who, bladder relieved, happily followed them through the massive front doors.

"Jesus, it's like being in a castle," Emily breathed, taking in the deer heads over the huge fireplace and the tapestries hanging over the reception desk.

"You're here for a week, I'm sure you'll get used to it," said Harry. "Let's check in."

The reception desk was manned by a young guy, younger than herself, Emily thought. He had bright blue eyes and a name tag that read James. He gave them a cheerful smile and Emily was suddenly struck by a thought.

This was where there was only one room available, she thought. This was where she and Harry would be forced much against their wishes to share a large, sagging double bed. A bed so cold that they'd have to snuggle together at night for warmth. And the snuggling would lead to other things and before she knew it the two of them would be getting married at this very hotel a year from now with her whole life turned upside down and sparkling with love.

"Here are your room keys," James was saying.

Emily looked down to see two very separate, very large keys with tags attached to them.

"I'm afraid I'm on my own just at the minute. Would you mind leaving your luggage here and I'll get it up to you in a few? In the meantime, go up the stairs and Ms. Lorde, your room will be to the right, Ms. Jackson, your room is to the left."

Emily's heart was still slowing down as she and Harry climbed the stairs.

"Thank you for the pleasant trip," Harry said as they reached the top of the enormous staircase. "I'm sure we'll speak later."

"Right," Emily said. It was all she could say. Harry was smiling at her and then turning and walking away and Emily was still half-lost in a romantic fantasy that was both unwanted and ridiculous.

"Idiot," she hissed at herself as she turned toward her own room. And she wondered where Savannah would be sleeping.

CHAPTER SEVEN

Harry looked around the room. It was enormous. Two double beds sat against one wall, two large windows looked over the carefully manicured lawns of the hotel. In the distance, she could see the shadows of mountains. Elsie grumbled something and made a bee-line for the dog bed that was in one corner. The hotel had thought of everything.

There was a knock at the door and Harry opened it to find James, the young receptionist, with her suitcase.

"Um, thanks," she said.

"No problemo," he grinned. "Everything up to scratch in here?"

Harry nodded as he came in and fussed a little with one of the curtains. "It's all brilliant," she said. "This is a lovely house."

"Been in the family for generations," James said, stepping back apparently satisfied with his curtain fussing.

"Wait, this is your house?"

"Well, it would have been," said James with a sniff. "But, well, you know what it's like nowadays."

"The economy strikes again."

"Something like that," James said. "Mind you, to be fair it'd have happened sooner or later anyway. Running a place like this is no joke."

"So you're selling up?" asked Harry, perching on the end of a bed and thinking what a sad thing that was.

"Maybe," he said. "There's some Americans interested, like always. But we'll see. This is supposed to be our last season though."

"Gosh," said Harry. Elsie turned around in her bed. "Oh, um, thanks for the dog bed, it was a thoughtful gesture."

"Anytime," James said. "And if there's anything you need, just phone down to reception. No request is too big or too small."

"Watch out, or I'll have you bringing roast dinosaur steaks to the room," joked Harry.

"And we'd do our best to provide them," James said, grin widening.

"Harry?"

Harry turned to see Gabe peeking around the door. "Gabe!" She stood up so that she could disappear into a hug as James saw himself out and closed the door behind him. "Sorry I'm a bit late."

"You're not late at all. I had reception phone me when you checked in, didn't want to miss you."

"This room is amazing, Gabe. Seriously. It's like being in a... a... a palace or something," she said, thinking of Emily.

"Pretty nice, huh?" he beamed. He patted the end of the bed. "Even got you an extra bed in here, just in case, you know, you made a friend." He waggled his eyebrows.

Harry laughed. "I'm pretty sure that if I made the kind of friend you're talking about then we'd only need one bed."

"Right," Gabe said, sitting down on the end of the bed. "You know, we need to get this figured out. You can't be going stag to weddings for the rest of your life."

"Why don't you worry about your own wedding for right now?"

"I am. But I'm also thinking about you, Harry. You're incredible and you deserve someone else incredible. I don't like thinking of you alone."

"I'm not alone," Harry said, sitting on the opposite bed. "I've got Elsie. Now you're back and I've got you, for my sins. I've got dad and plenty of friends and—"

"And that's not what I'm talking about," Gabe said seriously.

Harry rolled her eyes because she'd heard this so many times before and she really was quite tired of it. She knew Gabe cared, but really, enough was enough.

"I told you I might be seeing someone," she said, crossing her fingers behind her back. It wasn't exactly a lie, she told herself. She might be seeing the lady from the dog bakery. She just might be not seeing her as well. That wasn't a lie, was it?

Gabe laughed and shook his head and Harry felt a prickle of anger.

"What, you don't believe that I could find a date?" she asked.

"Harry, I've known you for too long, I know what happens to you, I know—"

"As a matter of fact, I met someone very nice on the train," she said quickly.

And then she half-regretted saying it. This was definitely not a lie. Emily was nice. She was lovely, in fact, and friendly as well, so there was that. Elsie liked her too. Not that she was interested in Emily, as was fully evident from the fact that she hadn't fallen over, said something immensely embarrassing, or in any other way made herself look like an idiot in front of her. But she was nice.

"Right," said Gabe as though he didn't believe her in the slightest. He went on before she could say anything else. "I've just come by to invite you to dinner."

"Okay," said Harry slowly.

"We've decided not to be super over the top about planning activities, there's plenty for people to do here. But I want you to meet Sab. So I thought that she and I could invite you to dinner, and then you can meet the rest of the family after. What do you think?"

He looked so sweetly nervous that Harry forgave him for not believing that she could meet someone herself. "Sounds perfect," she said.

"About seven?" he asked, getting up.

"Can't wait."

"In the meantime, enjoy the rich life," he grinned. "And don't let Elsie near those chocolates."

Harry whipped round to see Elsie curiously nosing at a box of complimentary chocolates on one of the bedside tables. "Elsie!" She stepped over to grab the dog's collar. "I swear, the one thing you're not allowed is the one thing you won't leave alone."

Gabe laughed. "Isn't that always the way? Forbidden fruit and all that. I've got to run. See you at dinner."

HARRY CALLED ELSIE to heel as they walked through the hotel foyer. Gabe had always had good taste. Gabe had always had money. Not that that had ever come between them. He wasn't a show off, and he certainly wasn't the kind of person who would make her feel lesser for not having what he had.

Still though, she felt mildly uncomfortable as she walked through the hotel. This place was way fancier than anywhere else she'd ever been. She stopped by a doorway to look around. She wondered if everyone here was for the wedding and thought that maybe they were.

Then she took a breath and sneezed so loudly that every eye in the foyer turned to her.

"Sorry, sorry," she said, catching her breath before sneezing again. "Damn flowers," she whispered, moving away from the display.

It was ages before dinner, but she couldn't exactly just sit in her room. And Gabe had said there was plenty to do, so she'd thought that she'd have a look around. Plus, Elsie could use the exercise after being on the train all day.

At the reception desk she spotted James. Maybe she should go ask him what there was for guests to occupy themselves with.

As she was about to move, she saw Emily coming down the stairs.

Ah, even better, a partner in crime to do something with. Maybe there was a snooker table. Did Americans play snooker? She thought they might not, but she could teach her. The idea of spending a little more time with Emily warmed up her insides.

She was about to go up to her, when Emily paused at the bottom of the stairs, her eyes on someone else. Harry followed her gaze.

The woman was tall, with long dark hair and an aquiline nose. She was also only about ten feet from Harry. Harry felt her stomach squeeze and her mouth go dry.

"Oh, what a cute dog," said the woman. "Can I pet her?" She bent down to stroke Elsie without waiting for permission. "What's her name?"

"Um, it's, er…" Harry's throat tightened and suddenly she just had to cough. She tried to do it quietly and quickly, but the tickle just got stronger. She began to cough and took a step backward, knocking into the flower display as she did.

The vase crashed to the floor, spilling water and flowers in a puddle around her feet. Through watering eyes, Harry stooped down and tried to pick up the flowers, still coughing.

"It's alright," Emily said, rushing over. "I got this."

Harry took a breath finally. She looked up to see the tall, dark-haired woman walking away, her attention taken by something else. She couldn't help but watch the sway of her hips.

"Yeah," Emily said, seeing what Harry was looking at. "That'd be Savannah."

"Savannah?" asked Harry, turning back to Emily.

"Sabrina's older sister, general femme fatale and sexy bad girl," Emily supplied, her eyes still firmly on Savannah's backside.

"Hmm, and not at all someone you have a crush on?" asked Harry in amusement.

"It's not a crush," Emily said, finally turning back to her as Savannah disappeared. "We're meant to be together."

"And I'm guessing that Savannah hasn't quite realized that yet?"

Emily grinned dark eyes glinting in the light. "She will," she said with assurance that Harry envied more than she could say. Emily's hand swept her blonde hair out of her face. "Actually, I was kind of hoping that this week would..."

"Push things into action?" Harry said.

"Something like that."

"Best of luck with that, then," Harry said. Privately she thought that Savannah didn't look at all like the kind of girl Emily should be chasing. She looked aloof, she looked like trouble. Emily looked like the very opposite of trouble.

"Want to grab a coffee?" Emily asked, depositing the last of the flowers back into the thankfully unbroken vase.

Harry was about to agree when a scream echoed through the hotel. A scream so loud that her hands automatically went to block her ears, and Elsie quivered by her side.

CHAPTER EIGHT

"**W**hat the hell is that?" Emily said.

But Harry had her hands over her ears and Elsie was cowering behind her legs. Emily looked around and saw Sara rushing down the stairs.

"What's going on?"

"That's Sab," Sara said.

Without a second thought, Emily followed Sara through one of the many corridors snaking off the hotel foyer until the screaming got louder. Just as they reached an open door, a scream was cut off and Emily felt her ears ring with the sudden silence.

"What's the matter?" gasped Sara, stepping into the room.

It was some kind of dressing room, or a place for waiting, something like that. Vases of flowers waited on a table, a large mirror hung on one wall, and a garment bag was lying across the back of a chair.

"It's all going to be fine," said Gabe, his face pale. He was holding Sabrina in his arms, her face hidden in his shirt.

"It won't be," she sobbed.

"It absolutely will," he said, stroking her hair. "If I have to go to London to get you a new dress, then I will."

She looked up now, face tear-stained, but eyes wide. "You would?"

"Obviously," he said with a grin.

Emily's heart just about melted. This was what she needed. Gabe would move the world for Sabrina and it made her feel all shaky just thinking about having someone like that.

"What the fuck is all the screaming about?" Savannah walked in at just that moment and Emily's breath caught in her throat.

"Well, Sabrina..." She trailed off. Actually, she had no idea what had happened.

Gabe sighed. "The dress."

"It's totally ruined," Sabrina said, tears in her voice again.

"I'm sure it's not," Emily said loyally. "It's probably just wrinkled from the journey, I'm sure we can fix it."

Gabe shook his head, but Emily didn't catch the motion fast enough. Sabrina dissolved into tears again.

"All this commotion over a dress?" Savannah said, rolling her eyes. "I just had a massage, but any hope I had of being relaxed this evening disappeared with all that stupid screaming."

Emily glanced at Sara. "Why don't we take a look?" Sara said, shrugging back at Emily.

Gabe stepped forward and unzipped the garment bag.

"How the hell did that happen?" Emily said. The white dress inside was now dappled with brown, a look so disgusting that it took Emily a second to realize that the stains were melted chocolate and not something altogether worse.

"We must have packed it wrong," Gabe said.

Sabrina hiccuped and Emily took a deep breath. There was no 'we' in this situation. She knew that Sabrina would never have let Gabe see the dress before the wedding. But he was taking on part of the blame for a mistake that couldn't be his just to avoid having Sab be to blame for everything. Her heart melted even further.

"Who the fuck would pack chocolate in a wedding dress bag?" Savannah said. "Idiot."

"I didn't!" said Sabrina. She looked up at Gabe. "I honestly didn't. I swear I didn't."

Sara was bending over the dress, turning the material toward the light. "It's fine," she said. "It's going to be fine."

"How can you say that?" wailed Sabrina.

Sara looked up. "Um, because I worked at a dry cleaners all the way through college, or are you forgetting? I've seen worse than this and I'm sure we can get it cleaned. The wedding isn't for days yet anyway."

"Do you really think...?" asked Gabe.

"Certain," sniffed Sara. She zipped up the bag and picked it up. "Leave it with me. I'll talk to reception and get this to the nearest dry cleaners and get it rushed. It'll be as good as new."

Sabrina clutched her youngest sister in a hug. "You're the best."

"Well, the competition isn't up to much," Sara said, poking her tongue out at Savannah over Sabrina's shoulder.

"Whatever," Savannah said. "I'm going to see if I can get a mud wrap before dinner."

"That's a great idea," said Gabe. "Why don't you take Sab, this afternoon's been stressful."

"Because she ruins my vibe and there's a guy working the massage table..." Savannah began. But Gabe gave her a look and she rolled her eyes again. "Fine. Come on then, bartered bride, let's go."

"Do you even know what bartered means?" Sabrina said, following her sister.

"It's the name of like an opera or something. That flute player I dated played in it," Savannah said.

"Alright, but bartered means traded or swapped for something, which is in no way relevant here."

"Huh, I thought it meant over-dramatic," said Savannah as their voices disappeared down the hall.

"Jesus," said Gabe, rubbing at his eyes.

"I'd better get this dress sorted," said Sara. She cradled the bag in her arms like it was a child as she left.

"I could have done without that," said Gabe.

"How did it happen?" Emily asked. She pulled herself up so that she was sitting on the edge of the table.

Gabe leaned back against the wall. "This is the staging

room, we're supposed to leave our outfits here to be pressed or whatever. We unpacked and came down to leave them, Sab unzipped her bag, and then boom, you know the rest."

"She didn't pack chocolate in the same suitcase though, let alone inside the garment bag," Emily said. She knew Sabrina too well for that, there was no way she'd do something that stupid.

Gabe looked thoughtful. "No, she didn't. I'm sure she didn't. Mind you, I suppose she's been stressed by the wedding plans and all, maybe a bit jet lagged, mistakes can happen."

"Not to Sabrina," Emily said. Because Sab was the mistake fixer, not the mistake maker.

"Then I've not got a clue what happened," Gabe said.

"You didn't leave the dress here alone, did you?" said Emily, her interest perked now. If there was one thing she loved almost as much as a good romance novel, it was a mystery.

"Nope," said Gabe.

"Oh." So much for that then.

"Of course, the garment bags were left alone on the plane," he added.

Right, thought Emily, of course they were. And they must have been left alone at other points during the last day or so. "What about on the train?"

"Stored right above our heads over our seats, and there was always someone around. Sav, Sab's parents, someone."

"The taxi?" tried Emily.

"In the boot, no way could anyone get to them."

"And the hotel?"

Gabe sighed. "I mean, yes, obviously, they were in our room. But there was always someone in or out, it'd be a risky thing to try and mess with the dress in there. Sab and I have been running in and out greeting guests all afternoon."

Emily nodded, brain turning all this over.

"Wait, do you think the dress was sabotaged?" asked Gabe, pushing back up off the wall.

"I don't know," she said honestly. "Maybe?"

"Jesus Christ." Gabe rubbed his face with his hands. "That's the last thing we need."

Emily wrinkled her nose. "Maybe it wasn't," she said, trying to stay upbeat. "Maybe it was just an absent minded mistake."

Gabe looked more hopeful at this. "Maybe so," he said. "Probably, actually. Sab's been stressed."

"Moving to a whole new country and getting married is pretty stressful." Emily paused. She needed to change the topic of conversation. She was certain that the dress had been sabotaged in some way. Why, she had no idea, but there was no way Sabrina would have done something dumb, stressed or not. "What do your parents think of all this?"

"Oh, uh, well, they're not around to see it, unfortunately," said Gabe. He looked away and Emily felt a spike of his pain.

"Neither will mine be," she said quietly.

He looked at her again now. "It's hard, isn't it?" he said. "Especially after a long time. You think that the grief is gone, that it's over with, but then there it is, rearing its ugly head again, just to remind you that it'll always be there."

Emily looked down at her hands, nodding because he was right.

"Still," he added. "My father would have hated the fuss and my mother would have complained about not getting married in a church, so at least I'm continuing to disappoint them in death just as in life."

Emily laughed. "I'm sure you were never a disappointment."

"Maybe not," Gabe said. "But maybe that was only because I tried so hard not to be. Which was stressful in itself."

"Just as long as you don't disappoint Sabrina," said Emily. "I think Sara and Savannah would poke your eyes out if you did, and I'd be forced to help."

"Mmm, you're a close bunch, aren't you?" He grinned at her. "And I like my eyes far too much to disappoint anyone. Plus, obviously, I adore Sab."

"You do, you're good for her." Emily sighed. "I just wish I could find someone like you."

He laughed. "I've got no brothers, I'm afraid."

"What about sisters?"

"Ah." He blushed.

Emily took pity on him. "It's alright, it's a heteronormative world, you're in the majority, you don't need to apologize."

"I get to be embarrassed though, right?"

"A little," she said, laughing.

Gabe checked his watch. "It's a couple of hours until dinner. I might go and get myself a drink. I feel like I deserve one after all this. Fancy joining me?"

Emily seriously considered it. Gabe was nice. She thought this was the first solo conversation she'd had with him. But she had other things on her mind. "I might go for a walk," she said airily. "Stretch my legs after all that time on the train. As long as you don't mind drinking alone?"

"Given that the hotel is packed with everyone that either Sab or I have ever known, I doubt I'll be alone for long. Enjoy your walk." He rubbed at his arms. "I'm going to pick up a sweater before I head to the bar. You might want to do the same. Evenings will get cold around here."

"Noted," Emily said with a grin.

He said his goodbyes and left, leaving Emily with the feeling that this weekend might be a little more interesting than she'd expected. She was one hundred percent sure that the dress had been sabotaged. Why and how, she didn't know. But maybe she could find out.

And there was only one person she could think of that might help her uncover the truth. Fortunately, the person in question came equipped with her very own bloodhound.

Emily pushed herself off the table. She needed to find Harry and Elsie.

CHAPTER NINE

Harry paced around the forecourt, phone in her hand. Elsie was running across the lawn in front of the hotel, having the time of her life.

"It's amazing, dad."

"Sounds like it," said her dad. "Sounds like a palace."

Harry laughed. "That's exactly what Emily said."

"And who's Emily."

"Just someone I met on the train." Elsie dropped a pine cone at Harry's feet and she picked it up, tossing it as far as she could.

"Mmmhmmm," said her father.

"What's that supposed to mean?"

"It's supposed to mean that this could go somewhere."

Harry snorted. "She's just a friend, dad. I literally just met her. She's nice. American. She's, um…" She tried to remember the relationship. "She's the bride's sister's best friend or something."

"And she's nice."

"Mmm," Harry said as Elsie raced after the pine cone to retrieve it.

"Well, she could be the one."

Harry sighed. "Let it go, dad, alright? I've got enough here with Gabe complaining that I'm forever alone."

There was a pause, then a sigh in return. "You're right, girl. I'm sorry. I'm supportive of all your choices. Even having your face eaten off by Elsie, or whatever it is you're afraid of."

Harry laughed. "I know, I know. Speaking of which, there's definitely something going on here."

"Oh yeah? Like what? The hotel is a front from the Mafia?"

"I really regret showing you The Sopranos," said Harry, picking up the now quite soggy pine cone. "No, actually, I'm not really sure what. But there was a lot of screaming a few minutes ago."

"A murder," her father said immediately.

"What a conclusion to jump to."

"You're in an isolated country hotel. It's a classic locked room mystery. Someone's killed the butler."

"I think you mean that the butler did it," Harry said with a laugh. "And I'm sure it's nothing like that. Probably some kind of accident." She looked up just in time to see Gabe come out of the front door and jog down the steps. "And here's Gabe, so I need to go."

"Glad you arrived safe, love. Keep me updated on the murder."

Harry was still laughing as she hung up.

"Dad?" asked Gabe.

"The one and only. He sends his regards."

"He could have come, you know."

"I know, and so does he. But he says he's getting on and doesn't like leaving London." Harry saw the creases of worry on Gabe's face. "Is everything alright?"

"Yeah," he said. "Yeah. Everything's fine. I'm a bit tired is all."

"Um, did you scream?"

He laughed at that, his eyes crinkling up in the corners in a familiar way. "No, that would have been Sabrina. But it's all under control now."

"What's under control now?"

He shrugged. "Just some trouble with the dress, that's all. Nothing for you to worry about. Have you written your speech?"

"Done and dusted," Harry said, petting Elsie's head. The pine cone seemed to have disintegrated at this point. "I am a professional, after all."

"I should have expected nothing less." Gabe looked out into

the woods surrounding the hotel. "Do you think I'm making a mistake?"

Harry, who'd been distracted by Elsie, did a double take. "You what?"

"A mistake," he said again. "Doing all this, doing it so fast."

"Why would you think that?"

He sighed and looked at her. "I'm not sure that I do. No, I don't. I love Sabrina and that's the end of it. Just... it feels like a lot of other people think that this is going too fast. And, well, with mum and dad gone it's not like I've had anyone to hold me back, if you know what I mean."

Harry cocked her head to one side, eyeing him. "Since when have you doubted your judgment, Gabriel Hamilton?"

He grinned at her. "Since never?"

"Damned right. Ignore what everyone else might think. If you're happy then that's what matters. And frankly, it's not like you're enacting the death penalty or anything, you're getting married."

"A lovely comparison, or anti-comparison."

"You know what I mean," Harry said, blushing. "I mean what you're doing can be undone if necessary."

"And now you're mentioning divorce, smooth, in excellent taste for a wedding," said Gabe, the corners of his mouth twitching.

Harry shook her head. "I give up. If you're happy, that's good enough for me and it should be good enough for everyone else."

"You're right, of course." He patted her shoulder. "I knew there was a reason I chose you for best man." He narrowed his eyes. "Your speech doesn't mention the death penalty or divorce, right?"

"Obviously not."

"As long as you're sure." He took her hand and squeezed it. "Thanks for coming, Harry. Thanks for being there for me. I really appreciate it." He smiled. "I just wish that I can do the same for you some time."

"You will."

He rolled his eyes. "That would require you going on a date. Or actually meeting someone."

Not again. Was this week just going to be a constant barrage of 'when are you going to get a girlfriend?' She got it, Gabe was happy and wanted her to be happy. But she couldn't take a whole week of this.

Then she saw Emily coming down the front steps, waving at her.

Unless... maybe she didn't have to take a whole week of this. Emily seemed nice and fun. Maybe she'd be willing to go along with a little... not deception exactly. Just a little white lie.

"I told you I met someone on the train," Harry said.

"Right..."

Oh crap, was she really going to do this. What if Emily wouldn't play along? But Emily was getting closer now, a huge grin on her face, if anything looking absolutely delighted to see Harry. So why not? The skeptical look on Gabe's face was enough to seal the deal.

"I did," said Harry. "She's right here."

Gabe glanced over. "Emily?"

Harry's heart thudded in her chest. She hadn't quite cottoned on to the fact that Gabe and Emily would probably know each other. Shit. What had she done?

* * *

Emily literally ran into Sara in the hotel lobby.

"Ow!"

"Where are you headed in such a hurry?" Sara said. She was still carrying the garment bag with the dress inside it.

"Nowhere," Emily said, still rubbing her head.

"If you're looking for Sav, she's probably still at the spa."

Emily opened her mouth to protest that she wasn't Sav's stalker and then realized that on another day at another time, Sara would have guessed totally correctly. "As it happens, I wasn't looking for her."

"Great," Sara said. "You're too good for her and you know it."

"She's your sister, you can't say that."

Sara laughed. "I can say that because she's my sister. Feel like a trip into town?"

"There's a town?" Emily asked.

"Um, no. Not exactly. It's a village maybe? Or perhaps a hamlet? I'm not sure what the difference is."

"Don't ask me," Emily said. "You're the English teacher."

"Trainee English teacher. And I'm off to find the local dry cleaner who sounded thrilled to help save a wedding over the phone."

"Sounds like fun, but I was actually looking for someone other than Savannah. Some girl I met on the train."

Sara's eyes lit up. "That sounds hopeful."

"Nothing like that," Emily said quickly. "She's fun though and nice."

Sara nodded. "Good. I'm glad. I was a bit worried that we'd be so busy with the bridesmaid stuff that you'd feel left out. I'm glad you made a new friend."

"Hey, I could have been a bridesmaid."

"Why aren't you?" Sara asked. "Is it because you secretly hate the dresses?"

"No, it just... It seemed like it should be you and Sav. Sisters, you know."

"You're practically a sister."

Emily didn't say that the 'practically' was the most important word in that sentence. She didn't want Sara to think that she felt left out because in truth she didn't mind it. She knew that she was loved and adored and she also knew that some things needed to be family things. Real family things.

"I gotta run," Sara said. "There's a taxi waiting."

She ran off to save the wedding dress and Emily searched for Harry until she finally saw her out on the front lawn. She grinned to herself and went off to speak to her.

But as she approached Harry and Gabe, who had been in deep

conversation, they both turned to look at her. She slowed her step. What was going on? Did she have bird poop in her hair or something?

Harry's eyes widened as though she was afraid or nervous, and Gabe's eyes narrowed as though he were suspicious or disbelieving.

"What?" Emily said.

Harry bit her lip. "Um, I was just telling Gabe that, um, that we met on the train."

"True," Emily said.

"And that, uh..."

"That you hit it off quite famously," Gabe threw in. "That the two of you are, you know, interested. Romantically. Or something."

Emily froze for a second.

A very brief second.

And in that second she remembered every romance novel she'd ever read. She remembered Savannah's eyelashes and the curve of her cheekbone. And she remembered just how jealous Savannah could get.

The idea came to her already fully formed.

Because this could really work. This could be exactly what she needed to make Savannah realize what she was missing out on. And she'd never have to say a word. All she'd have to do was... well... this.

She gave it zero more thought.

She stepped in to where Harry was standing, snaked her hand around her waist, grinned at her, then at Gabe, then shrugged. "I thought we were keeping it secret, but if we're not, then yes, we met on the train and we're interested." She let her eyes run up and down Harry's body. "Very interested," she drawled.

Harry let out a big breath next to her and seemed to relax.

And Gabe stared at them both for so long that Emily seriously thought about offering him some eye drops.

Then he started to laugh.

CHAPTER TEN

Harry glared at Gabe crossly. "It's not funny."

"Are you kidding..." Then his laughter sounded tinny, and then it stopped. "Wait, are you... you're serious?"

"As a heart attack," Emily said, smiling perkily.

Harry felt Emily's hand tighten around her waist. A second ago she'd been willing to spill the truth, to say it was all a prank, but right this second, with Emily's hand right there, she just wasn't able to.

No, strike that, she didn't want to. Gabe was her best friend and she loved him but his insistence that she found someone was verging on bullying at this point, whether he meant it to or not, and she'd had enough. She draped an arm over Emily's shoulder.

"You mean the two of you are..." Gabe didn't seem able to finish a sentence.

Harry shrugged. "Yes, the two of us are... whatever." Her voice quivered a little. "I mean, beginning stages." Emily tightened her arm around Harry's waist. "But we're definitely onto something."

Gabe looked from one to the other and Harry could tell that he didn't quite know what to believe.

"I just came to see if you and Elsie wanted to take a walk with me," Emily said, turning to Harry, dark eyes dancing.

Harry relaxed a little. "Absolutely. Elsie would love it. Right now?"

"Unless you're doing something else?"

"Don't hold back on my account," said Gabe. "I've got plenty to do. Just don't wander too far, I don't want to have to send search parties out."

"Righty-o," said Harry as Emily looped one arm through hers and whistled to Elsie.

The whole time they were walking across the lawn she could feel Gabe's eyes on her back.

"So," Emily said, once they reached the edge of the trees. "What was all that about?"

Harry groaned and told her. "But you don't have to do anything," she finished with. "It's just me being stupid, I'll tell him the truth when we get back."

Emily leaned her head to one side and stopped, looking at Harry. "I don't think we should," she said.

"But—"

"No, this is important to you. You don't want to be bothered with people constantly questioning you all week about your relationship status, I get that. It's tiresome. We're both single. Why don't we have a fun week pretending we're together?"

Harry's eyes narrowed. "What's in this for you?"

Emily sighed and found a convenient fallen tree to sit down on. "It's like this," she began.

Three minutes later, Harry was shaking her head in disbelief. "You mean you've been in love with Savannah for almost two decades?"

"As long as I've known what love was, I suppose," Emily admitted. "I mean, it's not like I haven't tried to have other relationships. It's not like I've been sitting at home alone seeing no one or anything. Just that Savannah had always been there, like some big swan gliding over my head or something. Don't you have someone like that?"

Harry felt herself flush. "Um, not really."

"Seriously? Come on, not a single crush."

She puffed out a breath. She might as well come clean. "Look, there's a problem with all of this. I don't actually know what I'm doing when it comes to, um, to dating and... and things."

Emily frowned. "You mean..."

Harry cleared her throat. "I mean that I've never actually dated a woman, nor kissed one, let alone anything more than that. So I'm not sure that I'm best placed to fake a relationship because honestly, I don't really know what one looks like."

Emily regarded her. "Has it ever occurred to you that that's why you're so nervous?"

"I suppose," Harry said, sitting down on the scratchy bark of the tree next to Emily. "But then it's like getting a job with no experience, isn't it? You need the experience to get the job, but you need the job to get the experience."

"I guess," Emily said thoughtfully. Then she sat up straighter. "Look, this could really work out for us both, I mean it, Harry. You'll get some practice at being in a relationship so that you're less nervous the next time you meet someone, and I'll get to show Savannah what she's missing out on and drive her straight into my arms. Come on, you gotta admit that sounds pretty good."

Harry shook her head doubtfully. "I don't know. I mean, you saw Gabe's reaction, he really didn't believe me."

Emily laughed and Harry looked up at the sound of it tinkling through the woods. "We'll just have to make them all believe it," she said, taking Harry's hand in her own.

For a second, Harry let their fingers intertwine. It felt nice, familiar, warm. Then Elsie came nosing around, a pine cone in her mouth. Emily let go of Harry's hand so that Elsie could drop the cone into her hand. Then she threw it and Elsie tore after it.

"Elsie likes you," Harry said.

"Makes a change," said Emily. She grinned. "I'm a vet, a lot of animals that I see are afraid of me, even though all I want to do is help."

"Elsie got into trouble the last time we went to the vet," confided Harry. "She licked his face so much he couldn't listen to her heart beat."

Emily laughed again. "Occupational hazard. And I'm not to be distracted. What do you say, Harry? Can we help each other out here?"

Why not? The idea had been crazy at first, but maybe Emily had a fair point. A little practice might be just what she needed to get a little more confidence. The only thing she wasn't so sure about was Emily's unshakable conviction that pretending to date someone else was going to make Savannah fall into her arms.

On the whole though... It wasn't all exactly a lie. Was it? She did like Emily. Emily seemed to like her just fine. Surely some relationships started off exactly like this. Arranged marriages, for a start.

"Why not," she said finally.

"Good," Emily said, putting her arm back through Harry's and pulling her close. "Because there's something else we need to talk about. How do you feel about mysteries?"

"UFO kind of mysteries or Agatha Christie kind of mysteries?"

"Um, Agatha Christie, I suppose, if I had to choose."

Harry listened carefully as Emily told her all about the dress.

"It could just have been an accident," she said doubtfully. "I mean, that would seem to be the most likely of explanations, wouldn't it?"

"Except I'm almost sure it wasn't," Emily said. "Sabrina wouldn't do something like that. This was sabotage."

"But how?" Harry asked. The log was beginning to get uncomfortable and slightly cold. "I mean, if the garment bag wasn't left alone, it hardly seems possible."

"Maybe someone did sneak into their room," Emily said. "It could have been done."

"In that case, whoever it is is about to get caught doing whatever it is they do next. It'd be a stupid criminal to do something like that in a room that has no fixed schedule, where someone could walk in at any time."

Emily pulled a face. "I guess. Alright, so we put that on the back burner for a while. I need to think about that one some more. But that doesn't stop us keeping an eye out for suspicious characters. And I'm sure something else is going to happen soon."

"Did you read a lot of Nancy Drew when you were a child?" Harry laughed.

"Yes," said Emily, grinning back.

Harry shook her head. "Nothing else is going to happen. This was an accident. Who would want to sabotage a wedding? It's not like it's a royal wedding or anything."

"Hmm. I hadn't exactly thought about suspects yet," Emily said, getting up and brushing off her jeans. "I don't suppose there are any exes around?"

"Yes," Harry said. "Me."

"You? But…" It took Emily a second to put the pieces together, then her eyes widened. "You and Gabe?"

Harry nodded.

Emily put her hands on her hips and for a second Harry could see the entire outline of her body, the way her waist curved in, the roundness of her hips. "Harry-I-don't-know-your-last-name, did you sabotage Sabrina's dress with chocolate?"

"No," Harry said firmly. "And it's Lorde, by the way."

"You're kidding," Emily said, holding out a hand and yanking Harry up off the fallen tree. "I've bagged myself a lord? How fortuitous."

"You know that's not how titles work, right," said Harry as they began to tromp back out of the woods.

Emily waved a hand as though that didn't matter. "I've got more important things to do than worry about the British aristocratic system," she said. "Such as mysteries to solve."

"I thought it was romance you loved, not mysteries."

"Why not both?" Emily said, hooking her arm back through Harry's. "And hey, at least it'll give us something to do. Unless you're interested in going to the spa every day."

"Um, not really."

"Didn't think so," Emily said, steering Harry back toward the hotel.

When they reached the front steps, Emily pulled her in closer. "You okay with this? Last chance to back out now."

Harry looked up at the big front doors. Gabe would be in there. The thought of not having to listen to him about her forever singledom for just a few days sounded pretty nice. Besides, in a way, she was doing him a favor. He had enough to worry about with the wedding and all, this way he wouldn't be worried about her too.

"Yes," she said. "Let's do it."

But when they ran into Gabe in the hotel foyer, he had bigger concerns than whether or not his best friend was finally dating.

"What's wrong?" Harry asked, seeing his pale face.

"It's the flower fridge," Gabe groaned. "It's completely kaput."

CHAPTER ELEVEN

"I don't understand," Harry said over breakfast. "What exactly is a flower fridge?"

"Um, a fridge that flowers go in," supplied Emily. "Rather obviously."

"And flowers need refrigeration, do they? Just pop them in next to the butter. Makes them rather hard to admire, I should imagine."

Emily put her fork down. "Flowers get refrigerated to keep them fresh. Say, for a wedding. They're taken out of the refrigerator before the wedding starts. Also rather obviously."

"Right," Harry said, looking somewhat unsure of things. "Alright, I suppose. But surely these things break down. I mean, it's not beyond the realms of possibility that a flower fridge might conk out of its own accord."

"No," said Emily, picking up her fork again. "But I do think we should check it out anyway. Just to be sure."

Harry looked far from excited about this and cut herself a piece of bacon. "Any thoughts on the dress mystery yet?"

"Give me a chance," Emily said. "It's not like I've had a lot of alone time to work on it."

The night before she and Harry had had dinner with Sabrina and Gabe. Dinner followed up by the others drinking a bottle of wine in the hotel's cozy lounge while she and Harry stuck to non-alcoholic cocktails. The late night coupled with her jet lag meant that she was hardly on top form today.

The good news of the evening was that Harry and Sabrina had got on famously, which Emily took to mean that Harry didn't find Sab attractive at all, which was probably a good thing given that she was marrying her best friend and all.

Sara and Savannah had been conspicuous by their absence. Sara in bed with a book and a headache and Savannah... doing whatever it was that Sav wanted to do. Starting an orgy in the snooker room perhaps. Which was a disappointment, because Emily had been looking forward to showing off her new girlfriend to gauge Sav's reactions.

"I was thinking," Harry said, interrupting Emily's thoughts. "There might have been a time when the dress was left alone."

"I thought you thought this was all a ridiculous Nancy Drew mystery."

"I do," grinned Harry. "But I also don't want to spend the day getting a mud wrap, whatever that is, so I'm going along with your plan."

"Again, rather obviously, it's when someone wraps you in mud. Do you have problems understanding things when they're put into plain language?"

Harry stuck her tongue out. "Why would someone want to be wrapped in mud?"

"It's good for your skin."

"Well then, go outside and roll around, there's plenty of mud out there and it won't cost two hundred pounds."

Emily laughed. "Fair point. Alright, alright. So, about the dress?"

"Mmm." Harry finished her mouthful and swallowed. "I was thinking that if Gabe and Sabrina's arrival was anything like ours, then their luggage might have been left behind while they went up to their room."

"Right, reception was short-handed yesterday," Emily said, remembering that they'd had to leave their cases downstairs.

"Meaning someone might have tampered with things then." Harry paused. "Although that only narrows it down to people with access to the hotel foyer which is, well, everyone."

Emily folded her napkin and put it on the table. "Still, at least we have opportunity and means."

"We're seriously lacking a motive though," Harry reminded her, sliding a piece of bacon under the table. Loud lip-smacking noises signaled that Elsie was very appreciative of the treat.

"It wouldn't be a mystery if we had all the answers," said Emily standing up. "Come on."

"Where are we off to?" asked Harry, stuffing a last piece of toast into her mouth.

"We're going to look at a flower fridge."

Harry groaned but got up anyway.

Out in the hotel foyer, Harry pulled Emily up short.

"What?" Emily hissed. She was anxious to get to the flower fridge. Anxious to prove that she was onto something here and definitely wasn't imagining anything.

"Strangers," Harry said, pointing.

Harry's hand was on her arm, which stopped Emily turning too quickly. Casually, she turned her head and saw three people, a man and two women, dressed in suits. "No idea who they are. You?"

"I called them strangers, remember?" said Harry. "And I've never seen them before unless they're some long lost relative."

"They don't look like relatives," frowned Emily.

The group nodded at something one of the women said, then moved off behind the reception desk.

"Staff of some kind," said Harry.

"Them?"

They turned around to see a young woman in a cleaner's uniform, duster in hand.

"Them's some fancy rich American company that might be going to buy the place."

Emily's stomach dropped. Not a suspect then. She smiled. "Thanks."

"No problem," said the woman, disappearing around a column to dust something out of sight.

"Nice thought though," Emily said to Harry. She wanted to encourage her. Harry grinned back at her and Emily couldn't help but smile too. Harry's grin was very contagious. Her dimple danced and her nose wrinkled up a little. "Come on then, we've got refrigerators to inspect."

EMILY ANGLED HER phone a little more so that the flashlight glowed onto the back of the fridge. "Look, right here."

Harry stuck her head back down. "I suppose," she said in a doubtful voice.

"What do you mean, you suppose? There are scratches there."

"Scratches around the screws that could have been used by any service person when taking the panel off the back of the fridge," Harry pointed out. "This doesn't prove anything." She sat back on her heels looking up at Emily. "I know you desperately want to have a mystery to solve here, but come on, both these things could be coincidences."

Emily leaned back against a metal counter. "Yeah, you're right, I guess. It's just... it doesn't feel right, you know? Like I know Sab loves that dress. I know she'd never do anything stupid with it. But... but maybe Gabe accidentally packed some chocolate into the wrong bag or something."

"Gabe wasn't on your flight," said Harry. "He came a week earlier. Would they really have been packing at the same time?"

"See?" said Emily, folding her arms. "It doesn't add up."

Harry sighed. "Look, I think the best thing for us to do is to keep an eye on things. I'm not convinced there's sabotage here and to be honest, the idea of sabotaging a wedding does seem pretty unbelievable. You still don't have any idea why someone would want to, do you?"

"No," Emily said. She sighed. "I just want to make sure everything's perfect. I feel like, I don't know, I feel like it's my job. I feel like I owe it to them all."

"Why?" Harry asked. She winced as she got back to her feet. "I mean, I know that you're a friend of the family but you can't owe them that much, surely."

Emily smiled. "You'd be surprised." In broad strokes, she told Harry just what the Laretto family had done for her, just how much she owed them.

"Wow," Harry said. "I, uh, I had no idea. That must have been so difficult." She reached out a hand as though to touch Emily, then thought better of it and pulled back.

"It was difficult. But I got through it with the help of them. And now, well, I suppose I'm looking for a way to pay things back, however small."

"Alright," said Harry. "Alright, I can appreciate that. We'll have eyes everywhere. We'll be like private detectives following a cheating husband. We'll make sure that no one does anything without us knowing about it."

"You might be getting slightly carried away," said Emily, turning to leave the small back room.

"I thought that was what you wanted?" said Harry, following her out into the corridor.

"It is, you're right, I'm sorry."

"Let's go rescue Elsie from my room and take her for a walk," Harry said. "We can check the perimeter and make sure there are no holes in the fences."

"Now you're just being ridiculous," grumbled Emily as she pushed through a swinging door that led back out into the hotel foyer.

Then she stopped, still.

"What?" hissed Harry, so close behind her that Emily could feel her warmth.

"Savannah," Emily said.

Harry put a hand on her shoulder. "You gave me a chance to back out, so I'm giving you one. You sure you want to do this?"

It would work. It had to work. It worked in romance novel after romance novel. It worked on TV and in the movies. It would work now. Emily nodded.

"Alright then, but you're going to have to take the lead, I've got no clue what I'm doing, remember?"

Emily reached back and grabbed Harry's hand. "We just have to walk through the foyer holding hands," she said. "It's not that hard. Let's go."

She practically dragged Harry through the door. But after walking almost half way through the foyer, Sav hadn't even turned their way.

"Say something," she whispered to Harry.

"Like what?" Harry whispered back.

Emily threw her head back and gave her very best fake laugh. From the corner of her eye, she could see Savannah turning to see what was going on.

Which was exactly when she heard Harry saying, "oops," just as her hand got yanked so hard that her shoulder almost pulled out of its socket.

"What are you doing?" she said, pulling Harry back upright again so fast that she shot up and they were nose to nose.

"I tripped," Harry said breathlessly. "I told you I'm no good when attractive women are around. This is the flaw in your plan."

Emily could feel Savannah's eyes on them.

More than that, she could feel Harry's fresh breath on her skin. She could see how beautifully pink Harry's lips were. Without thinking about it, she tilted her head, leaned in a little.

"Got yourself a wedding date finally," Savannah said, clapping a hand on Emily's shoulder so fast that she jumped about a foot in the air. "Good work, Jackson. Let me know if you spot a suitable contender for me."

And then she was walking away and Emily was left standing far too close to Harry.

CHAPTER TWELVE

E mily smelled rather predictably of vanilla. She was also, Harry noticed now, quite pretty. Which was odd because normally, being quite pretty would result in Harry doing something unspeakably stupid in front of her. But Emily's kind of pretty seemed to be alright. Safe, in a way. Her eyes were dark and kind, and sort of heavy-lidded in a way that made Harry's stomach squirm.

"Jesus," Emily said, taking a step back.

Harry wrinkled her nose. "That didn't quite work out as planned then?"

Emily took a deep breath. "Not exactly." She tilted her head to one side, looking after Savannah. "But maybe it's just going to take a little time."

"Or maybe," Harry felt forced to point out, "it's just a ridiculous plan."

"Is not."

Harry scratched her head. "Listen, if I were Savannah, I'd have exactly the same reaction as she just did, whether I liked you or not. I'd be happy that someone close to me had found someone."

"Ah, but you're not Savannah. You're..." Emily sighed. "You're kinder. And nicer."

Harry frowned at this. "Hold on, so she's not actually that nice? But you still like her?"

"She's... she's special. She's Savannah. It's hard to explain."

Harry looked thoughtfully at the door Savannah had just disappeared through. "I don't understand. But I suppose I don't have to."

"The heart wants what the heart wants."

Harry snorted. "The heart seems to have been reading too many bad boy romances. Not all arseholes have a vulnerable heart of gold, you know?"

"What would you know about it?" snapped Emily. Then she closed her eyes for a second. "Sorry, that was out of line."

Harry nodded. "Yeah, it was. But so was I. Sorry too."

Emily grinned up at her. "Our first lover's tiff."

"Who's first lover's tiff?" Harry looked up to see long dark hair hanging over the banister and a crooked smile.

"Harry, meet Sara, my best friend," said Emily. She cleared her throat. "And Sara, meet Harry, my, um…"

"Current love interest?" supplied Harry.

Sara squealed and rocketed down the stairs to grasp Harry into a hug. "For real? Gabe said something but I didn't believe it. Honestly, I get one headache and suddenly everyone's partnering up. It's lovely to meet you, Harry."

Harry stared over her head at Emily who shrugged and looked at least moderately guilty.

"I was coming to see if anyone wanted to play croquet," Sara said, letting Harry go.

"Absolutely," said Emily.

Harry rubbed her nose and looked at where Elsie was sitting waiting on the landing of the stairs. "Actually, I think I'm going to go upstairs and clean up a bit before lunch."

"Aw," said Sara. "Come on, it'll be fun. Besides, I've got no idea how to play croquet."

"Me neither," admitted Emily.

"Which makes three of us," said Harry. "Just because I'm English doesn't mean I know how to play."

"I bet you understand cricket though," said Sara.

Harry laughed. "As it happens, I do. But a dog that likes chasing combined with a game that involves hitting small balls doesn't seem like a match in heaven. And since this is the first time we'll all be having lunch together, I want to make a good impression, so the two of you are going to have to figure it out alone."

There was a brief awkward pause when Harry considered how to say goodbye to Emily. A hug? A kiss on the cheek? More? Then Emily patted her arm and linked arms with Sara before turning to go.

"I think there are flamingos involved," she said as they were leaving.

"That was Alice in Wonderland," Harry shouted after them, then shook her head and went to reclaim Elsie from the landing.

This really was a ridiculous idea, she thought as she headed to her room. A stupid and ridiculous idea that secretly she was quite enjoying. It filled the time and was definitely better than going to a spa. And Emily was good company.

The idea of it all was ridiculous, but there was also, she could see now, a slight danger.

For example, faking it in front of Emily's best friend seemed uncomfortable. Not that she wasn't doing the same to Gabe.

And then there was what had just happened downstairs.

Not that Harry was any expert on matters at all, but she truly thought that perhaps she and Emily had just almost sort of kissed.

There was something in the way Emily had moved her head.

She sat down on the bed and began to take her shoes off while Elsie flopped into her bed.

Would that be such a bad thing though? She supposed not given that she was supposed to be accruing experience here. And kissing Emily would surely be nice. She was pretty and her lips were pink and plump. She smelled nice so probably she tasted nice too.

Harry sighed. Savannah's reaction wasn't ideal. She had a feeling that this whole affair wasn't going to work out the way Emily wanted it to at all. But then, that really wasn't her problem, was it?

She unbuttoned her pants and stood up to slip them off, hands skating over her skin as she did so.

Emily was attractive though, wasn't she? In a weird, not-scary kind of way.

Harry gave a shudder, then dismissed all thought of the matter.

She needed a shower.

HARRY SLIPPED INTO the dining room almost unseen. She was just about to grab herself a seat at one of the outside tables when Gabe waved her over.

She groaned.

The place was full of guests and the top table was on a small stage. It would be like eating at Versailles or something, the whole court gathered to watch the king have lunch.

But this was Gabe's week, so she obediently went over to the top table, Elsie following behind, and took the empty seat next to Gabe.

"You're the best man, Harry, you have to sit up here."

She stuck her tongue out at him then grinned. "Putting me on display is evil."

He leaned in. "Having to make polite small talk with relatives is evil, trust me, I've been doing it for the last two days. How are you holding up?"

"Fine," Harry said airily as a waiter poured her some wine.

"And, um, Emily?"

His big blue eyes looked so sorry that she forgave him his initial reaction. After all, could she really blame him for not believing something that was in fact not true at all? "She's fine," said Harry, looking down the table to where Emily's blond head was bent next to Sara's dark one.

"Um, she's really nice, Harry. I'm sorry about before. I just... I suppose I'm not used to you being with someone. It was a bit of a shock. But Emily is lovely. Just..." He sighed. "Do you know what you're doing?"

"Obviously not," Harry said, grabbing a bread roll. She was starving. Somewhere around her feet, Elsie shuffled around and then slipped out from under the table.

For a second, Harry considered going with her, but Elsie was smart, she probably just had to go for a wee.

Gabe grinned at her. "Obviously not," he said.

"If you're about to give me the birds and the bees talk…"

"I'm not," Gabe said. "But I will remind you that after this week, Emily has to go home. And home is a long way away from London. I don't want you getting heart-broken."

"I'm responsible for my own heart," said Harry crisply.

He laid a hand on her arm. "I just meant…"

"Oh, I know." Harry sighed. "You're just being caring, I know. But really, everything's fine."

Just then, there was the sound of a raised voice from the other end of the table. Both Harry and Gabe craned their necks to see a late middle-aged American woman arguing with the waiter. He seemed to be reluctant to pour her a drink, which given her red cheeks and slurred words was probably a good thing.

"I expect better service than this," she was practically shouting.

"Sabrina's aunt by marriage," Gabe whispered to Harry. "The mouse-like bloke to her right is her long suffering husband."

Long-suffering he might be, but at some point, the short man stood up, remonstrated with the waiter, and then removed his wife's wine glass, handing it over to the slightly stunned waiter.

The woman now turned her attentions to her husband, beginning to argue with him in what she obviously thought was a whisper. The words were loud enough that other people in the dining room were beginning to stare.

"Gabe," Sabrina said, leaning over to where Gabe and Harry were watching wide-eyed.

"Right," he said, wiping his fingers on a napkin and getting up. "I'll take care of it."

The lunch, after the excitement of the argument, was pleasant enough. Sabrina was lovely, Harry truly liked her, and the food was excellent.

She was practically groaning with fullness when she stood up. "I'd better go find Elsie," she said to Gabe and Sabrina. "She's probably asleep on a couch somewhere. I'll join you in the bar for a coffee in a while, if that's alright?"

"Brilliant," Gabe grinned.

"I want to hear more stories about the trouble Gabe got into at university," Sab said.

"Don't worry," Harry said. "I've got a whole store cupboard full of them."

She saw Elsie the second she came out of the restaurant into the foyer. Her rapidly wagging tail was hard to miss. She was snuffling around something at the top of the stairs, where a long curtain swept the floor.

"Else," Harry called.

But the dog ignored her.

"Come on, Elsie," she said, climbing the stairs.

Then she saw what Elsie was doing and she screamed.

CHAPTER THIRTEEN

Emily's stomach dropped when she heard the scream. She immediately knew it was Harry. There was something in the heart-rending quality of it that made her recognize who it was instantly. She pushed her chair back so quickly it toppled over and rushed out of the dining room.

Harry was on the stairs, her back to everyone, not screaming now, but the silence was worse than the sound of screams.

Hurrying, Emily ran up the stairs to see Harry on her knees, cradling a confused looking Elsie to her chest.

"What is it? What happened?" Emily asked.

Harry sobbed. "Chocolate," was the only word she could get out.

Emily looked quickly at Elsie, the tell tale signs of her snack tracing the golden fur around her muzzle. A solid wave of calm came over her.

"When?"

"Uh, just now, I think, she was still eating it when I came up," choked Harry.

"Don't worry," Emily said. "It's going to be fine. I'm a vet, remember? I got this. How much has she eaten?"

Elsie looked up with big brown eyes, ironically the exact color of the chocolate she'd just eaten.

"I don't know," Harry said, starting to regain control of herself.

"How old is she?"

Harry took a breath. "Ten or thereabouts."

"Right," Emily said, coming to a decision.

She stood up, peered over the banister. People had gathered there, curious as to what was happening.

"There's nothing to see here," she said. "Just a dog-related incident, everything's fine."

People started to mumble and drift off and Emily caught sight of James close to his reception desk.

"You," she said.

"Me?" asked James. Then he remembered himself and straightened up. "Right, me. What can I get you, madam?"

"Get me a pot of mustard from the kitchen, a teaspoon, and a big bowl of fresh, cool water and bring them both outside."

"Right away," he said, running off.

"Come on," Emily said to Harry. "She's fine right now, let's take her out to the front lawn."

Harry was shaking when she stood up and Emily put an arm around her waist, helping her down the stairs as carefully as she could, Elsie following, tail still wagging and looking very confused.

"It's going to be fine," said Emily as they came out into the bright sun of the afternoon. "Trust me, it's all going to be okay. This won't be pleasant, but you've got to trust me to look after Elsie, okay?"

Harry nodded numbly just as James rushed out with the required ingredients. "Anything else, ma'am?" he asked.

"No, thank you," said Emily. "And if I were you, I'd get inside. This isn't going to be nice."

Harry moaned and Emily laughed a little.

"Harry, it's fine. All I'm going to do is induce vomiting. I normally wouldn't worry too much about such a big dog eating a small amount of chocolate. But given Elsie's age and the fact that we don't know how much she had, this is a sensible precaution to take. She won't have had time to digest any if we can get her to throw it up now."

Harry nodded, eyeing the mustard jar.

"Trust me," Emily said again.

She eyed Elsie, making an educated guess as to how much she weighed, scraped a heaping teaspoon of mustard and took the dog under her arm. Carefully, gently, she force fed poor Elsie a suitable amount of mustard, then freed her.

Elsie, looking distinctly sorry for herself, immediately disappeared into the bushes, and then came the sound of coughing. Emily peeked and then nodded.

"It's fine, she's bringing it up now. It doesn't look like she ate much."

"Jesus," Harry said. She dropped to the grass, looking like she'd just run a marathon. "Mustard? Really?"

"Not exactly the vet school recommended method, but I've seen it done before."

"Really?" Harry asked.

"Come, Elsie," Emily said, pushing the bowl of water to a very regretful looking dog. "Really." She was quiet for a second, then added: "By my father."

"Was he a vet too?"

She nodded.

Harry reached out and took her hand silently. The moment might have been romantic were it not for the loud, messy lapping of Elsie at her water bowl.

"We used to have this little poodle called Cat," said Emily, feeling the memory even now, smelling the scent of wet fur.

"Cat?"

"Hey, I was three when we got her," Emily protested. "And then one Sunday afternoon my mom saw her chewing on something that she thought was rat poison from the garden next door. She went crazy, and my dad came running out with a squeezy bottle of mustard and did his thing." She smiled. "I knew right then that I wanted to be a vet."

"I'm glad that you did become one."

"Turned out that what she'd been chewing on was some dumb kid's toy and not a rat poison box at all. She got a lot of treats that afternoon," Emily laughed.

Harry squeezed her hand and for a long time they sat on the lawn in the sunshine watching Elsie drink, hand in hand, as the breeze flowed over them.

And Emily thought that maybe this wasn't so bad. That actually, this was quite nice. That Harry was, in fact, the nicest person she'd met for a very long time. Too long.

Then she thought something else.

"Where did Elsie find the chocolate?"

* * *

Harry held back the curtain at the top of the stairs and the remains of the chocolate box were easy to see. Chewed through and covered in Elsie's saliva, that box was clearly recognizable as one of the complimentary ones in every room.

"I'll kill him," Harry said through gritted teeth.

"Who exactly?" Emily said, squatting on the floor next to the evidence and looking up at Harry.

"Our little wedding saboteur, whoever he is," Harry said defiantly. "Mess with Elsie and you mess with me. When we find him I'm going to scoop his eyeballs out with a rusty spoon."

"So you agree there is a saboteur then?" Emily said. "This isn't just a bunch of coincidences?"

Harry sat down on the top stair and Emily spun around so that she was sitting right next to her. Harry's heart hurt. The thought that something could have happened to her beloved Elsie made her feel shaky and sick inside. A shakiness and sickness that only stopped when Emily put her warm hand on Harry's knee.

"Elsie is going to be absolutely fine," she said. "I promise you that. She might be sulky and feel a bit sorry for herself. As long as you wait a couple of hours she can eat her normal food. Just keep an eye on her. But she's alright."

"I know," Harry said, her breath coming in a gasp, her chest feeling tight. "But I... I don't know what I'd do without her."

Emily put an arm around her shoulders, pulling her in closely. Harry smelled fabric softener on Emily's shirt, could hear her heart beating. Suddenly her skin tingled all over, her pulse started to quicken. But not in an embarrassing way, she didn't feel clumsy or out of place. She felt like she might belong here.

"You're going to be fine," Emily said, reaching up and cupping Harry's face, her thumb wiping across a cheekbone.

Harry's breath caught in her throat, she turned slightly, sat up, and then Emily's face was there, Emily's lips were there.

Harry had to hold her breath now as Emily's face came ever closer, as Emily's lips brushed against her forehead. She had to hold her breath and tell herself that this was nothing, meant nothing, even as her body responded and her heart yelled that this was what was supposed to happen, this was what was meant to be.

"Sorry," Emily said, pulling back.

"No, no apologies," Harry said, voice deeper and hoarser than usual. She bit her lip, her hand on Emily's arm, still close, too close.

"Sav was walking by down in the foyer," Emily said.

Harry's breath came back in such a rush it was like being punched in the stomach. She almost gasped with it. "Right," she said, drawing back. "Of course. No problem."

Because Emily loved Savannah and this was all fake and that was how things were supposed to be. Silly girl.

Harry was about to make her excuses, about to leave, when she felt a wet nose sniffing at her ankle. "Elsie," she cried, reaching down and hugging the dog.

"I told you she'd be fine," said Emily. "And I'm going to be the voice of reason this time and say that I don't think our saboteur deliberately fed Elsie chocolate."

"You don't?" Harry said, currently busy having half her skin licked off by Elsie.

Emily shook her head. "I think this was probably an accident. But this is a handy place to dump a box of chocolates that you no longer need. Say, after sticking a few into a garment bag containing a wedding dress that you're carrying upstairs."

Elsie lay on the step at Harry's feet and Harry considered this. "Possible," she said. "Actually, very possible." She looked over at the remains of the box. "But those boxes are in every room, there's probably a cupboard full of them somewhere in the hotel, and I'm sure I saw some in the bar as well. It's not like this narrows down our suspect list at all."

"We don't even have a suspect list," Emily pointed out.

"Which seems to be more and more of a problem." Harry sighed. "Listen, I want to catch the guy that did this, whether they wanted to hurt Elsie or not, the fact is that they did."

"Alright," Emily said reasonably. "In that case, all we need is to come up with a list of people that don't want this wedding to happen. Any ideas?"

CHAPTER FOURTEEN

"I'm not sure I want this wedding to happen." Gabe's face looked awful, like he'd just eaten a bad oyster or confessed his worst sins. Which, in a way, Harry supposed that he had.

"What are you talking about?"

Gabe looked behind him. They were walking through the forest and up into the foothills, a trek that the hotel promised was both 'beautiful' and 'achievable.' Harry wasn't so sure about some of the party members. Achievable for her wasn't necessarily achievable for Sabrina's aunt who'd already had several top-ups from her hip flask, or indeed for Savannah, who was attempting the hike in three inch heels.

"I meant what I said," he said, lowering his voice slightly. "I'm not sure I want this to happen. It's all just so... big."

Harry put her arm through his as the path grew muddier. "You're just getting cold feet, surely?" she said.

"I don't know, Harry. It's all sitting in my stomach like a stone this morning."

"Well, let's break it down." Harry was always the reasonable one. "Do you love Sabrina?"

"With all my heart," Gabe said immediately.

"Alright then, so it's not the actual getting married that's bothering you, it's the way it's being done."

"Huh," said Gabe. "Yes, I suppose you're right actually."

"Listen, this is all... extra," Harry said. "It's icing on the cake, it's the free biscuit that comes with your coffee. And a lot of it is about pleasing other people. Given your own way I'm fairly sure that you'd have scooped Sabrina off to a registry office and been done with it."

"Probably," admitted Gabe.

"All of this is just letting other people make a few decisions, that's all. It's about letting others think that they're contributing. In a way, it's letting other people live vicariously for just a little while through you two. Because secretly they, we, are all very, very jealous."

Gabe snorted a laugh. "You are?"

"Of course," Harry said solemnly. "You and Sab have the dream. True love and all that. We all want to witness it, to be part of it for a few days. That's all. So don't let it worry you too much. Maybe even try and have a bit more fun with it."

Gabe was quiet for a long time and Harry started to wonder. He couldn't be sabotaging his own wedding, could he? No, she decided. Not Gabe. He was too honorable for that. If he really didn't want to get married, he'd be making announcements and apologies, not sneaking around.

She was sure he was just nervous and nothing else. If she weren't, she'd be helping him make his escape right now. Suddenly, she sneezed.

"Bless you," Gabe said. "And thank you."

"For what?"

"For being the voice of reason like always." He pressed her arm against his side. "It's a shame we didn't work out, Harry. We balance each other nicely. But I'm damn glad that I got you for a friend in the end."

Harry rolled her eyes. "I couldn't get rid of you, you just kept hanging on."

Gabe shook his head. "You know, that's the problem with you, Harry. You never think you're good enough. You don't see what everyone else does. That I'm the lucky bastard here to have someone like you, not the other way around. You should work on that. You're special, Harry, and should appreciate it."

At that moment, Elsie came running out of the undergrowth, half covered in mud, jumping up at Harry and leaving muddy footprints on her jeans. And Harry was so glad to see her healthy and happy that she could only laugh.

"DEFINITELY NOT GABE," she said as Emily huffed next to her.

They were climbing now, firmly in the middle of the pack, but far enough away from the others that no one could hear what they were saying.

"Who said it could be Gabe?" Emily asked through deep breaths.

Harry shrugged. "Just thought I'd check. I knew he was feeling a bit nervous, but it's just cold feet. He doesn't like all the fuss really."

"Great," said Emily, pausing with her hands on her hips. "So we can rule out Gabe. The only ex here is you, and I assume we can rule out both you and me. So that's three out of... how many people are here? A great start."

"You're being sarcastic," Harry said. The air was chill and it nipped at her nose slightly even though the sun was high in the sky.

"I'm being exhausted," said Emily. "Whose idea was this? A team-bonding hike through the Himalayas?

"Are you tired?" asked Harry. She looked up at the rest of the path. There wasn't far to go until they crested a hill, Gabe was practically there already.

"Tired? I'm half dead," Emily complained. "Where's a handsome prince when you need one to carry you away?"

Harry eyed the path, then Emily, then shrugged. "You Americans use your cars too much."

"You British seem to like forced death marches."

"No one forced you to come," Harry said, turning her back on Emily. "Come on, up you get."

"Up I get where?" asked Emily suspiciously.

"Piggy back," said Harry. She turned her head so she could look over her shoulder at Emily. "We're fresh out of handsome princes, all we've got is princesses, so I'll have to do."

Emily narrowed her eyes for a second, then grinned. "You asked for it," she said.

She practically jumped onto Harry's back and Harry took a second to get used to the weight, to her changed center of gravity. Then she started to move. Emily was warm against her, her heart beat bumping through Harry's back. Harry took a deep breath, half to give her the energy to walk the hill, half to inhale the scent of Emily that was rather intoxicating. Then she sneezed.

"Ugh, hay fever," she said, letting go of one of Emily's legs to get a tissue. "Sorry."

"Hay fever?" asked Emily, confused.

"Allergies."

"Then why didn't you say so?"

Harry grunted. "Because despite what you might think, we do have a language of our own here, and since you're in my country, you should get used to it."

"You're English, not Scottish," pointed out Emily.

"And you'll be tipped off the top of a mountain in a second."

"Fine," said Emily. She leaned in and propped her chin on Harry's shoulder, lips dangerously close to Harry's ear.

Harry could hear her breathing, could feel her core start to contract. This was nice. But no different from being with any friend, she reminded herself. Except she was starting to suspect that perhaps Emily was a little different.

Maybe it had to do with her being American. They were more open, more friendly, which probably made them easy to be around, right?

"Savannah's back there jealous as all hell," Emily said, her breath tickling Harry's ear.

"Because she doesn't have some schmuck to carry her," Harry said. "Honestly, Emily, this is the worst plan ever. I don't think

Savannah even notices what we're doing half the time."

"She does," Emily said confidently. "Trust me. She'll get there. Once somebody else has something then she finds out how much she wants it herself, it's just how her brain works."

"She sounds so charming," said Harry.

"Save your breath for climbing."

For a few minutes they walked in silence, Emily's weight bumping against Harry's back in a way that made Harry's stomach feel strange.

"What about the men in suits?"

Emily jumped a little in a way that made Harry think that she might have been falling asleep. "Men in suits? Like Will Smith?"

"That was Men in Black," Harry said. "No, I meant those Americans."

"Narrows it down, most of us are American." Then Emily caught on. "Oh, you mean those two women and that guy, the ones the cleaning lady said were fancy Americans who might buy the hotel?"

"Right," said Harry.

"Um, what about them?"

"Well, I was just thinking that they could be suspects too. I mean, maybe they're trying to make the place look bad so that the price gets dropped or something?" She had trouble working out the details. Mostly because Emily was entirely too close to her.

"Great," groaned Emily. "Just what we need. Even more suspects."

Harry laughed and then so did Emily, and the sound rang in Harry's ear.

It was another hour before the hotel finally came back in sight. They were slip-sliding down a muddy slope when Emily said, "this arrangement seems to be working more in my favor than yours at the moment."

"Huh?" Harry was concentrating on not falling on her backside. She was also thankful that Emily was now moving under her own steam.

"I mean, you're not getting a lot out of this right now," said Emily, watching her feet. "I did promise you some experience, didn't I?"

"Did you?" croaked Harry, mouth dry.

Emily stopped. They were ahead now, everyone else had dropped behind, slowing as they grew tired. "I did. I said that you might be nervous because you had no experience and that if you pretended to be my girlfriend then you'd get more experience. But you haven't exactly had any, have you?"

Harry's breath started to jump in and out of her lungs again.

"I do like you, Harry," Emily went on.

"Um, good?"

Emily stepped closer. "You said you've never kissed a girl though, right?"

"Yes, um, no," squeaked Harry. She suddenly had to pee and her knees felt funny.

"Would you like to?" Emily came an inch closer.

"Um…"

"Race you to the hotel," Gabe said, breaking through the trees.

Harry caught her breath in relief. "You're on," she said, practically taking flight.

She pounded her way across the lawn, Elsie miles ahead, forcing herself to run so fast that her brain couldn't think of anything other than where her next breath was coming from. She was running so fast that even the front steps did little to slow her.

She finally screeched to a halt a mere centimeter from where a large puddle of water glimmered on the hotel's tiled foyer floor.

"Jesus," she panted. "Someone could seriously hurt themselves on that."

But there wasn't a Wet Floor sign in sight.

CHAPTER FIFTEEN

E mily let the hot shower cascade gloriously over her skin. Honestly, whoever thought that walking a thousand miles as part of a wedding week deserved to be shot.

Mind you, perhaps just at the moment she deserved to be shot as well. Just to put her out of her misery.

"You've never been kissed," she mumbled to herself. "Would you like to be?"

What the hell had she been thinking?

No, that was kind of unfair. The part of her that had been thinking had been thinking that so far this arrangement was working a lot better for her than for Harry. Unfortunately, there'd been another part of her that really hadn't been thinking much at all. The part that had jumped in there with the offer before her brain could interfere and let her think better of it.

She groaned and water bubbled out of her mouth.

Now Harry thought she was some kind of sex-crazed madwoman and would never want to go anywhere with her ever again.

Which was a shame because she enjoyed Harry's company. She was funny, if a little too logical sometimes. She was caring and sweet. She was definitely smart. And the way her eyes twinkled when she wanted to laugh was just adorable.

Yeah, alright, she was alone in the shower. She could admit to herself that under normal circumstances she'd probably hit on

Harry and have her evil way with her. It was just too romantic not to. A summer wedding at a secluded castle, a beautiful foreigner, what romance lover wouldn't love that opportunity?

But this wasn't normal circumstances. This was her one and possibly only chance, to persuade Savannah Laretto that they could and should and would make a go of things. It was a chance to get what she'd always dreamed of.

Not that her plans were currently going so great.

With a sigh, she switched the water off and stepped out of the shower. Whatever else Scotland was famous for, water pressure wasn't it. She grabbed a towel, missing her heavy pressure shower from back home.

Of course, there was always the chance that Harry had been so distracted by yet another sabotage attempt that she hadn't noticed Emily's clumsy attempts to kiss her. Alright, that was too much to hope for. But maybe she'd forget about it in the aftermath of finding half a lake in the hotel foyer without a Wet Floor sign in sight.

Not that Harry saw it as anything other than an accident, of course.

"This isn't America," she'd said when Emily had pointed out that this could just be another way to impact the wedding. Brides with broken legs didn't walk down aisles. "We're not all litigation happy over here, if someone forgets a Wet Floor sign, then it's generally just an honest mistake."

But there'd been water everywhere and Emily wasn't buying it.

Nor, she reminded herself, had she come up with a credible theory as to who would want to derail the wedding or why.

Which, to be scrupulously fair, she wasn't one hundred percent sure was happening.

Mostly because when she tried to concentrate and come up with theories she ended up thinking about what Harry would say. And then how Harry would look when she was saying it.

Which all led to the inescapable conclusion that actually, she rather liked Harry.

She finished drying off. Another time and another place, she reminded herself. She had a mission in mind right now and Harry was only a tangential part of that.

The sound of knocking on her room door made her wrap her towel hastily around herself. She paused just before she opened up and tugged the towel down just a little, enough to show her cleavage. After all, Harry could be wanting a de-brief.

She was busy sniggering to herself about the implications of 'de-briefing' Harry when Sara opened the door and waltzed right in.

"Make yourself at home," Emily said.

Sara grinned. "I haven't seen you for about a million hours. I missed you."

"You've been busy with wedding stuff, it's perfectly fine."

"It's not fine that I missed you. Anyway, they're making me insane."

Emily didn't even have to ask who 'they' were. "That bad, huh?"

"Bad enough that we're all going drinking. There's a little bar downstairs with a jukebox and everything. So get yourself glammed up. We need to let off a little steam."

Emily, who had really been itching to get to work on cracking her little mystery whilst possibly avoiding Harry and any memory she might have of a clumsy attempt at a kiss, looked longingly at her bed. A notebook and fancy pen lay there, as well as her half-finished romance novel from the train.

"Oh Em, come on, please?" Sara groaned. "We need you. You're like our buffer. Things are better when you're there."

"Fine, let me get dressed at least," Emily said, giving in because Sara looked exhausted and besides, she told herself, she might get a few clues if she could interview some witnesses and suspects. And the Laretto girls could be either. Or both. Or neither.

"You can invite Harry," Sara said with a grin.

"Oh, so that's why you're here, to get gossip."

Sara stuck her tongue out. "I'm your best friend. It's not

gossip, it's a shared secret or something. And she seems very nice. Lovely, actually."

"She is," Emily said, pulling underwear on underneath her towel. "She's very lovely. And kind. And clever."

"Mmmhmmm." Sara made kissing faces. "You know, only you could come to a castle for a week and fall in love. I suppose she's a secret princess or something, is she?"

"Not as far as I know," said Emily, getting her jeans from a drawer. "But then if she is a secret princess, I suppose that the clue's in the name and I probably wouldn't know about it, would I?"

"Touchy," said Sara. "Fine, we don't have to talk about her."

Emily sighed and scrubbed at her face with her hands. "Sorry. Sorry, I'm just... Overwhelmed a little."

"By Harry?"

Emily laughed. "God, no. By this whole wedding sabotage thing."

Sara frowned then lifted one eyebrow. "Sabotage thing?"

Emily sat down on the edge of the bed and explained, both of Sara's eyebrows rising higher and higher as she did so.

"So that's what you've been doing," she said, when Emily was done. "Investigating." She paused. "You don't really think that someone's trying to stop the wedding, do you?"

"Do you?" Emily said. "I mean, look at the facts."

"An accident with a wedding dress, a broken fridge, and some water on the floor don't really add up to much," Sara said doubtfully.

For the first time, Emily had doubts of her own. "I suppose they don't."

"So there's no need for you to go all Nancy Drew over things."

"What about Sab's dress though, you know she wouldn't be so careless."

"Ordinarily, no, but then, well, she's been pretty stressed recently."

"She has?" Emily asked. She should have noticed. She should have been paying more attention to the actual bride rather than playing at detective.

Sara pulled a face. "Actually, that's kind of why Sav and I thought we should get her a few drinks. It might open her up a bit. I'm wondering if she's starting to regret all this."

Emily couldn't help her heart skipping a beat at Sav's name. She nodded. "Right, yeah, of course." She stood up again and started getting dressed faster.

"But you should definitely invite Harry," Sara said. "She seems really cool."

"And you're super supportive."

"I'm your bestie, it's my job. Besides, it's nice to see you fawning over someone that isn't Sav."

"I never fawn," Emily said, face burning because she was dangerously close to lying to Sara and she really didn't want to.

"Whatever. It's still awesome and you're still lucky. And it's super romantic, which we both know is by far the most important thing in any relationship for you."

It was Emily's turn to stick her tongue out. "I'm not quite that superficial."

It was romantic though, wasn't it? Meeting a stranger, a week to build a relationship in a secluded hotel, the threat of being torn apart by distance looming at the end of that week. Emily shivered at the idea of it.

Of course, it was no more romantic than finally getting together with her best friend's sister and becoming a real member of the family she'd always been slightly on the outside of. That was romance too. Real Hallmark stuff. Well, other than the gay bit, Hallmark wasn't big on the gay thing. Maybe if Sav were a tall, dark, muscled baker with penis things might be a little more palatable for that Hallmark made for TV special.

"Are you coming or what?" Sara asked, lying back on the bed and picking up Emily's romance novel.

"I've still got to do my face and dry my hair."

"Fine," grunted Sara, turning a page. "But if you're not done by the time I finish the spicy parts then I'm going without you."

Emily rolled her eyes and then got down to making herself

look good.

"YOU COULD HAVE called her or something," Sara was pestering as they got to the top of the stairs.

"We're in a hotel," Emily said. "It's not like we're not going to bump into Harry at some point."

"You know, for someone who's madly in love with a mysterious foreigner, you're pretty reluctant to invite her to our little soiree."

Emily sighed. It was true. She was still squirming in embarrassment about offering to kiss Harry. Not her finest moment.

"But it matters not," chirped Sara, practically bouncing down the next three stairs. "She's appeared anyway."

Emily looked over to where Sara was heading.

Harry lounged against one of the columns in the foyer. One long leg crossed over the other, her hair still slicked back from the shower and her profile sharp and clean of makeup.

And Emily felt her traitorous heart beat faster, felt warmth seeping between her legs, felt her breath catch in her throat.

Harry really was terribly attractive. She cringed internally. She just hoped that the woman had come down with some kind of amnesia or something, anything to make her forget what had happened the last time they saw each other.

Harry looked up, spotted her and grinned, and then Emily had no choice but to head in her direction.

CHAPTER SIXTEEN

E mily in tight jeans and a top that slipped provocatively over one shoulder was not exactly what Harry had been expecting. In fact, the sight made her feel slightly warm. Warm enough that she wondered whether she should have taken a longer shower and gone straight to bed instead of coming down again.

But she did have business, she reminded herself. The thought scratched in her head. Business that she'd got back to in an effort to thoroughly ignore the proposition that Emily had surprised her with a few hours earlier.

Logically, it made sense. She should kiss Emily and be done with it. Get some experience. Get the job done. But then... it was Emily and for some reason Harry didn't quite know how she felt about the whole thing.

So instead of dealing with it, she'd put herself to work. It was not an attempt to placate Emily with information. Not at all. She wasn't making up for not responding to the kiss invitation by plying Emily with clues.

Except she probably was, which made her groan inside.

"You look like you ate a bad hot dog," Emily said, coming down the last of the stairs.

"You look like..." Harry bit off anything else she was going to say. "You look nice," she went with, mostly because it was true and a little bit because she thought she'd probably hurt Emily's feelings before and she didn't want to do it again.

"Thanks," Emily beamed.

"And, we've got something to talk about. You know, with the case." The words sounded stupid even as they left her mouth. But Emily's eyes lit up.

"Nope," Sara said, coming literally between them. "Emily's told me about all this and it's bullshit. Who would want to sabotage my sister's wedding? Come on guys. Enough games, let's get down to some serious business. Drinking."

Harry shot a look at Emily who shrugged as Sara linked one arm through Emily's and the other through Harry's and escorted them off down a short corridor.

"In here," she said, standing back.

"She's not an alcoholic, I swear," Emily whispered to Harry as they both tried to get through the door at once.

Harry, whose leg had just brushed against Emily's igniting a weird tingling feeling, jumped back. "Glad to hear it," she said. "Um, I don't actually drink, if that's alright?"

"Alright?" Emily asked, going through the door and letting Harry follow her. "It's a positive bonus. I get tired of baby-sitting these three when they get into their dad's wine collection." She grinned at Harry. "Don't drink either. Excepting the odd glass of champagne on special occasions."

"Same," Harry grinned back. So Emily wasn't insulted or put off or whatever else. A knot that had formed in her stomach eased a little. "And I really do need to talk to you about something."

"They'll be two glasses in in a half hour and we can talk about anything you want," Emily said.

The bar was small, eight tables, maybe ten, and an old fashioned jukebox in one corner that Savannah was already standing in front of. Sabrina was lolling on a couch that formed part of a booth. It was dark enough inside that Harry could almost forget that it wasn't even dinner time yet.

"Do you think food is going to feature in this evening?" she asked Emily.

"I doubt it," Emily sighed. "But we can probably sneak off and get some later. These three need to have a 'come to Jesus' moment."

"What's that?" Harry asked.

"It's this thing they do when one of them is stressed or whatever. They sit down, open a bottle of wine, and argue and cry and laugh until they're feeling relieved and slightly hungover. It's quite sweet to watch as long as you accept that they do love each other and they're not going to murder a sibling."

"Ah," said Harry, thinking about her own siblings, both of whom were quite nice and very ordinary people that she got along with just fine. Neither one of which she would dream of opening a bottle of wine with, and not just because she didn't drink.

"I don't know," Sabrina was saying. "I just have a feeling."

"A feeling about what?" asked Emily, sitting down on the opposite side of the booth and dragging Harry with her.

"Sab's convinced that the wedding is bad luck," Savannah said, returning from the jukebox and shoving Sabrina to one side so she could slide into the booth. "Which I've already told her is superstitious nonsense."

"But my dress," moaned Sabrina. "And then the flower fridge."

Harry bit her tongue to prevent herself mentioning the wet foyer floor.

"Both of which are bad luck," Sara said, dragging up a chair. "And both of which are bullshit reasons for you to be complaining. What's the real story?"

Sabrina took a breath and then looked down at her hands. "I just… is this too fast?"

Harry almost snorted but managed to stop herself just in time. So Gabe wasn't the only one with cold feet.

"That depends," said Sav, pouring herself a drink from the already opened wine bottle. "Do you love him? If yes, then no, it's not too fast. If no, it's definitely too fast. And if you're not sure, um…"

"If you're not sure, ask Emily, she's the romance expert," Sara said, pulling the wine bottle away from her sister.

"Go on then," Sabrina said, looking at Emily. "How am I supposed to know that this is love?"

"Your knees shake, you feel warm inside, your mouth gets dry, your pulse pounds," Emily said immediately.

Harry laughed and everyone turned to her. "Sorry, it's just... I'm pretty sure that's just attraction or something. It's not love."

"Yeah?" asked Sabrina looking interested. "What's love then?"

Harry shrugged. "Being complete with someone, I think. Having something happen, good or bad, and the only thing you want to do is tell that person. Wanting to wake up next to them. Wanting to hold their hand."

"Being eighty then," said Sara, with an eye roll. "And you're an idiot, Sab. You adore Gabe, we all know you do, and being nervous is fine, it's normal."

Sabrina grinned. "Yeah, I suppose I do really. I mean, I do definitely. It's just... this is all a lot."

"We told you to elope," Savannah said.

"And I'm beginning to wish I'd listened," responded Sabrina.

"Man, I love this song," Savannah said as something pounding and rock-like came on the speakers. She got up and started to gyrate her hips as Sara and Sabrina started to bicker over whether or not they liked the wine they were drinking.

Harry saw her chance and turned to Emily, whose eyes were firmly on Savannah. So much for being heart-broken about Harry not wanting to kiss her then. Or not knowing how to respond, to be more accurate. "Hey, do you want to hear what I've got to say or not?"

Emily blinked then turned to Harry. "I don't know. Maybe Sara's right, this is all just bad luck."

"No," Harry said. "I think you're right." Emily frowned at her. "I know, I know what I said. But I've done a bit of digging and actually, I think you might be on to something."

"Like what?" Emily asked, attention firmly turning away from Savannah now.

"Like I talked to that nice cleaner we saw the other day. And she said that the foyer is mopped in the early morning and that there was no reason for it to be wet. Even if it had been mopped, she was adamant that Wet Floor signs would be put up, the boss insists on it."

"She have any idea what might have happened then?" Emily asked.

"Her suggestion was a guest must have spilled something," said Harry. "But whoever it was must have been carrying an entire barrel of water to get a puddle that big, and that doesn't sound like a guest to me."

Emily nodded. "Agreed. Which means someone did it deliberately. Not only that, but someone who could walk through the hotel carrying that amount of water and not have it seem odd."

"Right," Harry said.

"Up you get." Savannah's hand was reaching down, grasping Emily's shoulder. "Come on, dance with me."

Harry saw Emily's face flush as she allowed herself to be stood up, and then Harry quickly moved to one side so that Emily could get out.

A second later, Savannah's gyrations were firmly centered around Emily, who looked like all her Christmases had come at once. Harry puffed out her cheeks. Maybe Emily's plan was working after all. Except...

Except Savannah wasn't looking at Emily at all. She was looking at the dark-haired bartender, almost daring him to say something as she rubbed herself against her sister's best friend. In turn, the bartender was leaning on his bar, eyes glued to the scene in front of him.

Savannah jerked her head and the bartender didn't hesitate to leave his position and come to join the two women. But the second he did, Savannah turned to him and began dancing with him instead.

For a long, agonizing second, Emily was dancing alone, not realizing that Savannah had ditched her. Harry cringed and didn't know what to do. She was on the verge of getting up and making an idiot of herself in an attempt to dance when Emily flopped down next to her.

Maybe it was relief that removed Harry's speech filter. Maybe it was disgust at seeing someone used so badly. Whichever, she spoke without thinking. "She doesn't deserve you."

"What?" Emily asked.

"Savannah," said Harry. "She's kind of..." She swallowed, reluctant to say it but knowing that now she had to. "She's kind of a bitch."

Emily quirked an eyebrow and shook her head. "Like you'd know anything about it, Little Miss I Haven't Even Been Kissed."

The words hit Harry like a gut punch.

She didn't need to leave though. Emily got up and stalked out, leaving Harry to baby-sit the Laretto girls.

CHAPTER
SEVENTEEN

T he hotel dining room laid on an evening buffet and Emily was trying hard to persuade herself to make healthy choices. Despite that, she ended up with fries and something that looked like a deep-fried donut.

She sat down at a table and started grumbling to herself as she ate the fries. How dare Harry? What qualified her to say anything about Savannah? Harry knew nothing about her, and certainly nothing about Savannah.

She was trying to persuade herself to get truly angry about it when Elsie appeared, tail wagging, followed closely by Harry.

"I thought you were keeping an eye on the girls," Emily snapped.

"They're grown ups, so I left them to their own devices," said Harry so nonchalantly that Emily wondered why she'd never done the same. Harry pulled out a chair.

"Did I invite you to sit down?" Emily said, but her heart wasn't really in it. She wasn't really angry, just a little hurt, a little bruised perhaps.

"Nope, but I'm doing it anyway," said Harry, putting her hands on the tabletop. "I owe you an apology."

"Right."

"No, I'm serious. I had no right to say that about your friend,

I don't know her, and I don't even know you very well. It wasn't my place and I'm sorry."

Emily looked at her for a moment, trying to see if she was sincere, waiting for the other shoe to drop, and when it didn't she felt herself start to blush. "I, uh, I shouldn't have said what I did either," she mumbled. "It was rude and I'm sorry."

"Okay," said Harry. "How about we're even then? We both pretend that the other didn't say what they said and move on?"

Emily laughed. "Alright." She picked up her knife, intending to cut into her deep-fried donut even though she wasn't feeling quite as upset anymore.

"Um, I'm not sure you want to do that."

"What?" Emily asked. "Why? Isn't it a donut?"

Harry snorted and then started to laugh, laughing so hard that she ended up hiccuping and had to drain a glass of water to speak again. "Um, not quite. It's a Scotch Egg."

Emily looked down at the spherical object on her plate. "An egg," she said doubtfully.

"Mmm," agreed Harry. "Not that it's necessarily bad, it's not, but it's probably not quite what you're expecting. Scotch eggs do seem to be something of a mystery to anyone not from the UK."

Carefully, slowly, Emily cut into the object, revealing a sort of savory bowling ball with layers of different colors. "Huh."

"Indeed," Harry said. "Try it."

Emily cut a slice and bit down on it. "It's like breakfast all in one bite."

"I suppose it is," Harry laughed.

Before Emily could take another slice, a figure appeared at the table. "Madame," the woman began.

"A glass of water, please," Emily said quickly. "Oh, and maybe a Coke. Harry?"

The woman cleared her throat. "Actually, I'm not a server. I was wondering how you're enjoying your meal?"

It was only then that Emily caught the American accent, she peered around the woman and saw the other two suited figures going from table to table as well. So the Americans were surveying the dining room, were they? For some inexplicable reason, she felt the need to defend the hotel, like she had some claim over it.

"It's lovely," she said quickly. Too quickly perhaps, because the woman frowned and looked like she was about to have follow up questions.

Before she could ask though, and before Emily could just blurt out that they should buy the lovely old hotel and be done with it, which was definitely none of her business, there was a loud clattering from across the dining room.

Everyone turned to where the bride's aunt had swept all the plates and silverware off her table and was currently pouring a glass of what looked like red wine over her husband.

"And don't think you're dragging that sorry ass into my bed tonight," she screamed as she turned and stalked out.

There was silence in the dining room.

"Wow," Harry said finally. "Looks like that spat got out of hand."

Emily, who was hurriedly feeding Elsie slices of Scotch Egg under the table, shrugged. "I've only met them once and he spent the whole time hovering over her convinced she was cheating with every single person she spoke to, women and children included. So I'm not inclined to be sympathetic."

"Fair," Harry said. "And also perhaps not the best example of a relationship."

"Definitely not," Emily grinned. "If you're looking for role models, I'd avoid them. But I like what's happening here."

"What's that?" Harry asked, raising an eyebrow.

Emily shrugged. "Us, this. I mean if we were in a relationship, I think this went pretty well. We had an argument, we both apologized, we cleared the air and we're moving on. That seems healthy to me."

"I guess." Harry's dark eyes were watching her.

"Just saying," said Emily. "You wanted experience, this was a healthy experience. I think."

"Right." Harry cleared her throat looking uncomfortable

enough that Emily wished she hadn't opened her mouth in the first place. "Um, changing the subject, I had a thought. We should probably talk to the hotel staff."

"About what?" asked Emily, head still in the clouds, thinking about Harry's eyes. They were so... expressive, that was the word. Expressive and soft and... and kind of sexy, to be honest.

"About the sabotage," filled in Harry. "About the wedding. I mean, if we're assuming that someone carried a huge vat of water into the foyer then either it was a member of staff who, I assume, could more easily get away with it, or they saw a guest doing it. It wouldn't exactly be discrete, would it?"

"Do they have dessert at that buffet?" Emily asked, craning her neck to look around.

"They do," said Harry. "And do they have something other than chips and Scotch Eggs?"

"There's some pizza that looks half-decent."

"Fantastic, I'm starving."

They both got up, Elsie trotting along behind them, to get back in line for the buffet.

"Excuse me, madam?"

Emily looked up to see the same suited American woman coming up to them. "Yes?"

"You can't have a dog in here, it's not hygienic."

"There's no sign saying we can't," Harry said cheerfully.

"I would have thought it was obvious," said the woman.

Emily glared at her. "Well it's not. And thankfully, you don't own the hotel yet, so if you've got a problem with it, you need to take it up with reception, not with us. Now, I'd thank you to leave us both alone."

The woman looked from one to the other, slightly stunned, then flounced off. Harry laughed. "Thanks," she said. "I rather like it when you use that sharp tongue to defend me. Defending my honor."

Emily flushed and felt a little warmer inside. "It was nothing," she said. She helped herself to a slice of pizza. "And you're right, we should talk to the staff, I think that's the way to go. We can start doing interviews tomorrow."

"Um, yes, alright," said Harry, taking a slice of Margherita for herself.

Emily paused and turned to look at Harry. "Thanks for doing this with me," she said. "I know... I know it's strange and I know I must sound crazy a lot of the time. But it's important to me that this wedding goes well. Sabrina deserves it."

"Gabe too," agreed Harry. "Even though they're both sounding like they've got cold feet."

"They probably should have eloped," Emily said, turning back to the dessert table.

"But then we'd never have met," laughed Harry.

And for a second, that was the worst thing that Emily could think of. After only three days she couldn't imagine her life without Harry in it. "We're still going to be friends though, right?" she said, taking a slice of cake. "I mean, after all this is over, we can still be friends."

"Of course," Harry said gently. She picked up Emily's plate and carried it with her own back to their little table, being sure to snag a sausage for Elsie on the way.

But they'd barely begun to eat when Gabe and Sara appeared, both looking frazzled and at the end of their tethers.

"Where have you two been? We've been looking for you for ages," Gabe said.

"Well, you found us in the dining room at dinner time, that doesn't seem much of a stretch," Harry said. "Fancy a sausage?"

"There's a problem," Sara said.

"Another?" asked Emily, sharing a glance with Harry whose eyes had widened.

"Aunt Lacey has thrown a fit."

"We know, we saw her pour wine over your uncle," said Harry.

"There's more to it than that," Gabe said. "She's now vowing to divorce him and is refusing to share a room with him."

"Sounds fair," Emily said, picking up her pizza.

"The hotel has no more spare rooms," said Gabe.

There was a long silence as everyone took in his words,

processed them, and realized what exactly was happening here.

Emily practically bit her tongue off. A one bed trope? Seriously? After they'd arrived at the hotel she'd assumed that romance novel idea was off the table. Now, apparently, it was back.

"It's no use looking at me," Sara said. "I'm already sharing with Savannah. Em, you've got a single room, so we figured we'd put Uncle Dirk in that and let Aunt Lacey stay where she is and hopefully calm down a little."

"And you've got a double," Gabe filled in, looking at Harry. "So, um, you two can bunk up together, can't you? I assume you don't mind since you're together anyway? It might only be for one night, things might be resolved by morning."

"Don't underestimate Aunt Lacey's capacity to carry a grudge," Sara said.

Emily looked at Harry.

"There are two beds," Harry said, determinedly not looking in Emily's direction at all. "So it'll be no problem."

Emily cleared her throat and Harry blushed.

"Even with one bed it would be no problem, of course," Harry hastily added. "Since we're, um, together and all."

Gabe grinned and Sara rolled her eyes. "Thank you," he said. He turned to Sara. "I'll get the uncle, you go placate the aunt." And they both hurried off.

Emily picked up her pizza and took a bite before Harry turned back to her. She quickly swallowed her mouthful. "So, we're stuck with each other for the night," she said with a wicked grin. She couldn't help it. It was too funny.

"In two beds," Harry said placing the emphasis on the word 'two'.

"Right," agreed Emily. "Two beds."

CHAPTER EIGHTEEN

E mily bumped a huge suitcase through the door then closed it behind her. "Alright, which bed is yours?"

"This one?" Harry said, pointing at the one by the window. Elsie gave her a look at then disappeared into her basket, burying her head between her paws. Harry kind of wished that she could do the same.

"Cool," said Emily, dragging her case over to the other bed, kicking her shoes off and climbing onto it. "So, at last we get some privacy."

"Privacy?" Harry practically squeaked. It would be good, she thought, if she could stop talking in questions.

"Um, to discuss the case," said Emily, pulling out a small notebook.

"Oh, yeah, right." The knot in Harry's stomach eased and she sat down on her own bed. "Alright then, what have we got?"

Emily peered at her notebook. "Not a lot."

"That's not true," Harry said. "We need to be logical about things."

"Seriously? Harry, at this point every person in the hotel is a suspect."

"Not true," Harry said again. "Think about it."

"Think about what?" Emily was beginning to get exasperated and it made Harry want to tease her more. She had red cheeks and her hair was curling around her face and her eyes were flashing and... and Harry felt far too warm.

Harry took a breath. "Okay, let's start from the beginning. The dress. We can rule out Sabrina, I suppose. She's unlikely to have sabotaged her own dress. Plus, we can rule out anyone that wasn't in the hotel at the time. Which means a fair few of the staff, I'm thinking, since cleaners and the like probably weren't around at that time in the afternoon."

"Okay," Emily said slowly.

"The flower fridge I'm not sure rules anyone out," Harry said, thinking aloud. "But if we're including the death-trap puddle in the foyer—"

"We are," Emily interrupted. "At least unless we have a reason not to, which we don't. So for now we're including it."

"Well then, there were a bunch of people with us on that hike, and everyone behind us has to be in the clear. Given that we were the first back into the hotel that means everyone on the hike has to be innocent."

Emily chewed on the end of her pen. "Good thinking." She darted a glance over at Harry. "You're quite good at this."

"You're not bad yourself," said Harry.

"No," Emily said, shaking her head. "This isn't my thing. Romance novels are my thing. Romance in general is my thing. The only reason I'm really doing this is because Gabe and Sab are the perfect couple and I need them to have a happy ending." She sniffed. "So, where do we go from here?"

Harry thought about this for a second, leaning back against the headboard of her bed. "Well, we can interview the hotel staff tomorrow," she said. "But I think our best bet is going to be catching someone red-handed."

Emily's eyes widened. "A stake out?"

Harry frowned at her. "Not what I said. But if we can figure out where the saboteur is likely to strike then we can lie in wait for them."

"Exactly, a stake out."

Harry sighed. "Whatever."

"How can we know where they're going to strike though?"

Emily asked plaintively.

"Well, now that the wedding's getting closer, there are only going to be so many opportunities. I'd guess the ballroom or wherever the reception is being held would be on my list, as would the chapel itself I suppose. We'd have to ask Gabe."

"Alright," Emily said, noting these options down in her book.

Harry closed her eyes and listened to the scratching of Emily's pen. It was a comforting noise. On the whole, she didn't really mind sharing her room. Now that the initial shock had worn off, it made sense really.

Apart from anything else, it would keep Gabe off her back. And it wasn't like anything was going to happen in here. There were two beds. Two. Separate. Emily was nice, kind, she seemed considerate, Harry couldn't think that she'd make a bad room-mate. Plus, they did have privacy, as Emily had pointed out.

This was important because Harry had promised herself that whenever she found out who had tried to poison Elsie, deliberately or otherwise, she was going to punch them. Not that she'd ever punched anyone before or had any clue how to go about it. But she assumed it was one of those instinctual things that she'd just know how to do once the moment arose.

She would defend Elsie's honor.

Like Emily had defended hers.

She opened her eyes again. Emily was leaning back in her own bed, the notebook closed now, staring off into the distance.

"Um, are you alright?" Harry asked.

"Mmm."

"Because we don't have to stay here. I mean, it's still pretty early I guess. We could take Elsie for a walk. Or go check on the girls in the bar. Or, um, or play snooker?"

Emily bit her lip then turned like she'd come to some kind of decision. "You were right."

"I was?" Harry asked, surprised and not a little confused. "Um, about what exactly?"

Emily sighed. "About Savannah. She is a... a bitch. You were right."

"No, no, I shouldn't have said it. I barely know the woman and I had no right—"

"I'm telling you that she is."

Harry sat up now, shuffling to sit on the edge of the bed. "Well if she is… not very nice, then I'm not sure I see the attraction." Maybe with her lack of experience there was something she was missing.

"I'm not always sure I do either," Emily said.

"I mean, you're lovely," said Harry. "You're nice and sweet and, well, just lovely. I think you probably deserve someone better than a person that treats you like Savannah does, like you're expendable."

Emily closed her eyes and smiled a little. "She was my first crush. The moment I was old enough to recognize what a crush was I fell a little bit in love with her. She was glamorous, older, she never played by the rules but she seemed to win anyway."

"That's not a good thing," Harry pointed out.

"Maybe not," Emily said. "But it is a sexy thing. And from then on, Sav was always there. I grew up around her. I grew up with the whole family. I think I thought of Sav as my way in, my way of really belonging, really being a part of the family. I don't know."

Harry didn't really know what to say to this. "I didn't mean to give you an existential crisis or anything."

Emily opened her eyes and laughed. "You didn't. I know, I've always known, I think, that Sav is wrong for me. It doesn't stop me wanting her though. I thought I'd grow out of all this, but I haven't."

"Maybe you need to get over her, rather than grow out of her," observed Harry.

"Savannah isn't interested in me, I know that in my brain. But my heart just won't listen. I need to move on, but I don't know how to," Emily said. She blinked and Harry thought she might cry.

"Listen, I'm the complete wrong person to have this conversation with. What do I know about relationships? You were right too."

"I was?"

"I've never even been kissed, I've no right to sit here and dispense advice or anything else. I've no idea what I'm doing."

"You were kissed by Gabe though, right? You said you were his ex."

Harry puffed a breath out and nodded. "Yes."

"How was that?" asked Emily with a look of amusement on her face.

"Wet but competent."

Emily snorted a laugh. "Not sure that's a compliment."

"And I meant that I hadn't been kissed by a girl, you know what I meant."

"I know." Emily sat up now too, turning to sit on the edge of her bed so that their knees almost touched. "What are you looking for?" she asked curiously.

Harry blew out another breath and ran her fingers through her hair. "The same as anyone, I suppose. Someone kind, nice, someone I connect with."

"You can do better than that," Emily pushed. "Come on. You've waited this long, you must be waiting for something, some sign or characteristic or something."

Harry couldn't look up. If she did, she knew she'd see Emily's eyes, knew that Emily would be watching her with that careful way she had, knew that Emily would be just a little bit too close.

"I suppose," she began, then took another deep breath. There was no point in lying about this, not if she wanted Emily's help, not if Emily was going to give her experience, help her be less nervous around other women. "I suppose I'm looking for someone like you," she said so fast that the words all came out bumping into each other.

She did look up now and Emily was looking at her, a strange look on her face that Harry couldn't decipher.

"Uh, I mean, I didn't mean exactly you," Harry said almost as fast as before. "I meant, um, just like you, I meant you're nice and sweet and, um..."

Emily smiled and shook her head. "Harry, sometimes it's better to just stop talking, you know? Ever heard that phrase that if you're in a hole you should stop digging?"

Harry kept her mouth shut and nodded.

"Good girl," said Emily. She shuffled forward a little. "Harry, I want to ask you something, and I want you to know that any answer is fine, I'm not going to be mad or disappointed in you or anything else. Is that okay?"

Harry nodded again.

"Harry, would you do me the honor of letting me be the first girl that you kiss?"

Harry couldn't open her mouth now if she tried. She could barely move. She nodded more out of habit than anything else, and then it was too late. Emily was already moving toward her, already tilting her head so that their lips could brush against each other.

Harry closed her eyes tight and then Emily's hand came up to cradle her cheek and Emily's lips pressed harder. Harry had to screw all her courage up so that she could relax.

Then it was happening.

Really happening.

Emily's lips were on hers and Harry's tongue was sliding into her mouth, and Emily's hand was moving to tangle in Harry's hair, and Harry's stomach was doing somersaults and her heart was threatening to break out of her chest and her pulse was alarmingly fast.

Which was precisely when Harry realized that she'd lied.

She didn't want someone like Emily.

She wanted Emily.

CHAPTER NINETEEN

It wasn't that the kiss made her feel like she'd never breathe again. It wasn't that angels sang or light shone down or the world suddenly clicked into place or anything like that at all. It was that for the first time in a long time, Emily felt at home.

She pulled back, not wanting to push matters, and Harry blinked up at her. For a second, Emily was going to say something, she didn't know what, but it felt important as it bubbled in her chest. Then Harry swallowed and Elsie whined and Harry said that she'd probably better take her out and Emily agreed and then everything was back to normal.

Except it wasn't quite.

It was like the world was on a slight tilt, not enough to really see, but enough that Emily's feet didn't touch the ground properly when she went to get into the shower. Enough that she felt just a little destabilized. Enough that when she heard Harry come back, she smiled to herself and started shampooing her hair.

And when she got back into the room and slipped under the sheets, Harry went into the bathroom and Emily closed her eyes and wondered if maybe this was the solution.

Not the solution to this week, not just a way to make Savannah jealous, but the solution to everything.

She'd been honest enough about the situation. She didn't know how to not be in love with Sav. She'd never lived that way.

But if Sav was the wrong person for her, as everyone else seemed to keep telling her, then maybe, just maybe Harry could be the one to help her get over Sav.

Did that make sense? She yawned.

Alright, maybe it wasn't a complete solution. For a start, she had no idea if it would work. For another thing, she had all of four days left with Harry. But Harry was sweet and lovely and kind. She was attractive and funny and all the important things.

And whilst that kiss hadn't exactly been a long-awaited for happening under twinkling stars that made Emily feel like she was the only person in the world, it had been so perfectly natural and almost familiar that it made Emily feel like she was the other half of someone in the world.

Harry crept out of the bathroom.

"I'm not asleep yet," Emily said.

"It's late," said Harry, climbing into her own bed. She flicked out the light. "Goodnight, Emily."

Emily grinned to herself. She might be onto something here. She could get used to this. But she wasn't about to scare the pants off Harry by saying anything right this second. "Goodnight, Harry."

There was a long minute where she could hear Harry breathing. "Thank you," Harry mumbled.

She wasn't about to ask for what. "You're welcome," she said softly.

And they fell asleep.

THE KISS WASN'T mentioned again the next morning. They woke up and blearily bumped around the room getting ready and had a cheerful breakfast. A particularly sweet blonde waitress made Harry spill orange juice all over the table, which made Emily laugh and Elsie bark.

"You shouldn't laugh at my misfortunes," Harry grumbled. But she was smiling as she said it and when Emily caught her eye, Harry blushed.

"It's rather endearing," Emily said.

"Maybe the first time. The thousandth time it's slightly less so," said Harry.

And Emily thought that she might want to be around for the thousandth time, just so she could tell Harry how endearing it still was.

"Do we have a plan for how all this is going to happen?" asked Harry, cracking a boiled egg.

Under a glittering Christmas tree in the snow, Emily thought. You'll go down on one knee and I'll manage to squeak out a yes before the tears come and... She cleared her throat. "For talking to the staff you mean?"

Harry nodded.

"Dunno," said Emily. "I suppose we start with the basics. I mean, we have three incidents and we can more or less isolate the times they happened. So if someone wasn't in the hotel when at least one of the things happened we can eliminate them."

"Right," Harry said through a mouthful of toast.

"And then we ask if they saw something, know something, you know, the usual cop questions."

"Maybe you know," Harry said, swallowing. "I've never been questioned by the police myself."

Emily rolled her eyes. "It was only once."

Harry's eyes widened. "What for?" she asked, sneaking a piece of sausage under the table to Elsie.

"I'm kidding," said Emily. "Seriously? You think I've been questioned by the cops?"

"I do barely know you," pointed out Harry.

"You know me better this morning than you did before," Emily said before she could stop herself. But that was as close as either of them came to mentioning the kiss. And Harry was already putting down her spoon and slurping up the rest of her tea.

"I suppose we should get on with things then," she said, pushing her chair back.

Meekly, Emily nodded, finished her juice, and followed Harry and Elsie out of the dining room.

"I really don't have the time," James said, leaning on the front desk.

"It's just a few questions," Emily cajoled. He smiled and his blue eyes sparkled and Emily thought how handsome a man he was.

"Alright then," he said, his Scottish accent light.

"We just want to know if you've seen anything you might think is suspicious?" asked Harry.

James laughed. "This is a hotel. You wouldn't believe some of the things that I've seen."

Harry rubbed her nose. "More along the lines of connected to the wedding," she said.

He shrugged. "Not really." His eyes were no longer on the pair of them though, he was looking at whatever was behind them.

Emily turned around to see the three Americans in suits coming through the front door. "Ah, business calls?"

James nodded. "Sorry," he said, pulling a face. "They are quite important though, I mean they could be buying the place, so..."

"So you need to play nice," Emily finished with a smile.

"Exactly," said James with an air of relief.

"He was around for all of the incidents," Harry said to Emily as they walked away. "But I suppose it doesn't make sense."

"You saw how he was about those American inspectors or whatever they are," Emily agreed.

"If he was the one sabotaging things then he'd blow any chance of those people giving the hotel a good report," Harry said. "Besides, he's a busy man, he barely stands still."

"Agreed," said Emily. "Which means we need to move on. Let's go through the downstairs rooms, there's sure to be cleaners and the like. They're likely to have seen some interesting stuff, let's see what we can find out."

TWO HOURS LATER and they'd been laughed at, pushed aside, and yelled at in Polish by the head of housekeeping.

"You know, this isn't as easy as I thought it might be," Emily said.

They were sitting on a leather upholstered bench in the foyer, exhausted.

"I'm beginning to be glad that Private Investigator wasn't one of my career choices," Harry agreed. "And I'm not sure that we've got anything particularly helpful."

Emily sighed. "I suppose we have to move on to plan B then."

"Plan B?"

"Stake outs," Emily said, relishing the words.

Harry groaned and Emily patted her hand and then stopped patting because the feeling of Harry's hand under hers was warm and soft and nice.

For a long moment they sat there, hand in hand.

"I'd better take Elsie for a wee," Harry said, stirring but not quite moving her hand.

Emily realized that her heart was beating a little harder, that she was smiling without thinking about it.

"Em, there you are," Sara said, rushing down the stairs behind them. "I've been looking everywhere for you. Come on, Sav's called a family meeting."

"A family meeting?" Emily asked, eyes darting to Harry.

"I've got to take Elsie out," said Harry, sliding her hand quickly out from under Emily's and standing up.

"Come on," said Sara impatiently, holding out her hand.

Emily shot one last glance after Harry's disappearing form before she allowed herself to be pulled up and dragged back to the little bar by Sara.

"Finally," Sav said when Sara opened the door.

Emily looked around. All the Larettos were there, mom and dad and with Sara all three daughters, and now Gabe too, smiling and uncomfortably squashed into a corner of a booth.

"What's going on?" Emily whispered to Sara as they took a seat.

Sara shrugged. "Who knows? It's Sav."

Sav was already grinning, her face practically splitting in two, and she clapped her hands together and squealed.

"Sorry, sorry, I'm just so excited," she said.

"About what?" asked Mrs. Laretto because she knew her oldest daughter too well and was more than suspicious by this point.

Savannah tossed her hair over her shoulder and then turned, gesturing with her head to someone. The tall, dark barman slid out from behind the bar. Emily's stomach squeezed and her legs started to feel funny.

"I'm excited," Savannah said, "because Tony and I have an announcement to make."

"Tony?" boomed Mr. Laretto.

"Announcement?" chorused Sara and Sabrina.

"Gods be praised she can't be pregnant," Emily overheard Mrs. Laretto mumble.

"Yes," Savannah said, high voice over-riding them all. "We're getting married."

There was a rumble that became a shout and Emily couldn't distinguish the voices one from the other anymore. All she could see was a circle of light, Sav and the bartender standing in it, eyes only for each other. Then her world was closing in and getting tighter and darker.

"I need air," she said, pushing past Sara.

But Sara was too busy yelling at her sister to notice the devastation on her best friend's face.

CHAPTER TWENTY

The grass was soft underfoot, but there was a sprinkling of brown leaves, crunchy enough to signal that autumn wasn't that far off. It was still warm though, the sun stroking Harry's skin as she walked. Elsie leaped playfully after a leaf and then chased after an invisible rabbit.

It had been... Harry didn't have a word for it. Incredible seemed too hard, amazing seemed too common, fantastic seemed too glitzy. The kiss hadn't been any of those things and yet it had been all of them and more.

"Not the world's best writer if I can't find a word for a simple kiss," she mumbled to herself as she walked.

It had been more than a simple kiss though, she knew that.

And it had been more than the kiss that had touched her. It had been what happened after. There had been no pressure, no strangeness, no nothing. Just her and Emily alone together, comfortable and, well, normal.

It all seemed so obvious now, so easy, and Harry wondered why it had been so hard with everyone else in the world.

She also wondered just what in the hell she was supposed to do now.

She could ask Gabe, of course, but then Gabe was so full-on about things and he was so busy with the wedding. Which left one other person that she could call. With a sigh, she picked up her phone.

"Harry! Fallen in a loch yet?"

"Not yet, dad," she said with a laugh. "I'll work on it though."

"Just as long as you don't get eaten by any monsters. How's the wedding?"

"They're not technically married yet. But everything seems to be going well."

As far as Harry could see, things were going pretty well. The guests that she'd seen seemed to be happy and content, Sab and Gabe had cold feet, but there was nothing wrong with that. Well, other than the sabotage, of course, but she really didn't want to get into that.

"Um, dad?"

"Yes?"

"Remember that thing that you said about mum, about being, well, like me, and about her not being nervous and stuff around you?"

"Yes."

Harry took a deep breath. "Well, was it true?"

Her father chuckled. "True as I live and breathe."

She took another deep breath before asking what was really on her mind. "Why do you think that was?"

There was a crackling pause as her father thought about this. "I think sometimes," he said, "that love isn't what you expect it to be. You know, all those fireworks and hearts pounding and all that. Like you see in the films. In fact, I think maybe very often it's not like that at all."

Harry sat on the edge of an old stone wall as Elsie galloped around the lawn.

"I think mostly," her father continued, "that love is like coming home. Like putting on a jacket you've had for years, one that fits you perfectly. Like sinking into an armchair that's spent forever forming perfectly to your frame. You know what I mean?"

Harry thought about kissing Emily, thought about how familiar it had felt even though it had been the first time. "Yes," she said slowly. "Yes, I think I do."

"And when you feel that comfortable, how can you be nervous?"

She shuffled on the wall to make herself more comfortable and bit her lip. How indeed? "So that's love then, is it?"

There was another pause. "Harry, something you want to tell me?"

She sighed. "I'm not sure."

She could hear his smile over the line. "If this Emily is something special, you make sure that you let her know that she is. Don't go over all useless and just hope that she'll realize. When something's right, you know it is. I've more than taught you the difference between right and wrong, Harriet Lorde. If this is right, then grab it with both hands and don't you ever let it go."

She swallowed back her tears knowing that he was thinking of the mother that she barely remembered.

"Time is short, Harry, so short that you won't believe the moment that it runs out. Don't waste it, girl."

Harry sniffed and sat up straighter. "I won't, dad."

He coughed and she knew he was covering up his own emotions. "More importantly," he said, sounding more robust, "how does Elsie feel about her?"

Harry grinned. "Elsie loves her."

"Well then, she must be alright, mustn't she?"

She said her goodbyes and hung up, putting her phone away and leaning back a little in the sunshine.

So there it was then. Not that she'd been in that much doubt.

This was something. Not just A something, but THE something. This could be everything. She should be nervous as anything, but she wasn't. She was quiet and still and content. She had no doubts that Emily had feelings too. Whether or not those feelings were strong enough, she had no idea. But she couldn't control that. All she could control was herself and what she did next.

She whistled. "Come on, Else," she called out.

The dog came running and trotted after Harry as she walked

all the way back to the hotel.

"AM I IN for another interrogation?" James grinned as Harry came up to the reception desk.

"Um, I don't think so?" offered Harry. "Not unless there's something you want to tell me?"

He laughed. "I don't think so either. Is there something I can help you with?"

"Maybe," she allowed.

She'd been thinking on her walk back. She liked Emily and her father was right, she should speak her mind, she should act on whatever this was. And for her, kissing Emily had been exactly like her father had said, comfortable and familiar and nice.

But Emily wasn't her. Emily was a romantic, an idealist. Emily read books with half-naked people on the covers and investigated mysteries and had her own ideas of what love looked like. So maybe the right way to do this was to do things Emily's way. At least a little.

"I was wondering if you could help me set up something a bit, um, a bit romantic?" she asked.

James's grin widened. "I'd be delighted. We do have a rose garden and I'd be—"

"No, no," Harry said quickly. "I get horrible hay fever."

"Ah, no flowers then," said James, nodding in understanding. "Well, how about our private dining room? I could have the chef whip up something a little special, get a table for two out in the conservatory area where you could look up at the stars, some candles?"

Harry nodded. It sounded pretty romantic to her. "Sounds good. Any way you can make that happen tonight?"

James blew out a breath but nodded. "Yeah, yeah, I think I can get it worked out."

They went over the details and swapped mobile numbers so that James didn't call the room with any questions and spoil the surprise, and then Harry practically bounded up the stairs with

Elsie in tow.

This was going to work, she felt it in her bones. She didn't exactly know what was going to happen or what she expected to happen. But she did know that she was doing the right thing, that she had to speak her feelings or regret it forever.

She burst into the room not expecting Emily to be there. Elsie trotted over to her bed and Harry had already closed the door before she realized she wasn't alone. Emily was there.

She was there and lying face down on her bed and sobbing like her world had come crashing down around her ears.

Harry gulped but didn't hesitate. She sat down on the edge of the bed, putting a hand between Emily's shoulder blades. "Hey," she said. "Hey, what's wrong?"

Emily shuddered, breathed deeply, and turned over. Her face was swollen, her eyes were red, there were snot marks above her lips and Harry wanted nothing more than to hold her tight as tight and make the hurt all go away.

"It's Savannah," Emily hiccuped, just about controlling herself. "She's... she's getting married."

She wailed and turned away again and Harry patted her back.

Plans had to change, she could see that. She could see that today was no time for declaring love or anything else. Hurriedly she texted James to cancel the whole thing and then turned back to Emily. She dragged a box of tissues from the night table and pulled one out.

"Hey, come on," she said. "Turn over, talk to me."

"How could she do this to me?" Emily cried, turning again.

Harry pushed the tissue into her hand. "She's not thinking of you."

Emily cried harder.

"Emily, you know I'm right. You know that Savannah isn't thinking about you. She's thinking about herself and I get the feeling that's something she does a lot. She's not considerate, she doesn't deserve you, and deep down you know that."

Emily snuffled into the tissue but her sobs quietened a little.

"Maybe this needs to happen," Harry said reasonably. "Maybe

she needs to be with someone else so that you can move on. You said you didn't know how to, you said you knew she really wasn't right for you."

"I know, I know," Emily said, voice choked. "But this... getting married, I mean..."

"Wait, just who exactly is she marrying?" Harry asked.

"The bartender from that bar we were at the other night."

Harry tried very, very hard to keep her face straight. "A man she met hours ago?"

Emily nodded and Harry sighed.

"It must hurt," she said. "Shall I run you a hot bath? And I'll call down to room service for a hot cup of tea."

Unbelievably, Emily chuckled at that. "That's the most English thing I've heard you say."

Harry smiled at her. "Maybe, but it'll make you feel better, trust me."

Emily sneaked her hand down and insinuated it into Harry's. Her fingers were hot and sticky and Harry clutched onto them. "Thanks, Harry," she said. "You're a good friend."

Harry kept her smile on and held onto Emily's hand. Perhaps friend was good? Perhaps friend was enough?

But in her heart she knew that it absolutely wasn't.

CHAPTER
TWENTY ONE

E mily carefully turned the door handle, hand on the door keeping it steady and silent as she opened it.

"Where are we going?" Harry hissed.

"Here," said Emily, finally opening the door fully.

Inside, the altar was already dressed, a white screen behind a dais, columns for flowerpots, the tiny chapel looked like it belonged in a fairy tale. Emily heard Harry's breath catch in her throat.

"And what exactly are we supposed to be doing?" asked Harry.

"Looking for clues," Emily said primly. "And... and anything else suspicious."

Harry stood at the head of the aisle looking at Emily with one raised eyebrow. Her hair was still damp from the shower and there were tiny gray smudges under her eyes from being up too late. Up too late comforting Emily.

"Clues."

"Or anything else suspicious," Emily nodded. "Go on then, you take that side, I'll take this one."

With one last despairing look, Harry shook her head and began strolling slowly down one side of the wooden pews.

"Imagine getting married in here," she said. "It's beautiful, isn't it?"

"Hush," Emily said. "We're not supposed to be in here."

But it was beautiful. Heart-breakingly beautiful, even in the cold bright light of morning. Sabrina would look so wonderful walking down this aisle, and Emily could already see Gabe waiting for her at the end. It was going to be the perfect wedding.

She could almost cry, except she was all cried out.

She was, she had to admit, slightly better this morning. It had been a shock, Sav announcing things like that. But then, that was Sav, wasn't it? Selfish, unconcerned with what others thought of her.

For so long she'd been a part of Emily's life, a part of the way she saw herself, that it was difficult to move on, difficult to say that this one-sided dream had come to an end. But it had to. Emily had known that for far longer than she cared to admit.

Maybe Sav would be happy with her bartender. Maybe the affair wouldn't last until the end of the week. But whatever happened, Emily was certain that she needed to get on with life, that she needed to let go of the idea of Sav.

"Wow," Harry said in the echoing emptiness of the chapel.

"What?" asked Emily, thinking she'd found something.

"Oh, sorry, nothing, just, well, just that the wedding programs are over here and they're really sweet, that's all."

"Oh," Emily said, continuing on with her own inspection.

But maybe everything wasn't lost. She had Harry, after all. Harry who had watched her cry, comforted her, been there. Harry who was fun and sweet and pretty and everything else. Harry who could be the help she needed to get over Sav.

Would that be such a bad thing? After all, Harry herself needed experience too. Perhaps they could both learn a thing or two from this. It wasn't like she'd be taking advantage. And there was plenty of chemistry there, she wouldn't deny that.

Alright, it wasn't fireworks and clashing cymbals kind of chemistry. But kissing Harry had been... tingly. That was the best word she had for it. It had made every fiber in her body tingle in a way that was far from unpleasant. Actually, in a way that had made her want to do it again but she'd been afraid that Harry would be overwhelmed.

Even now she was a little afraid that Harry would be skittish and nervous and that she might screw things up by saying the wrong thing.

"Nothing here," Harry said, reaching the front of the chapel.

Emily ducked her head down and took a look under the pews on her side and shrugged. "Nothing here either," she said, joining Harry.

"It'd help if I knew what we were looking for."

"Not a clue," Emily said with a grin. "I just thought that this could be an obvious place to create trouble if you wanted to stop a wedding, that's all."

"Well, there's nothing that I can see. Unless whoever it is is planning on doing the whole objecting thing."

"You know, I don't think that works outside of the movies," said Emily.

"I wouldn't bet on it. And you're not to try it."

"It is kind of romantic though" Emily said. "Someone so in love with you that they can't stand to see you marry someone else."

"So they humiliate you in front of all your family and friends and stop the wedding that you've spent months and thousands of pounds planning?" asked Harry. "That doesn't sound romantic, that sounds selfish. If someone I loved was getting married I'd hope that I'd be happy that they were happy and that would be enough for me."

"Really?" Emily asked. They were standing close enough together that she could smell Harry, the leather and spice smell of her, the slight tinge of wet dog, the essence of Harry. It wasn't unpleasant. In fact, it was kind of comforting.

"Really." The light caught Harry's hair, making red highlights shine in the dark.

"You really are too good to be true, aren't you?" Emily said, captivated for a second by the sight of the light on Harry. "You really are a good person."

"I should hope I am. I try to be."

"And it's totally unremarkable to you," Emily breathed, thinking that Savannah would never say anything even close to this. That perhaps Harry was the best person that she knew.

"What does that mean?" Harry asked just as there was a noise at the front door.

"Quick," said Emily. "Get behind here."

They leaped behind the altar screen, standing as still as they could while the chapel door opened and someone came in. There was the sound of two men chatting and then thumps as something was deposited on the ground. Harry peeked around the screen.

"It's only the flowers being delivered," she hissed.

"Shh!"

There was a brief pause, then the sound of the door closing. "It's fine, they're gone."

"But they might come back," Emily said.

"So might the saboteur," said Harry. "Which reminds me of the main weakness in our investigation here. We still have absolutely no idea who might be to blame for any of this. And I'm thinking that we might not be great detectives."

"These things take time."

"The wedding isn't that far away."

"Well, as long as we keep everyone safe, isn't that what matters?" Emily asked.

"I'm not so sure. I want to catch whoever's responsible for all this. Especially whoever made Elsie eat that chocolate."

"I know," Emily said. They were closer now, both sheltering behind the screen, the warmth of Harry's body noticeable.

"I just... I don't think we're doing the greatest job, that's all."

"Well, we'll just have to try harder," Emily said, trying and failing to ignore the fact that Harry's arm was brushing against her. She cleared her throat. "Um, there's the reception room as well. We should check that out."

"Right," Harry said. "I suppose. You'll have to let me take Else out for a walk first though, we can't leave her locked up in the room all day."

"Fine, fine," Emily said, getting just a scooch closer to see if Harry's arm really was as warm and soft as she could remember.

Harry paused and looked down at her, blushed a bright red and immediately turned away again. "And you didn't answer my question, did you?"

"What question was that?" asked Emily, watching her lips and very much wanting to kiss them again.

"You said that me being a good person was totally unremarkable to me, and I asked you what that was supposed to mean," Harry said, still not looking at her.

Emily bit her lip but very, very slowly slid her fingers into Harry's. "I think it means that I'm starting to realize that maybe, perhaps, being a good person is a very nice thing indeed."

She heard Harry swallow.

"Even if that good person doesn't, oh, I don't know... doesn't shower you with roses or whisk you onto the dance floor for an Argentinian tango or fill your bathroom with candles and rose petals?" Harry finally asked, eyes firmly on the screen in front of her.

"What?" Emily said. "Why... no, never mind. Yes, even if the good person doesn't do those things then it's still very nice that they're a very good person. And perhaps filling up a hot bath when someone is upset is more important than filling the tub with rose petals."

"More practical too," said Harry.

They were quiet for a long minute, Emily's fingers all tangled in with Harry's.

"I think you're a very nice person too," Harry said eventually. She coughed a little. "Um, actually, I was thinking that maybe... maybe I might like you. Sort of a lot."

Emily's heart skipped a beat. Literally skipped a beat so that she was frozen to the floor.

Harry's eyes darted to her. "And I know you're in love with Savannah and that you're heart-broken and all right now and that I have no right to say anything at all and I really shouldn't.

It's just that... it's just that I'm afraid this might be my only chance and you're literally the only woman that I've never done anything completely stupid in front of and—"

The only way to stop her was with a kiss. So that's exactly what Emily did. She pulled her in and crashed her lips against Harry's, stopping the flow of words and instead kissing her until all thoughts of anything other than the kiss were gone.

When they finally broke apart, both panting a little, Harry looked slightly stunned.

"Sorry," said Emily. "But I was afraid you'd never shut up."

Harry nodded, still stunned into silence.

"And you might be right that this isn't exactly the best timing. But you're also right that this is a limited time opportunity. You're right that we have feelings, whatever they might be, and that we could explore them. I'm not promising anything, we might not be a match made in heaven or anything."

"You definitely make my legs feel wobbly," Harry said uncertainly.

"A good sign," Emily laughed. She reached up and ran a hand over Harry's almost dry curls. "I think I'm trying to say that I like you, Harry."

Harry looked down, her eyes dark and soft, her cheeks flushed just a little pink. "I like you too," she said seriously.

So seriously that Emily had to kiss her again.

CHAPTER
TWENTY TWO

Harry's lips were bruised from kissing Emily in the chapel and she could still taste her if she concentrated. Which made it rather hard to concentrate on anything else. Yet something was nagging at her attention as the two of them walked down a back corridor of the hotel.

"We'll just check the reception hall," Emily was saying.

"Mmm," said Harry. "And then what?" She was teasing and couldn't help it. It was like something had taken over her body. All she could think about was kissing Emily again.

Emily turned around, eyes sparkling, a small smile on her lips. "Well, then we can take Elsie for a walk, of course."

"Aha," Harry breathed. Emily was standing awfully close again. "A walk."

"In the secluded woods," added Emily, moving in a little closer.

Harry dared herself to put her hand on Emily's waist and Emily's smile widened.

"Of course, we could stay here," she said in a husky voice. "I mean, in our room."

"Rather than in a damp corridor," said Harry. Her stomach was tightening, her pulse was pounding, she could feel her skin flushing. "I see."

The thought of Emily upstairs. The thought of Emily on a bed. The thought of Emily doing anything at all right now, short of leading a fox hunt or something else unspeakable, made her feel terribly breathless.

Emily stepped back again, resting a hand on Harry's arm. "Too much?" she said. "Coming on too strong?"

Harry appreciated her concern. "Um, not sure?" she answered honestly. "I mean, I like the idea, I just…"

"It's just a bit much."

"The idea is a bit much," Harry agreed. "But then the reality, well, I'm not so sure about that." She let her hand drift to the small of Emily's back, experimenting with pulling her closer and finding that she liked it, liked the power, liked the way Emily's eyes widened a touch when she took control.

"We can be as slow as you like, slow, cool, chill, I swear," said Emily, voice quivering slightly.

Which was when Harry's brain finally decided to kick into gear. "Chill," she said, hand dropping away from Emily.

"What?"

Harry looked around at the silver boxes lining the corridor. "Chill. These things are all catering fridges, set up and ready for the caterers to store food for the reception." She opened a door, then another, and a third, before sighing in relief.

"Okay, and?" Emily asked thoroughly confused.

"I wrote a catering handbook a few years back," said Harry, looking at the gauge on the front of the fridge and seeing exactly what had been nagging at her. She pressed a button and then moved to the next fridge doing the same thing.

"What are you doing?"

"These fridges, they're all set to ten degrees," Harry said.

"Not anymore they're not," said Emily, looking at what Harry was doing to the third and then the fourth fridge.

"Because the maximum temperature for a catering fridge is eight," explained Harry, working her way down the line. "Anything above that is in what they call the danger zone."

"Seriously? An Archer reference?"

Harry stopped and looked at Emily. "Well, yes, but I didn't expect you to watch it, and also probably not the important thing here."

"I'm full of unexpected surprises, just one of which is that I find Archer hilarious. And what exactly is the important thing here?"

"The fact that it looks very much like someone is trying to give the entire wedding party food poisoning," said Harry, setting the dial on the last fridge. She sighed and rubbed her face. "Or perhaps not. Perhaps I'm being over-cautious. Maybe the fridges are set higher because there's no food in them yet. But then the food should be coming any minute and—"

"And you should trust your instincts," Emily said. "We'll need to come back and check on these later to make sure that no one's screwed with the temperatures again."

Harry nodded.

"Let's go check the reception hall anyway," said Emily, looping her arm through Harry's. "And nice catch there with the refrigerators."

Harry smiled as she let Emily lead her away.

They snuck in through the back door of a large hall, already set up with small round tables and centerpieces, a dancefloor in the middle.

"Oops," said Emily almost immediately.

She tugged on Harry's arm and pulled her down behind a table, crawling under the tablecloth and gesturing for Harry to join her just as the sound of voices came from one of the sound doors.

"Excellent event space," said one of the voices. An American, Harry thought. One of Sabrina's relatives? "Easy to rent out and make a fair amount of money. Puts this place firmly on the conference circuit, I should expect," the voice went on.

No, not a relative. One of the trio of inspectors looking to buy the hotel, she thought.

"According to the plans, there's another space next door," said another voice as the sound of footsteps began to fade.

Harry took a deep breath to ask Emily if they could get out from under the table and immediately sneezed.

She clapped a hand over her mouth and nose. Emily's face went white and her hand clutched at Harry's arm.

"Did you hear that?" asked the first voice from just inside the room.

"Probably nothing," said the second voice and the footsteps began to move again.

"Jesus," Emily breathed.

"Hay fever," said Harry. She pulled a face. "Sorry."

"Not your fault," Emily said. She was grinning now. "We did almost get busted though. It's not a successful stakeout if you get made."

There was something about being in close quarters in the half-light under the table. Something about being so close to someone that Harry had only just discovered made her heart beat strangely. Something about feeling so comfortable, so familiar with someone that she could have known her all her life.

"Is it a successful stake out if you make out though?" she asked, eyebrow raised.

Emily snorted a laugh. "That's a terrible joke, Harry."

Harry grinned back. "It is. But it's also a fair point. And an earnest question since I do want our stake out to be successful." She shuffled a little closer. "We don't want to run any risks now, do we?"

Emily's head was tilting, Harry's hand was moving up to the back of Emily's neck, their lips were tantalizingly close when there was the sound of a door being flung open and then slammed closed again.

Harry practically jumped back.

"See, completely empty," Savannah's voice said. "I told you it would be."

There was the sound of a man laughing and then a rustling which Harry thought might mean that Savannah and whoever she was with were doing something Harry would rather be doing herself at this point.

"It's not my fault I share a room with my stupid sister," Savannah was saying. "And it might be helpful if you lived a little closer to the hotel so we could go there."

"Yeah, not close enough for a lunchtime quickie," the man said.

The bartender. It must be the bartender. Savannah's erstwhile fiancé. Harry darted a worried glance at Emily, but Emily had her eyes closed and Harry put a hand over hers. How could they get out of this? The last thing she wanted was for Emily to overhear whatever was about to happen.

"Bit fancy in here though, don't you think?" the bartender said. "Not exactly cozy, is it?"

"It is empty though," said Savannah. "Or empty enough until my stupid sister gets stupid married anyway."

The bartender chuckled uncertainly. "You should be happy for your sister, shouldn't you?"

"I'm the eldest," Sav said firmly. "This should be me, not her."

"Well, it'll be you soon enough, love. Might not be as fancy as all this though," the bartender said.

But Harry was already thinking, the wheels already turning.

Of all the people they'd thought could be responsible for the sabotage, there were a handful that had never even entered the running. And Savannah was one of those. But here she was loudly admitting that she was jealous of her sister's wedding.

Harry turned to Emily, whose eyes were open now.

"Did you hear that?" she hissed.

Emily nodded, blew out a breath, then whispered back: "She said as much before. At the station when we were on our way here."

Harry took this in, biting her lip. "You didn't say anything?"

Emily closed her eyes again.

"Come on, there's a cupboard over here, it's a bit more cozy, innit?" the bartender's voice said.

There was the sound of squealing and then movement, then another door opened and closed and Harry knew that the room was empty again.

With careful movements, she got out from under the table.

Emily had known that Savannah was jealous of Sabrina, making her the ideal suspect. Yet she'd said nothing about it. Why? Because she was in love with Sav? Because she wanted to protect her?

Which was fine, Harry supposed. Fine and yet it was just a reminder of the fact that Emily was fixated on someone else, someone who wasn't Harry. Someone who could potentially be the one who'd arranged for Elsie to eat the chocolate, accidentally or not.

Her head was spinning and she was starting to feel just a little bit sick.

Emily was coming up from under the table, looking shame-faced and embarrassed. "Harry," she began.

Harry shook her head. She didn't want to have this conversation now. Not until she'd had a bit of time to think. Not until she'd digested this new information.

"I, uh, I need to take Elsie for a walk," she said calmly.

"Harry..."

"Sorry," said Harry, looking away. "I can't do this just now."

And she walked quickly out of the room before Emily could say anything else.

CHAPTER TWENTY THREE

Emily looked out of the window. Harry was slowly tramping through the orange leaves that littered the green lawn, Elsie joyfully jumping at birds, and Emily's heart was hurting. She tapped her fingers on the windowsill, thinking to herself. But she knew exactly what she needed to do, there was only one thing that could be done.

With a sigh she stood up from the window seat and walked out of the hotel. The day was warm but not hot, and she could hear the clack of croquet balls from the other side of the hotel. She put her hands in her pockets as she approached Harry.

"I'm sorry."

Harry turned around quickly seeming surprised to see her. "Sorry?"

"I'm sorry," Emily said again. "I know how that looked and I apologize for it. If it's alright with you, I'd like to talk about it."

Harry stood there looking at her. Finally she blew out a breath. "You Americans really are forward, aren't you?"

"Would you prefer not to talk about it?" Emily asked.

"I'm not sure I gave it a lot of thought, I sort of assumed that we'd both sulk about it for a while and then bring it up in an awkward way or just pretend it didn't happen at all."

"Huh. That seems... unhealthy."

"I didn't say it was healthy," said Harry, turning and continuing her walk. "Although I can see how your way might be faster in the long run."

Emily skipped a step to keep up with her, feeling the comfort of being by Harry's side. There was something about her, something that felt like home. She felt better just being next to her. "I honestly forgot that Sav had said anything about being jealous of Sabrina until I heard her just now."

Harry nodded. "Alright, I suppose I can buy that. But you have to see how it looks from my point of view. You adore Savannah, you've been in love with her for years, and it just feels like you might cover up something if you thought that Sav was involved."

"I see that. But then why would I investigate it in the first place if I thought Sav was to blame? Not that I do, by the way."

"Fair point," Harry said, crossing the tree line into the woods. "I suppose I could also be coming from a place of jealousy myself." She looked down at Emily and smiled a little. "I mean, it's not like I don't have a horse in this race."

"Are you calling me a horse?"

Harry grinned and just kept walking. "Convince me that she's not involved," she said.

"We're going to circle back to the horse thing," Emily said, thinking about how she was going to explain this. "It's the relationship that they have. They're sisters."

"Meaning what?" asked Harry.

"Meaning that I've seen them practically scratch each other's eyes out over a pair of earrings," said Emily. "And then I've seen them team up against a guy that pinched Sabrina's ass and scare him so bad he literally ran out of the bar we were in."

"I'd have liked to have seen that."

Emily smiled. "It was pretty funny. But my point is that they snipe and bitch at each other, all three of them, it's what they do. At heart though, there's nothing they wouldn't do for each other and I'd trust any one of them with my life, not just Sara. And yes, that includes Sav."

She cleared her throat and knew that she needed to be even more honest.

"Sav saved me, in a way," she said quietly. "After my parents died, I, uh, I had some troubles." The cool breeze blew on her face. "I had trouble leaving the house, really doing anything. In the end, Mrs. Laretto made a psychologist's appointment for me. But it was Sav that persuaded me to go. She said it'd be like being a Kardashian, like being rich. And it was Sav that went with me to my sessions. It was Sav that was there for me."

They walked quietly for a long minute or so, and then Emily felt Harry's fingers creep into her own.

"I think I understand," Harry said softly. "I'm going to ask this just once. You're sure that Savannah has nothing to do with all this sabotage?"

"I'm a hundred percent sure. And I'm a hundred percent sure Sav would stab whoever is responsible with a rusty spoon if she found them first."

"Heard," said Harry.

"And now back to the horse thing," Emily said.

Harry stopped, looking down at her with a concerned look. "I wasn't actually calling you a horse, you know that, right?"

Emily laughed. "I'm very well aware of that. But I also know what you actually meant. You meant that what just happened was a reminder of the fact that I have, as you say, spent most of my adult life in love with Savannah. And now... Now you and I are... whatever we are."

"An eloquent way of putting things."

"There's no point in putting labels on things that haven't earned them yet," Emily said as she started to walk again.

"Fair." Harry followed her.

"I can't promise you anything Harry. We're practically strangers even though it doesn't feel like it sometimes. All I can tell you is that I do really like you. Regardless of anyone else who's around I feel like you and I have a connection."

"Okay," Harry said. "Okay. I feel that way too."

"Savannah is no good for me. Savannah..." Putting this into

words was weirdly hurtful, strangely painful and yet sort of cathartic as well. "Savannah is not right for me. She was a fantasy, a romantic ideal, and one that I need to work to get rid of. But I am working on it. I know that there isn't going to be some sort of fairy tale happy ending here. I suppose I've always known it but I needed these few days to put everything into perspective."

Harry squeezed her hand. "It must be difficult."

"It is difficult," Emily agreed. "But less difficult than I thought. Especially since you're here."

"Ah yes, me, the great heart-breaker."

Emily laughed. "Harry, you are a heart-breaker, or you could be if you let yourself. You're the perfect woman, you're smart and funny and single and you've even got a great dog."

"I also have a tendency to pour cups of tea on people and sometimes to fall down stairs," Harry said.

"I'd call those in-built entertainment options rather than flaws," Emily said. "But you have a lot to give Harry, if you only had the confidence to see it."

Harry stopped again, pulling on Emily's hand to stop her too. "Maybe I'm starting to see it a little," she said, blushing. "Maybe you're helping me see it a little. I mean, if someone like you can be interested in me, I can't be all that bad, can I?"

Emily laughed again and shook her head. "No, you're not all that bad Harry."

"Good to know."

Emily reached up and cupped Harry's face with her hand. "You're more than not all that bad," she said, voice lowering. "You're a lot of good, Harry Lorde."

Harry's eyes got darker and Emily pulled her head down until their lips were brushing. Then Harry was putting her hands in Emily's hair and deepening the kiss, mouth searching hungrily. Emily found herself hiccuping with laughter as Harry backed her up against a tree.

"Funny?" Harry asked, drawing back and looking confused.

"Not funny like that, just... Yes, funny," Emily said. "But in a good way." The bark of the tree was rough on her back and she took hold of Harry's hips, pulling her in closer. "In a very good way," she assured her.

Harry's grin was crooked but it faded as Emily gently pushed her hands up Harry's shirt, feeling soft skin and tight muscle. Harry groaned and Emily felt her heart pulsing between her legs.

"Harry," she murmured.

"Mmm?" Harry's eyes had closed.

"Do you think we might go back to the hotel?"

"Mmm." Harry's eyes were still closed. A second later they flashed open. "Back to the hotel?"

Emily nodded. "Only if you want to."

Harry was already letting her go, whistling for Elsie. She took a step away then turned back to Emily. "Would it be terribly unromantic if I offered to race you there?"

"That depends whether you're chivalrous enough to let me win," Emily said.

"All's fair in love and war," Harry said as she took off after Elsie, tearing through the trees and back out onto the lawn.

Emily laughed and followed, pumping her arms and legs hard to catch up.

They were neck and neck as they approached the steps of the hotel at which point they both slowed down, aware that chasing through a luxury hotel probably wasn't a great idea.

"Where are you two rushing off to?" Gabe asked, coming out of the front door with his arm around Sabrina's shoulders.

Emily and Harry both stopped and looked at each other, neither answering.

Gabe rolled his eyes. "Just don't forget that it's the rehearsal dinner tonight. You're both required to be in attendance."

"Right, yes," Harry said.

"Mmmhmm," agreed Emily.

Gabe shared an amused look with Sabrina. "Carry on then," he said and the couple walked away.

"Rehearsal dinner," Emily said.

"Not for hours," Harry said.

Emily swallowed and looked up at the hotel. Hours. Hours that could be well spent. "Race you?"

But Harry was already disappearing up the stairs.

CHAPTER TWENTY FOUR

Emily raced into the bedroom closely followed by Elsie who made a dive for her basket. Harry was last through the door and she slammed it behind her, leaning back on it and panting. Emily kicked off her shoes and threw herself on the bed.

Harry caught her breath and then lost it again as she looked at Emily, blonde hair tangled on the pillow, lips smiling. Suddenly, she was shy, unsure.

"It's alright," Emily said. "We do this at your pace. In fact, we don't do anything if that's what you want."

"No," Harry said firmly. "That's not what I want. Not at all what I want." She could feel her blood pulsing, could feel her heart beating, could feel the warmth in her stomach. She wanted this. She just wasn't sure where to start, that was all.

Emily smiled. "Then why don't you come over here and we'll figure out together what we both want."

"I just… I don't know where to start," Harry said, moving to sit on the bed next to Emily.

Emily sat up. "Usually, we start with a kiss," she said, coming in closer.

"That I can do," Harry smiled. She brushed her lips against Emily's, lightly at first, tentatively, then a little harder.

Emily responded immediately, hands coming up to cup Harry's face and then to tangle in her hair, pulling her closer. Harry was intoxicated with her, the smell of her, the taste of her. She found that she was pushing back, that Emily was lying down, and that Harry herself was unbelievably lying next to her on the bed.

"Slowly," Emily said, breaking the kiss.

Harry looked into her brown eyes and then kissed her again, wanting so much to move slowly and yet wanting all of this all at once. She pulled back again. "Could I, uh, take off your t-shirt? Maybe mine too?" she asked cautiously.

Emily grinned. "Race you?" she asked.

Harry laughed and flicked one button on her shirt open before yanking it off over her head, only to throw it down and see that Emily had beaten her and was lying down again. She lost her breath again. The curve of Emily's waist, the swell of her breasts in their simple bra. Harry's hands started to shake.

"It's alright," Emily said calmly. "I won't break, I'm not fragile."

"I have no idea what I'm doing," Harry said, voice shaking as well.

"It's not rocket science," Emily laughed. "You do what you would do to yourself, or what you think you'd enjoy, that's all. And if something is wrong or I'd prefer something else then I'll tell you, I'll guide you."

Harry nodded but still didn't move. Emily took her hand and pulled it up, placing it on her stomach. "Kiss me again."

Doing as she was told, Harry let the warmth of Emily's skin move through her hand. She was aching with need now, a need she had no clue how to sate. Emily wriggled and Harry pulled back to see that she was taking off her bra.

Her breasts were full, her nipples the same pink as her half-open lips.

"Touch me," Emily said.

Carefully, Harry moved her hand up, let it flow over the curve of Emily's breast, let it brush over a tight nipple and Emily gasped.

"Too much?" Harry snatched her hand away, but Emily caught it.

"Not enough," Emily said, replacing Harry's hand. "Circle the nipple gently, then pinch it, not too hard."

Harry did so and was rewarded by another gasp. She studied Emily's face carefully, seeing the flush of her cheeks, the way her lips were swelling. So she did it again. And then, daring, she lowered her face and allowed her tongue to do the job. Emily pressed up, pushing her breast into Harry's mouth and Harry thought she might die of over-excited suffocation.

"Harry," Emily groaned.

Harry flicked the nipple with her tongue and let her opposite hand clutch Emily's waist, pulling her closer. For long moments she lay by Emily's side, taking first one breast then the other, hearing Emily groan, hearing her heart throb, feeling her pushing up in response.

Until she was hardly breathing herself.

Until Emily was sweating, the taste salty on her skin, and was grabbing Harry's hand and forcing it downward.

"Please," Emily said.

Trembling, Harry unbuttoned her jeans. With a quick movement, Emily slid them off, kicking them off the end of the bed, taking her underwear with them.

"You too," she said, eyes only half-open, breath coming quick and sharp.

Harry stood up, pulling off her own pants and knickers, unable to believe what she was seeing. Emily was lightly tanned, the hair between her legs was a darker triangle than Harry had been expecting. And all Harry could think about was that Emily's skin was about the softest thing she'd ever touched.

"Come on," Emily said, beckoning her back to bed. "Lie beside me."

Harry lay beside her, barely touching her. She wanted this, she told herself. She wanted it badly. And she couldn't let Emily do all the work. Slowly, she put her hand back on Emily's stomach. "Is this okay?"

Emily moaned and nodded so Harry let her hand stray further down, over the slight curve of stomach, stopping just short of wiry hair. Emily moaned again and opened her eyes.

"Harry? You can stop if you want to."

But Harry honestly didn't think she could. She let her hand move again and Emily parted her legs, her knees falling to either side so that she was open and ready and Harry could smell her, the musky scent of her. She felt herself swelling inside and squeezed her legs together.

"May I?" she asked, voice husky.

In response, Emily pushed her hips up and Harry's hand slid over her mound, resting between her legs. Harry's mouth was dry. Her fingers knew what to do though, they'd done it often enough to herself. Gently, she parted Emily, felt for the warm wetness that she knew would be there and almost came herself when she felt it.

Emily was breathing hard and fast, her eyes were closed, her cheeks flushed pink and Harry couldn't take it anymore, couldn't take the tension of it, the anxiety, the anticipation.

She pulled her fingers upwards, dragging wetness with them, until she met a hard bump and then she began to circle it. Emily's hips pushed up again, rising to meet her hand in a rhythm that Harry couldn't know and yet, quite impossibly, did.

Rough hands pulled her down, pushing her mouth towards a breast. And Harry had no hesitation now. She let her fingers work as her tongue lapped at Emily's nipple and heard a gasp and then a long, long moan.

Against her body, the muscles in Emily's stomach tensed, her hips rose and thrust against Harry's hand, and Harry could feel the tension building and building and knew what was about to happen. She found that she was moaning too, that she was burning inside, so close to exploding herself.

One of Emily's hands wrapped in Harry's hair, holding her close, the other clamped over her busy hand, holding it tight against her, and she cried out and shook, trembling against Harry.

Harry stayed as still as she could, waiting, panting, until Emily sank back to the bed.

"Jesus."

Harry took that as a sign that she could move. She looked up, grinning. "Not bad for a beginner?"

Emily swallowed, eyes still glazed over. "Not bad for an expert," she said.

Harry's grin widened.

"Oh, don't look so satisfied with yourself," Emily laughed. "And get your ass over here."

"What does my arse have to do with things?"

"Just move," Emily said. "Here, like this, straddle me." She pulled Harry's leg over her, helping her to sit.

"Why like this?" asked Harry, slightly confused sitting atop of Emily.

"So I can watch you," Emily said.

"Watch me do what?"

Emily's hands were on her waist now. Harry forgot how to breathe. Then the same hands were tugging at the edge of the sports bra she was wearing. Harry struggled to take it off, sweaty and breathless. Emily's hands found her small breasts, cupped them, covered them, her hands brushing against nipples that Harry hadn't known were sensitive at all.

"Watch you come," Emily said hoarsely.

Her eyes were darker again, her breath coming faster again and Harry didn't understand why, Then she remembered how turned on she'd gotten touching Emily and thought the same thing might be happening to Emily. Which confused her slightly, she'd never thought of herself as sexy.

"You're beautiful," Emily said. "And sexy as hell."

"I am?"

Emily shook her head and said nothing, instead letting one of her hands drift down until it rested on her own stomach close enough to Harry's center that she could almost feel it.

"May I?" Emily asked.

Dumb, Harry nodded.

Gently, Emily slid her hand under Harry. Then just as gently she maneuvered herself until she was in just the right position so that her fingers teased Harry's entrance.

Harry gasped and moved automatically, finding that Emily's palm was pressed hard against her. Then she understood. Understood and instinctively moved, rocking back and forth as Emily's fingers slid into her and her palm provided friction.

She moved in ways she hadn't known that she could, feeling the heat building up inside her, feeling her breath leave her body, feeling every muscle tighten inside her.

Until she was throbbing and sighing and laughing and coming all at the same time, and collapsing on top of Emily.

"Not bad for a first time, right?" Emily whispered into her ear.

"I've got nothing to compare it to," Harry answered honestly.

"Oh," Emily said. "I think we can work on that, don't you?"

Harry glanced at her watch. The afternoon was only half over. "I think I could pencil you in for a couple more hours."

"Pencil me in?" Emily asked, eyes getting big and round. Then she flipped, expertly bringing Harry onto her back. "Pencil me in, huh? You're going to pay for that."

And Harry gasped as Emily slid down between her legs and thought that this was a price very much worth paying indeed.

CHAPTER
TWENTY FIVE

Harry's legs burned in an uncomfortably pleasant way. She kept smiling to herself unnecessarily and she was sure that people could tell by looking at her. She felt subtly different and yet the same. And, she had to admit, she felt... happy. Was that the word?

It had to be the word, that full feeling of laughter and smiles and comfort. This had to be happiness.

At the same time, she was scolding herself to calm down, to stay realistic. Because at the end of the day, Emily had to go home and then what?

And then something would happen, a voice at the back of her head told her. All those movies and books couldn't be wrong. Love would win through, it always did. Maybe Emily would get a job here, or an up until now unknown rich aunt would bequeath Harry loads of money and she'd move there.

Something like that.

Elsie's tail beat the floor next to her and Harry put out a hand to stroke her head.

Emily was responding to a disaster call from Sara, something about bangs gone wrong, which Harry had thought was some sort of firework emergency until she remembered that Americans called a fringe bangs. The confusion wasn't completely cleared, since she didn't remember Sara having a fringe, but then perhaps that was the emergency.

Whatever the reason, Harry was now dressed up nicely, freshly showered and clean. Elsie was freshly walked and respectably tidy if not a hundred percent clean, Harry thought as she picked a piece of pine cone from the dog's coat. And both were sitting quietly on a bench enjoying the evening warmth and waiting for an appropriate time to go in for the rehearsal dinner.

"There you are."

Gabe's voice boomed from behind her and a second later he was plopping down onto the bench beside her. Harry was already grinning, ready to tell him the whole truth, ready to let him in on her secrets, but when she saw his face she closed her mouth.

"Harry, I hate to say it, but you're slacking a bit in the best man department."

"I am?" Harry said, instantly knowing that it was true. "Yes, I am, aren't I?"

Gabe laid a hand on her leg and patted it. "It's alright. I know you've been… busy, shall we say? I didn't want to interrupt young love and all that."

"But you needed me," said Harry with a sigh. He was right, she should have been paying more attention to him, this was his week after all.

"Oh, I didn't want to be a third wheel. We all know what it's like to have someone new and exciting. I'm honestly happy for you, Harry. And Emily seems nice."

"She is," Harry said, not letting herself gush. "She's very nice."

Gabe grunted.

"That's not the problem, is it?" Harry said suddenly sitting up straighter. "You haven't found someone new and exciting, have you?"

"Lord no," said Gabe. He was staring out over the lawn. "Not at all."

Harry let out a breath. "Good, because all this looks like it cost a bomb and I'm not sure I could deal with having everything called off. Besides, you and Sabrina look happy together."

"We are." He tapped his fingers together, a habit he had when he was worried. "We really are. I love her, I know I do. I don't know why I'm so nervous and jittery about everything, I just am. I have no idea whether that's normal or not."

Harry bit her lip.

"I do know that I'd have appreciated a bit more support from you, Harry, to be honest."

She flushed bright red. Half of her was annoyed, the other half guilty, and she couldn't decide which half to go with. Yes, she should have been spending more time with Gabe. But also, she'd been investigating who was sabotaging his wedding, for god's sake.

Except that sounded ridiculous, even in her head. And had she really been investigating, or had she just been so caught up in Emily that she'd forgotten why she was really supposed to be here?

She didn't know what to say, so she shut down and said nothing.

"Harry, you're all I've got," Gabe said not looking at her. "That sounds pathetic, but it's somewhat true. Ma and Pa are gone, I've got no siblings, you're my family, Harry."

All her anger drained away. She stretched and put an arm around him. "You're right. And I'm here for you, Gabe. Promise. I've been a bit shit, it won't happen again."

He grinned at her. "You were probably better off with Emily than listening to my constant worrying. And she's a damn sight prettier than I am."

"She is," allowed Harry. "But you're my best friend and I wouldn't have it any other way."

"Good." He drew back a little. "Hold on a sec. Harry Lorde, are you… are you glowing?"

"I don't know what you're talking about," Harry said primly.

"You are, aren't you?" Gabe said. He shook his head. "I know I doubted this at the beginning, but Harry, you're in love, aren't you? Aren't you?"

She shifted on the bench.

"Oh Harry, that's wonderful." Gabe grabbed her and hugged her tight.

"Hey, I didn't admit to anything," Harry said. Except the words didn't feel as wrong as she'd thought they would.

Gabe drew back. "Alright, do you think of her face constantly?"

"Um, sometimes, I suppose."

"Can you not keep your hands off her?"

"Gabe! I'm a grown adult and can fully control myself, thank you very much."

"That's a point," Gabe said, narrowing his eyes. "You haven't fallen downstairs in front of her or anything of that nature, have you?"

"I spilled a cup of tea on her on the train," Harry said. "But that was mostly because there was this really pretty blonde woman coming the other way up the aisle."

"That's a bit... odd." Gabe frowned. "Even since I've known you, you've conspired to look foolish in front of anyone even remotely attractive."

Harry shrugged. "Emily makes me feel comfortable, I suppose."

He watched her. "She feels like home, doesn't she?"

Harry nodded.

Gabe wrapped his arm around her and pulled her in until her head was on his shoulder. The sun was beginning to set and the sky was orange and the air smelled clean.

"It's a good thing, Harry, this falling in love. It's messy sometimes, confusing definitely, and occasionally incredibly painful. But in the end, when the pieces all slide together, it's miraculous and wonderful and the most stunningly beautiful thing you've ever seen. And the best part is, it can happen to anyone. Not just rich and beautiful people, but to an ordinary Joe on the street. We all share it, no matter where you're from or who you are. It's like this beautiful meal that we all get a part of."

"You make it sound so perfect," Harry said.

Gabe snorted. "It's definitely not perfect. Sab snores like an elephant."

"She does?"

"She does. But it doesn't seem to matter. I think that's how you know it's love. The little things are important, and yes, the snoring irritates me, but it pales in comparison to anything else, you know?"

"Maybe I'm starting to understand."

"This wedding has me at sixes and sevens," Gabe said uncertainly. "I feel like it's a lot of pressure and I'm afraid of a million things. I'm afraid of not being the man that Sab needs me to be. I'm afraid that I'm going to bawl like a baby when she walks down the aisle. I'm afraid that she's going to change her mind and not walk down the aisle at all." He sighed. "All I want is to wake up and already be married."

Harry took his hand. "Come on then, let's get you married. Or at least rehearsed to get married. I'm a little confused about what's happening tonight. Are we rehearsing having dinner or what?"

Gabe laughed. "The celebrant is going to walk us all through what we have to do and then we get to eat. It'll be fun, I hope."

"Then lead on, MacDuff," Harry said, pulling him up off the bench. "Elsie and I are right here with you." She hooked her arm into his. "Did I tell you that I got a bow tie for Else so that she'll look the part."

Gabe laughed. "You didn't, she must hate it."

They walked arm in arm into the hotel and Harry tried to give her full attention to Gabe and what was happening. But at the back of her mind she could only think one thing.

She was in love with Emily.

Everything Gabe had said made sense.

And she wasn't afraid, far from it. She was excited and happy and thought she might burst with the truth of it.

Harry Lorde in love, who would have thought?

THE EVENING WAS kind of fun. Watching Sabrina boss her sisters down the aisle made Harry understand better what Emily had tried to explain about their sniping relationship. Watching Gabe try to dance his first dance with Sab was flat out hilarious. And watching the entire rehearsal was touching in a way that Harry didn't know she could be touched.

Add in the fact that Emily was only ever a heartbeat away, that they shared fleeting smiles and brushed hands whenever they could, and Harry was starting to think that maybe life couldn't get better.

Well, maybe it could a little. Maybe it was time she told Emily exactly how she felt. Maybe she needed to share this excitement with Emily herself.

All she needed was an opportunity to do so.

So when Emily appeared behind her chair and hissed into her ear, Harry almost thought that she might be about to declare love as well. Except when she turned around, Emily's face was annoyed, angry even.

"What?" Harry asked.

"I just checked the refrigerators. The temp was up again."

Harry scraped her chair back. The meal was coming to an end. Several people had already gone up to bed. She glanced over to where Gabe was sitting with Sab, halfway through a glass of wine and already looking sleepy. Then she nodded.

"Let me say good night and then we'll deal with it."

"Deal with it how?" asked Emily.

Harry shrugged. "We're going to have to keep watch all night, aren't we?"

CHAPTER
TWENTY SIX

"I can't believe we're going to stay awake all night watching over refrigerators," Emily grumbled.

"Try and pretend that you're Nancy Drew," Harry said, sliding down the wall and sitting next to her.

"I'm not feeling very teenage detective right now," said Emily, her hand creeping around Harry's back and circling her waist. "I'm definitely feeling much more adult than that."

Harry laughed. "Interesting things do happen in the dark, you know."

"If memory serves me right, interesting things happened in the light this afternoon."

She didn't know what she'd expected. Maybe nothing. Harry had been a virgin, after all. All she'd known was that she wanted her, that being with Harry made her feel good. And then being with Harry had made her feel really good. Especially good.

Except it wasn't just the physical things, was it? Sitting right here on the cool tiled floor of a dark corridor keeping watch over some stupid refrigerators felt pretty good too. Which all added up to something. Feelings, that's what it added up to.

Feelings that were... not exactly unwelcome now that she came to think about it.

Alright, so she'd wanted her big moment, her kiss under the

Christmas tree, her boombox out in the yard, her kisscam at the big football game. But it seemed like love had perhaps snuck up on her, crept in like a thief in the night until it was just standing over her bed waiting to be noticed.

Emily's heart skipped a beat and Harry snuggled in closer to her.

Was it so bad?

Not at all. Not in the slightest, actually.

Of course, there was the question of what exactly she should do about it. She'd be leaving the entire country pretty soon and that was non-negotiable. But love overcame bigger obstacles than that, didn't it?

She squeezed Harry a little tighter. Was she sure?

Who could be sure though? She knew that she definitely wanted more of Harry, she didn't want to say goodbye for good. She closed her eyes and tried thinking about Savannah. A small shiver of desire went through her, but then Harry was letting a hand trail across her thigh, so that could be the cause.

Either way, she and Harry were going to have to have a conversation. Was a cool, dark corridor an appropriate place for a State of the Relationship talk?

"I'm assuming that you don't go around fighting crime when you're at home," Harry said, interrupting Emily's thoughts.

Emily laughed. "No, not generally."

"So what do you do then?" Harry asked, turning slightly so that her breath was warm on Emily's cheek.

"I told you, I'm a vet. I go to work in the morning in a great little clinic that I love. Then I come home in the evening and do the normal stuff. Go to the gym, see friends. I like cooking."

"See, that's something I'd never have known about you," Harry said. "Being in a hotel and all there hasn't been much need for cooking."

"What about you then?" Emily asked, starting to enjoy this game. Harry had a point, they barely knew each other in real life.

Harry shrugged. "I'm a freelance writer. I spend a lot of time at my desk or researching things. When I'm not writing I'm walking Elsie or seeing friends, the usual. I like reading, though not much crime or romance, I prefer a good thriller. And, um, let me see... I like roller skating."

"For real?" Emily laughed.

"For real," Harry said, her voice lower. "And this stake out is going to be a huge bust if we don't keep it down, we're scaring off all the criminals."

There were five fridges in total. Three close to where they were sitting, and two further away down the corridor, but still in sight.

"And you don't... you don't live with anyone or anything like that?" Harry whispered quite anxiously.

Emily squeezed her again. "If you're asking whether I'm a cad and cheating already, the answer's no. I'm not going to pretend that I've sat around waiting for Sav to notice me my whole life. There have been others. But no one currently."

She scratched her nose, nervous to say what she wanted to say next.

"And um, I know that you haven't been with anyone, but would there be room in your life for someone do you think? I mean, one day?"

The question hung in the air and Emily almost wished that she could pull it back in and unsay it because Harry's silence went on far too long.

"You don't have to answer," Emily whispered sadly after a few seconds.

"Shh," Harry said. A hand clutched at Emily's hand. "Hush, look, there, there's someone coming, isn't there?"

Emily squinted into the darkness and saw movement. "Yes, yes, I think there is." She looked up at Harry. "What are we going to do?"

"Wait," breather Harry. "Just wait."

The figure loomed through the darkness and Emily felt Harry stiffen beside her. Then there was a burst of movement. The figure stopped and tapped at the gauge on the front of the furthest fridge and Harry exploded into action.

Before Emily could even stand up, Harry was racing down the hall, barreling into the dark figure who made an 'oof' sound as Harry hit him.

"What do I do?" Emily said, racing up to them.

"How about you let me go?" said a voice from under Harry that sounded vaguely familiar.

"How about I don't," Harry said. She struggled up, the man's wrists pinned together by her hands. "Told you I liked a good thriller," she grinned up at Emily.

But Emily was already beginning to recognize who Harry was holding. "You," she said.

"Yeah, me," said the bartender.

"It's the bartender," Emily helpfully told Harry.

"The bartender did it?" asked Harry. "Not as catchy as the butler did it, but it'll do."

"I didn't do anything, and I do have a name, you know."

"You do?" asked Harry and Emily at the same time.

"It's Tony, and if you'll let me actually sit up I'll tell you whatever it is you want to know, because I honestly haven't done a fucking thing."

"IT'S THE STAFF room," Tony said grudgingly showing them into a room lined with lockers on two sides and a kitchenette opposite them. "Want a cuppa?"

"Wouldn't say no," Harry said just as Emily elbowed her.

"What if it's poisoned?" Emily hissed.

"Jesus," Tony rolled his eyes. "I told you. I've done nothing. Sit down and let me put the kettle on and you can tell me what the hell the two of you are up to."

Emily narrowed her eyes. "You first, scumbag."

"Unnecessary," said Harry.

Tony sat down and held up both hands. "Alright, alright, I'll admit it. It's not serious."

"What's not serious?" Emily asked.

Tony looked confused. "The fling," he said. "That's all it is, a fling. I mean, I'm a red-blooded man, and you'd be surprised how often the tourists throw themselves at me, it's not really my fault."

Emily privately thought that Tony wouldn't exactly discourage someone hitting on him. "A fling. With Savannah, I assume." She cleared her throat. "You do know that she's going around telling everyone that you're engaged."

Tony at least had the grace to look shame-faced. "Yeah, well, I had a few too many, and she was upset about her sister's wedding and all, and, well, it sort of just happened." He cheered up a little. "But she's back off to America soon, so it won't be a problem."

"Won't be a problem?" Emily shrieked. "What about her? What about her feelings?"

Tony rolled his eyes again. "It's not like she loves me. She just wanted someone to show off at the wedding. She's good fun is Sav, but she's not exactly the marrying type, is she? She made me promise to take my shirt off at the reception when we dance so people can see my muscles."

Emily was about to open her mouth but Harry put a hand on her arm. "Can we get to the point here. You were messing with the fridge in the corridor, why?"

"Because someone else has," Tony responded immediately.

Harry looked at Emily puzzled, then turned back to Tony. "What do you mean?"

"Exactly what I said. Some bugger's been messing with the fridges, turning the temperatures up and such."

"And you care about this because?" asked Emily.

"Listen, I might not be rich like you lot, but I've got a job I'm proud of. Tending bar isn't as easy as you might think. Anyway, I'm in charge of the bar at the wedding tomorrow and some of my stuff will be in those fridges. Drink garnishes and the like, plus my ice will be in those freezers. So yeah, I've got an interest in keeping the fridges running like they're supposed to."

Emily blew out a breath. She didn't like the guy, but he obviously wasn't the person they were looking for. "Any idea who's been messing with the refrigerators?" she asked.

"Not a monkey's. Could be anyone I suppose. Could be you two for that matter."

"It's not us," Harry said. "We were doing the same as you, keeping an eye on things. There have been a few things going on, some kind of sabotage of the wedding, we've been... investigating."

"Regular little Miss Marple, aren't you?" Tony sniffed. "Now, if you don't mind, I'm going back to work. Some of us have a job to do." He eyed the two women. "I'll be looking after the fridges."

He pushed his chair back and left.

"Do we trust him?" Harry asked Emily.

"Yes," Emily said reluctantly. "He's not exactly a charmer, but I think he's telling the truth."

"So what now?" Harry asked. She was sitting under the light so that it caught the red highlights in her hair. Her eyes looked heavy with tiredness and Emily could swear that her lips were still swollen from kissing.

"Now I think I take you to bed," Emily said.

Harry's eyebrows rose. "That's an idea I could get behind."

Emily stood up and gestured for Harry to go through the door first. There'd be time for conversations later, she told herself. In the meantime, there were more important things to do. Like watching Harry's behind as she walked through the door. Emily's lips twitched into a smile. She could get quite addicted to Harry Lorde.

CHAPTER TWENTY SEVEN

"You look so beautiful," Mrs. Laretto was already crying.

Emily could see Sabrina's reflection in the mirror and she did look beautiful. Her dress was clean again, she was positively glowing, and she seemed calm enough sitting on the edge of a hotel bed.

"Stay still," said the hairdresser with a growl.

Emily let her head be dragged back as the woman aggressively combed her hair.

"Yeah, you look okay," Savannah said, looking at Sabrina critically. "A bit pale though."

"Mom," Sabrina said. "Sav's starting again."

"Savannah, if you don't have anything nice to say today of all days then I don't know what to do with you," said their mother.

"Have her adopted," offered Sara.

"She's too old," Sabrina said. "Unfortunately."

Savannah stuck her bottom lip out and for a second Emily actually thought that she might fight this one out. Then she smiled a little.

"Yeah, you look good, sis," she said, coming to sit next to Sabrina on the bed. "Really good."

"Thank you," Sabrina said grudgingly.

Sav looked down at the floor. "You're lucky."

"I know, I know, big fancy wedding and coming all the way to Scotland and all the rest of it," said Sabrina.

"No, I meant you're lucky with Gabe," said Savannah. "He's nice. And he obviously loves you. I hope that one day I find someone who loves me as much as Gabe loves you."

Sabrina was quiet for a second, then she pulled Sav in close. "You will."

Emily blinked back tears, only partially because the hairdresser seemed to be pulling her hair out at the roots. Savannah was a good person at heart, she'd always known that. Maybe she was starting to grow up a little now.

And oddly that felt… neutral.

She was glad for Sav, glad for the others. But there was no resounding applause or anything, no desire to jump straight into Sav's arms. She took a breath, then another, both breaths coming easily, no sign of it catching in her throat or butterflies in her stomach.

Then she thought of Harry and her stomach responded by doing a somersault and when she looked in the mirror again she was grinning.

There. That had to prove it. She and Harry were meant to be, right? Well, other than the fact that a couple of days from now they'd be an ocean apart. Her stomach somersaulted again, this time backward, and her grin faded.

"That's the best I can do," the hairdresser said.

Emily looked in the mirror. Her blonde hair was scraped back, her eyes looked too big with make-up, her nose looked too sharp. She looked almost like someone else altogether.

"Sabrina Laretto!" screeched Mrs. Laretto.

Emily spun around in time to see Sabrina let go of Savannah to reveal a streak of Sav's foundation on the shoulder of her previously white dress.

"It's fine, it's fine," Emily said.

"Oh shit," Savannah said.

"Club soda," Mrs. Laretto said.

"I'll get it," said Emily, going to the door.

"I'll help," said Sav, running after her.

* * *

"How are you this old having been to boarding school, university, and several finance jobs, and you still make a pig's ear of tying a decent tie?" Harry asked.

Gabe snorted. "My dad tied my tie on my first day of school and I never untied it."

"You mean you didn't wash your tie for twelve years?"

"No," Gabe said indignantly. "We didn't have to wear a uniform for sixth form."

"So ten years then?"

"Maybe."

"Gabriel Hamilton, you're a pig," Harry said fondly, finishing his tie by straightening it up.

"I am rather, aren't I?" Gabe said cheerfully. "Makes you wonder how I bagged someone as amazing as Sab really."

"Got over your cold feet then have you?" asked Harry, turning to the mirror and straightening her own tie.

"I don't like all the fuss," Gabe said, standing behind her and putting his hands on her shoulders. "And I don't like feeling alone in all this, without my parents. But then I realized that it's one day out of my life. I love Sab and I'll do anything to be with her. And, well..." He stopped for a second.

To her horror, Harry saw a glint in his eyes. He wasn't going to cry, was he? What was she supposed to do?

He sniffed. "I've got you and Elsie standing by, so I'm not alone, am I?"

For an instant, Harry regretted every second she'd spent away from him this week. She should have paid more attention. But he'd always seemed so busy with Sabrina's family. On instinct, she turned around and wrapped her arms around his stolid middle, hugging him tight.

"You've always got me," she mumbled into his shirt.

"Hey, steady on there old chap," Gabe said. But his arms were around her too and he clasped her to him for a long second before letting her go. "Oh, bugger."

"What?" Harry asked, leaning back.

"I've left the boutonnieres in the fridge downstairs."

"I'll go get them," Harry said. "You keep an eye on Elsie."

Elsie was lying on the floor, her bow tie already tied. She opened one eye and looked at them both before settling down to sleep again.

"Alright, but the flower fridge is broken, remember? So they're on a shelf in one of the catering fridges in the corridor behind the reception room."

"I know where the fridges are," Harry called as she left. And she made a note to herself to check the temperatures while she was there.

❈ ❈ ❈

"He's not here." Sav tapped her fingers on the bar.

"I'm sure he'll be back in a minute. I mean, he's got to be preparing for the reception." Emily looked around the room. It was ready, or more or less. The tables were set, the flowers were fresh. Only the guests and the bartender were missing.

It was odd to think that just a few hours from now Sabrina would be married.

"Listen," Sav said. "I need you to do something for me."

"Mmm?" said Emily, only half listening.

"Kiss me."

It took a second for those words to sink in and when they did, Emily was quite sure her brain hadn't processed them correctly. "What?"

Sav sighed. "Tony's losing interest. I'm not an idiot, I know we're not really getting married. But I'm not letting him dump me, no way. So here's the deal: you kiss me. He sees, gets jealous, then a few hours from now I get to dump him. See? Plus, you get to kiss me, so..."

"So what exactly?" Emily asked, still in shock.

"So don't pretend like you haven't wanted to do it for years," Sav said. She batted her eyelashes. "Come on, Em. Do it for me. I'm not gonna let a bartender dump me. I need to get him all excited, then I dump him, that's how it works."

Emily, who had never actually seen someone bat their eyelashes before, was somewhat in shock.

Savannah rolled her eyes. "Emily Jackson, I want you to kiss me," she declared.

"This is—"

"I know you want to, I know you've always wanted to, I'm offering you a golden opportunity, a one time deal."

"Harry," Emily managed to squeak out.

"Like she'll ever have to know."

Emily closed her eyes. She hated that this was happening. A week ago she'd have jumped at the chance, but now...

Savannah stepping in closer, put a hand on her waist, and Emily wasn't made of stone, her skin started to prickle.

"Kiss me, Emily Jackson," Savannah murmured.

✳ ✳ ✳

For a start, she was eavesdropping, which never led to any good, Harry certainly knew that. But then, who made that rule exactly?

There obviously had to be occasions when overhearing information was to someone's advantage. Like... like if Lincoln had overheard his assassin bragging about what he was going to do, for example. Or if... She struggled to think of another example. Probably because her brain was shrieking for her attention, trying to get her to focus.

It wasn't meant to be this way. But then, what ever was?

She'd come downstairs, cut through the back corridor of

the hotel toward the fridges, before remembering that going back through the reception hall would be faster. Now she had the delicate boutonnieres in her hand and she was leaning up against a cracked open door seeing and hearing something that she really shouldn't be.

"Emily Jackson, I want you to kiss me," Savannah had said. Her voice was high and piercing, easy to hear, easy to understand.

So Harry had peeked. She'd peeked and heard and she knew that she wasn't supposed to know. She knew that Emily hadn't actually kissed her. At least not yet. It didn't matter though, did it? Because she'd been deluding herself for long enough.

She wasn't being over-dramatic here. She wasn't going to flounce out of the hotel. She wasn't going to throw a fit. But she was, for the first time this week, going to be wholly logical and sensible about things.

Whatever she had with Emily, it wasn't destined to last. And whether Emily kissed Savannah or not, it didn't really matter. What mattered was that there would always be a Savannah, or someone like her, and Emily would always have that choice. And Harry wouldn't be second best.

Besides, how could she stop any of this? A couple of days from now, she and Emily would be heading their separate ways and then what?

So it was all in all better that she stopped dreaming. Stopped pretending. This had been nice, was nice, but it would end when they both walked out of this hotel.

Harry took a deep breath and looked at the flowers in her hands. So delicate, so fragile. Then she walked away, not waiting to see whether Emily kissed Savannah or not. Because it really didn't matter.

CHAPTER TWENTY EIGHT

S urprisingly, the wedding itself went off without a hitch. Unsurprisingly, Emily cried her eyes out and had to retire to her room to re-paint her face before the reception started in earnest.

As she carefully re-applied her mascara she thought about how beautiful Sabrina had looked, she'd thought about how romantic it all was, and, oddly, she'd thought about Harry. Because if there was one thing that not kissing Savannah had taught her, it was that her feelings for Harry ran far deeper than she'd imagined.

Not that she hadn't been tempted. She was only human, after all. And she'd been in love with Savannah for decades. Or perhaps in lust, or maybe in some in-between kind of fantasy world. She wasn't quite sure, but she was sure that, just like that, it was all over.

When she'd walked away from Savannah she'd felt a weight leave her shoulders, she'd felt lighter and younger than she'd felt in forever. And she couldn't wait to tell Harry about it.

Of course, by the time they'd solved the problem of Sabrina's messy dress, yet again, time was getting shorter and shorter. And then she'd had to go to the little chapel, and she'd seen Harry waiting at the altar with Gabe and her heart had exploded with pride. Then she'd seen Sab finally walk down the aisle, followed by Sara and Savannah looking like little angels, and the tears had started.

All of which meant that she hadn't had a chance to say a word to Harry all afternoon. She looked around, Elsie's basket was empty in the corner, she'd sort of been hoping that Harry would slope off upstairs for a break and they'd see each other, but to no end.

She checked herself over in the mirror one more time and smiled, smiled because she couldn't help it, because the thought of just seeing Harry made her smile, and then she got up to go downstairs.

The reception room looked different now the lights were dimmed and the place was full. Tony was tending bar, Savannah was draped over said bar, the happy couple were at the top table, along with Sara who rolled her eyes in Emily's direction, and Elsie, who was staring hopefully at a plate of chicken wings. But no Harry.

Frustrated, Emily went to get herself a drink. "Just a Coke," she told Tony.

"Put a bit of excitement in there for you?" he offered.

She shook her head but smiled anyway. It was his way of forgiving her for the night before, she could see that. "Nah, I'm good, thanks."

"Fridges are all alright," he said as he popped the cap on a glass bottle. "Been watching them myself."

"Cool," said Emily, turning to survey as much of the room as she could.

"Your partner in crime is over there," Tony said, pointing with one hand while handing her the Coke with the other.

"Dance with me," Savannah said, sliding around the bar.

"The dancing hasn't started yet," Emily pointed out.

Sav sighed. "I know that. I meant later. Have a dance with me. Please?"

Again, Emily got the impression that this was some kind of apology. Sav was trying her best. She nodded. "I'll think about it, alright?" She was rewarded by a bright flash of a smile and she grinned in return. "I only said I'd think about it."

"Fine, go, think," Sav laughed. "I'll see you later."

But Emily was already heading in Harry's direction.

Even from all the way across the room she'd recognize her. The long, lanky body, the way she seemed so at ease in her suit, the way it fitted her just so. Harry was no typical woman, but then Emily had always seen that at least, she'd known from the start that Harry was someone special.

Maybe she hadn't quite known how special she was though. Maybe she'd down-played things, maybe she'd been so caught up in Savannah still that she'd missed what she should have seen from the very beginning. Harry was the special kind of special. The kind that came along once in a lifetime.

The kind that Emily was more and more sure that she shouldn't let go.

Fine, there were going to be practicalities and logistics and at some point someone was going to have to move. But those things didn't need to happen in a day. First, she had to be honest with herself and honest with Harry about what was going on here.

"Hi," she said, sidling up to Harry.

"Hi," Harry said, smiling back at her.

"Um… what's a girl like you doing in a place like this?" Emily tried.

Harry laughed. "Smooth, very smooth."

"I try," said Emily. She leaned against the wall next to Harry. "So, the wedding went well."

"No sabotage," agreed Harry. "Which is a good thing. I thought it was beautiful. I might have had to blink a tear away."

"The cool, logical Harry Lorde?" teased Emily. "No way."

"Yes," Harry said, her voice tinged with something that Emily didn't quite understand. "Yes, I think I did. It's beautiful, isn't it? When the world lines up like that, when things really come together. I don't think I've ever seen Gabe so happy."

"Sabrina neither."

Harry smiled. "He's been without a family for so long, it makes me happy to see him starting a new one."

"It's a bit soon for that."

"Do you think?" Harry asked, watching the bride and groom. "I think there'll be little footsteps sooner rather than later."

Emily blew out a breath and sucked in another one. "Listen, Harry, I think we should talk."

Harry looked down at her and nodded. "Yes, I rather think we should." She sighed. "I'll be honest, I was sort of thinking that perhaps we could just leave things, but that wouldn't be right, would it."

"Leave things?" Emily asked confused.

"Come on, over here," said Harry. She pointed them over to a small table that was still unoccupied. It was in the far corner away from the festivities, and they had some amount of privacy.

Emily took another of those deep breaths and wondered just where to begin. Did she start by saying the L word? No, it was far too soon for that. That would definitely freak Harry out. But she couldn't stand by and not admit to deeper feelings. Perhaps she could tell Harry that she really liked her? Or that she had feelings?

That sounded pathetic. She took her seat and turned it a little so that she was facing Harry. The words would come, she thought, if she'd learned one thing from all those romance novels it was that at the right time, the words would just appear.

"I heard," Harry said.

"What?" Emily blinked, unsure of what was happening.

Harry laid a hand on hers. "I was getting flowers from the fridges and I overheard you and Savannah in here earlier. I shouldn't have eavesdropped, but I did anyway, mostly. I won't apologize for it, because it made me realize something."

Emily's entire body started to tremble. Please let it be the right thing, she prayed. Please let Harry have realized what I realized. But she knew in her heart that Harry hadn't.

"Harry, it was nothing, just Sav being an idiot, I didn't even—"

"It doesn't matter," Harry said. "I didn't stick around long enough to see what happened at the end, but it honestly doesn't matter, Emily."

"Of course it matters! I didn't kiss Savannah, I swear I didn't."

"No, it doesn't matter." Harry shuffled her chair in. "Emily, I've had an amazing time. I'll never forget this, how could I? You have been patient and kind and amazing, and you're beautiful and a truly good person."

"Then why are you dumping me?" Emily couldn't help but say.

Harry smiled wryly. "Let's not call it dumping. It's not really, because let's be honest, we were never really together, not just for these few days. We've had a lovely time, Emily, but life is going to get in the way."

Emily blinked, feeling tears threatening again.

"That's what I realized when I saw you and Savannah. You have a whole life back home, one that includes her in one way or another, and I have a whole life here, and those lives are very different. Very different from a week-long fantasy in the Scottish highlands."

Emily's stomach flipped over and she stared miserably at their clasped hands. "Harry, I think we can try," she began.

Harry squeezed her hand. "Maybe we could. But why? Why spoil this lovely week by eking it out into months of long distance nonsense? We barely know each other, Emily. We've never seen each other in our real lives. It's better this way."

Maybe she was right, Emily thought. Maybe this was the right thing to do. Maybe they shouldn't ruin things. She looked up at Harry's sweet serious face and tried to imagine not seeing it again. She couldn't. But then again, could she imagine seeing it every morning?

"Don't let's end this being angry or sad with each other," Harry said quietly. "Let's be friends, let's have fun here, and let's never forget."

Emily laughed sadly. "You know, for someone with no relationship experience, you're doing pretty well with the whole break-up thing."

"I'm just being realistic," Harry said. "I treasure what we had, I truly do. But it's almost time to go back to real life. Because that's what life is, real, no matter what all those romance novels might have taught you."

Emily took a breath. "This isn't what I wanted to happen."

"You can't go into something planning for the end already," Harry said. "And I do hope you understand. I'm not angry with you or anything."

"I understand," Emily said.

But her eyes were on the top table, watching Gabe and Sab feed each other pieces of chicken, watching as they smiled and laughed, so perfect together, so happy. They'd had their fairy tale ending. They'd met abroad and overcome obstacles and made their dreams come true.

So why exactly couldn't she and Harry?

She was just about to ask Harry that exact question when there was a loud crack and a shriek. They both turned just as the large wedding cake on its own small table began to tilt and then to slide.

CHAPTER TWENTY NINE

Harry watched on in horror as Savannah's shadow blocked the tilting wedding cake from view for a moment. It took a second for her to realize that the cake had stopped sliding, that Sav must be holding the table up somehow. Then a dozen people, Emily among them, rushed to save the cake and Harry was left sitting alone.

Yet another sabotage attempt. She supposed it didn't matter that much anymore, after all, Gabe and Sabrina were married now and she and Emily were just friends. Friends that probably shouldn't spend time running Nancy Drew investigations and spending too much time together.

Elsie yipped and Harry patted her knee so that the dog rested her front paws on her leg. "Where've you been?" she asked. "Begging for chicken, I assume?"

Elsie's big brown eyes looked up at her and Harry patted her head. Her and Elsie. That's how it should be. Elsie was a sure thing, a dead cert. Rely on Elsie and she'd never be let down.

Which made her think that maybe her eavesdropping had done more harm than good. Maybe that was what had provoked all this more than the whole real life interfering thing.

"I did the right thing," Harry told Elsie. "I definitely did."

The host of people trying to save the cake let out a cheer and then there was a round of applause. Harry looked over to see that the cake had been carried successfully to a new table.

"Thank god for that," Gabe said, pulling out the chair next to her and sitting down. "I thought that cake was a goner for a second there."

"But it looks like a successful rescue was made," Harry said, trying to cheer herself up for Gabe's sake. This was his day.

"Indeed it was. I wish it hadn't happened though. Sab already thinks the wedding's been cursed somehow."

Harry shook her head. "No, someone's been sabotaging it. I'm sure of that now."

Gabe looked at her and frowned. "Seriously? Who would do that?"

Harry shrugged. "Not a clue. But the important thing is that the wedding is done, you're safely married and whoever it was that was messing with things has failed in their mission, right?"

"I suppose," said Gabe, looking doubtful about that.

"But you are safely married," Harry said softly. "Congratulations."

"I am, aren't I?" A grin spread across Gabe's face. "It feels odd... Complete somehow, if that makes sense? Sort of like I'm fulfilling some kind of destiny, like in a fantasy novel. Like this was all supposed to happen and now I'm ready to live happily ever after." He laughed at himself. "And I sound like an idiot."

"You sound like a man in love," Harry said stoutly. "And I like your tender side, so don't be an arse about it and pretend like you're not feeling anything."

Gabe shot her a sideways look. "You saw the tears then?"

Harry nodded. She'd had to bite her own lip when she saw Gabe's eyes sparkling at the altar. "And there's nothing wrong with them. There's nothing wrong with showing emotion." She smiled at him. "Though I suppose Sabrina won't let you forget that."

"No," Gabe said. "I'm sure she won't. She keeps me in line, I like that. She doesn't let me get away with nonsense."

"She's good for you."

"Which is the point, isn't it?" asked Gabe, turning to her. "Finding someone who's good for you. Finding someone who doesn't just make you a better person but who makes you want to be a better person."

Harry nodded slowly. "Yes, yes, I suppose it is."

She looked back at the wedding cake. Savannah was being toasted, lauded for saving the cake. Idly she wondered if Emily had been wrong. Sure, Sav had saved the cake. But had it been a feint? Maybe she was closer than she'd meant to be when sabotaging the table and had had to save the cake in order to save face?

Or perhaps a part of Harry still wanted Sav to be guilty of the sabotage because... because she was jealous, she realized. Not because Emily still loved Sav, although maybe she did. But because Sav had had Emily's attentions for so long, had bathed in her presence for so long, and had been able to grow so accustomed to her that she could ignore her.

Harry shook her head at her own stupidity. Being jealous when she wasn't even in a relationship was foolish.

"Penny for your thoughts?" Gabe asked.

"They're worth more than that," responded Harry automatically, a running joke she and Gabe had had since college.

"I'll give you tuppence, final offer," grinned Gabe.

For a second, Harry considered confiding in him. But this was supposed to be his day. She shouldn't bring him down. "Nothing," she said. "Nothing."

He quirked an eyebrow and looked like he was going to push matters but then he grinned at something. "Hey, look."

She followed where he was pointing.

"It looks like you're going to get your room back," he said.

Two figures were clutched in each others' arms, dancing to the quiet music that the DJ had started to play. Harry squinted and made out the faces of Aunt Lacey and Uncle Dirk, apparently reconciled. And then, to her horror, she felt her eyes filling up with tears.

"Oh, Jesus," Gabe said, plucking a napkin from the table. "Oh, come on, Harry, don't cry."

"I'm not," Harry said, sniffing and furiously wiping her eyes with the napkin.

"Yes, you most certainly are." Gabe hesitated. "Um, it's not because... It's not because I got married, right? You're not about to declare your undying love for me or anything, are you?"

This made Harry laugh through her diminishing tears. "You should be so lucky."

Gabe looked slightly relieved. "There is still the penis thing," he said.

"I should hope so," said Harry. "Sab will have a disappointing wedding night if not."

"So what is it?" Gabe asked, leaning forward. Then he caught sight of the dancing couple again and put two and two together. "Ah, you and Emily."

Harry nodded. "We are no more."

"I'm sorry, Harry, truly I am. She seemed really nice."

"And I didn't fall down stairs in front of her or anything," added Harry.

"Want to tell me what happened?"

Harry let her breath escape. "I ended things," she said simply. "It's for the best. She's about to fly back off to America, I'm here. It was fun, but this was a holiday romance, I shouldn't pretend it was anything more."

Gabe pressed his lips together and raised his eyebrows.

"I know, I know," Harry said. "But you and Sabrina had longer together than a week. And this really is for the best. It's not like we're fated mates or anything."

Gabe shook his head. "You can be a bit of an idiot, Harry."

Harry felt stung. "So can you."

"No, I mean it," Gabe said. "You're making a martyr of yourself, you're making yourself miserable for no reason other than something that might happen in the future, and that's stupid."

"Avoiding pain, avoiding the inevitable decline of the

relationship, avoiding drawing things out is stupid?"

"We all die at the end," said Gabe. "If that's the way you're going to look at things, then why bother getting out of bed at all? There's no happy ever after, there's only happy for now. And if you're going to turn away the first woman that's ever made you happy, then you're stupider than I gave you credit for."

"Cheers," Harry said. "Thanks very much."

Gabe took a breath and she didn't know if he was going to apologize or keep going, and she didn't find out because Sab appeared at his side.

"Come on, husband," she drawled. "It's first dance time, and then I can finally get out of this dress."

"That sounds promising," Gabe said, taking her hand and standing up. He looked back at Harry, but Sabrina was dragging him away already, and he didn't have time to say more.

Which was probably for the best because Harry really didn't want to argue with him. Around her, people began to collect around the dance floor and she realized that other than the immediate family she really didn't know anyone. She'd spent all her time with Emily.

Elsie sighed and lay down at her feet and Harry closed her eyes. This had all been experience, she told herself. Experience was good. And ending things with Emily was good, the right thing.

So why did it feel so terrible? Why did she feel lonely and sad and like going back to her life in London wasn't as tempting as it normally was? She thought about calling her dad, but it was getting late and he'd be watching Eastenders by now.

Savannah was still standing by the cake table. Harry watched her. Had she really been so jealous of her sister getting married that she'd tried to ruin it all?

She was the only suspect that they had, that Harry had, and she couldn't shake the feeling that Emily had hidden her motive to protect her.

It just all made so much sense. Sav had had plenty of opportunities to get around the hotel as both a member of the bridal party and someone involved with a member of staff.

Then two things happened at once.

Harry saw James in his smart suit come to congratulate the bride and groom and present them with a large knife to cut the cake with. She saw his eyes tighten as Savannah loudly regaled him with the tale of saving the cake. And then, behind all this, she saw the large room door open and three silhouettes appear, two women and a man.

Suddenly, she knew what had been happening.

She looked around, trying to find Emily in the crowds of people, but she couldn't see her anywhere.

Elsie grumbled and shifted at her feet, opening one eye before going back to sleep. And Harry nodded. It didn't matter, did it? Whatever the truth was wasn't important now. She had no one to share it with.

For a moment she could imagine Emily sitting next to her, her eyes wide as Harry explained her theory. Then she shook her head and the image was gone. Emily wasn't there and wouldn't be there. Harry's eyes burned again and she screwed up Gabe's napkin and held on tight to stop herself crying.

CHAPTER THIRTY

E mily wished she drank. It would give her something to do with her hands, and drowning her sorrows in sparkling water wasn't particularly effective. She sat at the bar and watched as people danced and chatted and laughed, and wondered why she felt so empty.

Harry was just being sensible. Sensible like she always was. And she was right. Continuing on with a long distance relationship based on the few days that they'd spent together was ridiculous. Totally crazy. Emily completely agreed with her in theory. In practice, however, things were different.

In practice, Emily wanted to hug Harry. She wanted to sit next to her and trade jokes. She wanted to pet Elsie's head and complain about eating chicken at a wedding and theorize about who had tried to destroy the cake and... And so many other things.

Which was weird because it was almost like she and Harry had known each other for their entire lives rather than just a few days.

To make things weirder, she was pretty sure she wanted to take Harry home with her, to pack her and Elsie in a suitcase and get them set up in her apartment and then just to go on living this wonderful charmed little life that they'd had for the last week.

She blew out a breath. But Harry was right. Harry was the

sensible one. These feelings would fade after a few days apart, right? And then... Then she'd be back to normal.

She just had to get through the next few hours, then the next day, then the next week, and she'd be back at work and back to her real life.

"Dance with me."

Savannah appeared out of nowhere and Emily looked up at her. Her dark hair was tangled artfully over one shoulder, her eyes were expertly made up. Her lips were pouty and kissable and right then, right there, Emily saw what she really was. A big, insecure kid.

"No, thank you."

"Come on, you promised."

"No, no I didn't," Emily said, just wanting to be left alone.

"Did so." Savannah put out a hand and tried to pull Emily off her bar stool, but Emily stayed put.

"I said no." Savannah pushed out her bottom lip and Emily shook her head. "You were right, you know, right to say that I'd always wanted to kiss you."

With this, Savannah grinned. "Who doesn't?"

"Me," Emily said. "Right now, I don't. Because I've had enough. Oh, I don't blame you for my stupid, teenage crush, that one's all on me. But I've defended you, Sav, defended you against all those people that said you'd never grow up, that you're a tease, that you're not good enough for me. All of that. I said you just needed time."

"Jesus, Emily—"

"But you've had time, haven't you? You've had time and you're still immature, you're still partying your life away and refusing to commit to anything sensible."

She stared hard at Savannah and then had a flash of memory. Savannah standing so close to the cake that she had to step in to save it. Which was heroic unless... Unless it was Savannah that had sabotaged the table in the first place. Savannah had been close enough to do that and perhaps she just hadn't gotten away in time and had been forced to save the cake or get caught.

Because Sav was jealous of Sabrina and Gabe, wasn't she? It was why she'd started this ridiculous charade with the bartender, it was why she was flirting around Emily, she was acting out like a child because she was jealous.

"You," Emily said, voice changing as she realized.

"Me what?" Savannah said. "Are you finally done insulting me, or do you have a few more things to say up your sleeve?"

"It was you," breathed Emily.

"What was me, for Christ's sake," Sav said, rolling her eyes. "The theft of the Mona Lisa? 9/11? Jack the Ripper? Sure, it was all me, blame me, that's what everyone does, I can take it, come on then."

"The wedding sabotage. The dress, the broken flower fridge, the temperature on the catering fridges, even the cake, that was all you. You were trying to destroy Sab's day."

"Why would I do that?"

Emily looked straight at her. "Because you're jealous. Because Sabrina has the life you can't have. Sensible, good, ambitious, and with a man who loves her for who she is."

For a long moment, Savannah stared at her, then tears glinted in her eyes, she tossed her hair over her shoulder, and she stalked off.

"Wow," Tony said, leaning over the bar. "Don't pull any punches, will ya?"

"What business of it is yours?" Emily snapped.

Tony shrugged. "It's not, particularly. But she didn't do it, you know."

"Do what?" Emily asked, eyes following Savannah as she left the hall.

"She was with me most of the night so she couldn't have messed with the fridge temps, and could you imagine Sav with screwdriver in hand sabotaging a flower fridge?" he chortled.

Emily's eyes opened wider. Fuck.

"You were too hard on her," Tony said, wiping a glass with a towel. "Sav is Sav, you can't blame a cat for being a cat. She is who she is, and maybe you all trying to change her isn't exactly the kind thing to do, you know? As for your theory that she's jealous, well..."

"She told me herself that she was," Emily put in.

"Yeah, jealous of the party and the attention maybe," Tony said. "But the rest of it? Despite this flimsy engagement I'm somehow involved in, I don't think Sav wants to get married at all. I think she's perfectly happy being herself and free."

Emily leaned on the bar and put her face in her hands. Shit. What had she done? She'd ruined a decent friendship because she was angry and upset about Harry.

Harry.

All this had been easier with Harry. Harry had talked her out of crazy ideas, Harry had been logical and sensible. Suddenly, she felt that her life was a little worse off without Harry in it.

"She won't have gone far," Tony said. "You could catch up with her and apologize."

"How do you know?" Emily said.

Tony grinned. "Because that door she left through goes to a storage cupboard."

Emily didn't even thank him, she raced off after Savannah, yanking open the door just as Sav was about to open it from the other side. Hurriedly, she pushed Sav back inside the stuffy closet.

"No, wait," she said. "Wait, I need to apologize. I'm an idiot and —"

"And you're upset because you've broken up with Harry," Savannah said. She sat down on a box of something and pulled Emily down next to her.

"A little. How did you know?"

Savannah sighed. "It's kind of obvious. You always get cranky when you break up with someone, and you're conjoined twin for the week is nowhere to be seen. By the way, you're wrong about all this. I didn't do anything to the wedding, I'd never ruin Sab's big day, and I hope you know that. She's my sister and I adore her. I'd do anything for her."

"I know," Emily said sadly. "I know."

"As for the rest of it, well, you might not entirely be wrong," Savannah said quietly. "People have told me similar things. I need to grow up, find what I want to do in life, whatever else. It's just... I don't want to. It doesn't feel like me. People are always trying to box me in and I hate it."

Emily felt Savannah take her hand.

"I'm me. I like being me. Sometimes I could make better decisions, and believe it or not, I'm working on it. But I just feel like I'm constantly not good enough. What you said back there didn't exactly help."

"I'm an asshole," Emily groaned. "I took out my feelings on you and that wasn't fair."

"It wasn't," agreed Savannah. "But it also wasn't entirely unfounded. I can be a bitch. I don't think. I do things, ask things without realizing the costs of those things. Like earlier today when I asked you to kiss me. That was a selfish thing to do."

"And calling you a saboteur wasn't?" Emily said. "I'm sorry, Sav, I truly am. I was the bitch, not you."

"We can both be bitches," Sav said. She leaned her head back against the wall. "I'm thinking about moving."

"You are?"

Sav nodded. "I've got a friend down in Miami with an interior design business. She's looking for some help and, well, as much as I love my family, I thought it might be a good idea to get out from under their shadows for a little while." She grinned at Emily. "Having sisters as perfect as Sara and Sabrina isn't easy, you know."

"I think that might be a good idea," Emily said, because it sounded like it, because maybe Sav needed space to grow up, to mature.

Savannah took a deep breath. "I'm sorry."

"About what?"

"About everything. About leading you on, teasing you, I suppose. I've always known that you had a crush on me."

"Way to make me feel better."

Savannah grinned. "If it's any consolation at all, if I could fall in love with anyone, I very much hope it'll be someone like you, Emily Jackson."

And it was enough. Emily felt like a tiny hole in her heart was being mended. She hadn't realized just how hurtful it was that Sav had never returned her affections.

"If it's any consolation to you, I very much hope that I fall in love with someone very much unlike you," Emily said, smiling. "You're one of a kind, Sav, and you shouldn't have to change to make other people happy."

Savannah nodded. "I suppose I should go cancel this stupid engagement and tell my parents that I'm moving to Miami, huh?"

"Probably," Emily said.

There was a pause.

"How about that dance first?" Savannah asked.

Emily bit her lip, thinking about Harry, thinking about how much she wanted to be in Harry's arms right now, talking this over with her, and how she wouldn't be, not ever again.

"Just as friends," Sav added.

And finally, as much as she hated dancing, Emily nodded. Because maybe some human contact was better than none at all.

"Oh, and you should really get back together with Harry. She was good for you," Savannah added.

CHAPTER
THIRTY ONE

arry searched the room but there was no sign of Emily. Elsie sighed and climbed into her basket and Harry shook her head.

"You're getting old, Else, if there's no party left in you."

She grabbed dry food from her bag and left Elsie with her food and water to rest before going back out into the hotel.

There was no point being petty about things, she'd decided. Certain things did matter, like the truth. And Harry couldn't think of anyone to tell about her deductions except Emily. Emily would know what to do with her thoughts. Emily would put things into order and decide who needed to be punished and how.

She wasn't going to feel sorry for herself, she wasn't going to cry. She had made this decision, the decision to be realistic and honest about the relationship, and the onus was on her. She and Emily might not be together, but the investigation they'd started had borne fruit.

Which was odd, because Harry could distinctly remember thinking all of this was silly and somewhat adolescent. She'd agreed to it only because Emily had drawn her into it. That and Emily had agreed to be her fake girlfriend to get Gabe off her back and...

And truth was important. She shouldn't have lied to Gabe, she shouldn't have gone on with this, and she shouldn't keep information that might be important to herself. End of story. Harry wasn't naturally a game-player and she didn't intend to start now. Open and honest, that was how it had to be.

She trotted back down the stairs and still there was no sign of Emily. Harry gritted her teeth. She must still be at the reception, even though Harry thought she'd looked through the entire crowd.

She pushed back into the hall, the music a little louder now, a little more exuberant, the lights lower. How was she supposed to find anyone here?

Methodically, her inner voice told her. She took a breath and then walked over to the bar. If she sat on a bar stool she'd be high enough to see across the room and at least she'd be comfortable while she scanned the crowds.

"This seat taken?" asked a voice after Harry had been looking for all of thirty seconds.

Harry looked to see Sara standing next to her, a smile on her face. Harry felt herself start to flush. "Oh, um, yeah, er…" She gestured toward the seat and succeeded in knocking over an empty glass that someone had left sitting on the bar.

She slid off her bar stool to pick up the glass and squatted down, standing up fast enough that she cracked heads with Sara who was also attempting to pick up the glass.

"Ow, shit," Harry said, clutching her head.

"Oooo, ouch," said Sara, rubbing at hers.

"I, uh, I'm sorry, I didn't mean…" Harry lost her tongue. Very, very carefully she put the glass back on the bar, far out of her reach.

"That was quite the introduction," said Sara, grinning and still rubbing her head. "Let me get you a drink."

"I should be buying the drinks," Harry said. "Not that I want to buy you a drink. I mean, I do want to, but not in a creepy way or any kind of sort of dating thing or anything, I—"

Sara held up her hand and gestured for the bartender. "What

are you having?"

"Coke?" Harry said, trusting herself with only the one word.

Sara ordered and Harry watched her. She was shorter than her sisters, but had the same crazy dark hair, the same deep, dark eyes, the same Roman nose. Harry swallowed because her mouth had gone dry.

"Here you go," Sara said, offering her the drink.

"Thanks," said Harry, immediately putting the drink down in case she spilled it all over Sara's front.

"Do I make you nervous?" asked Sara, slipping onto the stool next to Harry's. "I really shouldn't. I'm not here to grill you about your intentions with Emily or anything, I swear."

Harry looked down at her hands. If she couldn't see Sara, things would be slightly better. "Um, it's not that. It's just…" She sighed. "I get like this when there's an attractive woman around. I always have done. It's nothing personal."

Sara laughed. "I suppose I should be flattered then." She paused for a second. "Hold on though, you're not like this when Em's around though."

Harry shook her head. "Emily's… different."

"But attractive?" asked Sara unsurely.

"Oh yes," Harry said looking up and then shifting so that she almost fell off her stool. "Definitely that. I didn't mean to imply…"

"It's alright," Sara said. "I think I get it. Emily's home."

Harry looked down at her hands again, it was safer that way. "What does that mean?"

"It's hard to explain," Sara said. "But I've always felt that way when she's around. There's something about her. Wherever she goes, she always feels like home. It's weird but comforting. Like you're safe when she's there, you know? Which is ridiculous because if anything, Emily's the one that needs to feel safe, not me. What with her history and all."

Harry nodded.

"You know about her parents and everything, right?"

Harry nodded again. She was starting to feel something

strange, something tight in her stomach, a feeling that she wanted to ignore but didn't think she should. But it was hard to identify.

"Maybe that's why Em is different," Sara said.

"She's special," Harry said.

"Damn right she is," laughed Sara. "And actually, that's sort of why I wanted to come and talk to you, if you don't mind."

"About what?" asked Harry. Sara obviously didn't know that she and Emily had split and Harry wasn't sure how to broach the subject.

"I've seen Emily with plenty of other people. I just... I want to make sure that you understand."

"Understand what?" asked Harry feeling more and more out of her depth here.

"Understand that... that she's maybe not what you think."

Harry looked up and Sara scratched her nose. "What do you mean?"

"It's easy to assume things. Like she reads all those romance books and you'd think she wants her big moment, a televised proposal or whatever. But she's not like that at all. Sometimes... sometimes she finds reality hard, because reality always has been hard for her, I think. So she squashes it away and finds comfort in romance."

"I see," Harry said. The stomach feeling was getting tighter. What was it?

"But what she really needs is someone to make reality easy for her, if you see what I mean? Someone to make real life nice enough and comfortable enough that she doesn't have to hide anywhere else."

It was wrongness, that's what it was. The stomach feeling was wrongness.

Harry let out a breath.

She couldn't do this. She wanted to do this, she wanted to call things off, she wanted to be sensible, she wanted both her and Emily to go back to their real lives. But she couldn't.

Sitting here, unable to look Sara in the face, just reminded her of what life was like with everyone that wasn't Emily. It reminded her of just how special Emily really was. And how much she didn't want to go back to how things were without Emily.

"I think I've fucked things up," she said, looking directly at Sara. "I think I've blown it."

Sara narrowed her eyes. "How?"

"I... I broke up with her. I told her we had to go back to real life and that this wouldn't work but..."

"But this is real life," Sara said gently. "Of course it is. Just because you're not at home doesn't mean that everything's a fantasy."

"What about the distance? What about—"

"Pshh," Sara interrupted. "What about the distance? It's an obstacle, sure, but you'll overcome it, that's the nature of obstacles. If you really want to, that is?"

Harry swallowed and tried to breathe. Did she really want it?

The question was so simple and so stupid she almost laughed. Of course she did, obviously she did.

"She's over there," Sara said helpfully, pointing to the dance floor.

Harry looked over to where Emily was in Savannah's arms and suddenly it did matter. The truth mattered. Emily hadn't kissed Savannah, but even if she had, Harry didn't think she would have minded. Because she knew in the same way that she knew how to breathe that Emily was where she belonged.

And if Emily was where she belonged, then Harry must be where Emily belonged.

That was the only logic to the whole situation.

She watched Emily and Savannah dance, watched how graceful they looked, watched how Emily laughed.

"Don't be fooled," Sara said in her ear. "It might seem romantic, being in love with your best friend's sister and all, but it's only a fantasy."

Harry nodded. "I get it," she said.

"So what are you going to do?" asked Sara.

Harry blew out a breath. "Win her back."

"Win her back?"

Harry nodded again. "She might not need the romance, but she wants it, she deserves it. And if romance is what she wants, then that's what I'm going to give her."

"Okay," Sara said slowly. "What exactly did you have in mind?"

Harry started to grin. "I think I might need your help."

CHAPTER
THIRTY TWO

E mily snuck up the stairs, careful to make sure that she didn't bump into Harry. She couldn't deal with that right now, she needed to get her head together. One of the advantages of not drinking was that with the wedding reception winding down, everyone else was in their own world.

With shaking hands, Emily opened the door to the room she shared with Harry and slipped inside. It was empty, except for Elsie who was snoring away in one corner.

"Hey, Else."

Quickly, she gathered together her stuff and crammed it back into her bag, bending to give Elsie a goodbye pat before she walked out.

While she didn't enjoy the fact that she was leaving this room, she did know that it had to be done. She needed a plan if she was going to persuade Harry to stick around for her, and one in the morning was no time to start negotiations.

She let out a breath as the room door closed behind her. For once, Sav had been right. Still, statistically, she was bound to be right some of the time, right? But Harry did make her a better person somehow. Calmer, happier, and as logical as all of Harry's reasons might seem, Emily had only just realized that she didn't need to take this lying down.

She had the right to argue in her favor.

Exhausted, she wanted to drag her suitcase into her own room, now reclaimed from the drunken aunt and cleaned. She slid the card key into the slot and the door beeped but didn't open. With a sigh, she pulled the card out, turned it over, and tried again. Another beep.

"For fuck's sake," she swore.

"Here, let me help." Gabe had appeared from down the hall, looking cheerful and tired but not all that worse for wear.

"Aren't you supposed to be, um, doing wedding stuff?" Emily said, blushing when she realized what she was implying.

"For your information, Sab is dancing with her sisters and having a whale of a time and I was sent to make sure that the room had been tidied after the rush of getting ready. Which it has. So I'm about to be 'doing wedding stuff' as you put it," said Gabe, inserting the key into the door and opening it. "There we go."

"Shit," Emily said. "I can't stop screwing things up today."

"Today?" asked Gabe, then his face changed. "Wait a second, Harry's full of doom and gloom as well. According to her, you two have broken up."

"She dumped me," Emily said, dragging her bag into the room and sitting on the end of the bed. "Sort of."

"Sort of?" Gabe came in, letting the door close behind him. "Why sort of?"

Emily shook her head. "It's all a bit of a mess. Um, well, at first we were just pretending because Harry needed some experience to make her less nervous and because people kept nagging her about being single."

"Me," Gabe said. "I kept nagging her."

"Er... yes. But then after a while we faked it until we made it, or I thought we did, and then things went great, and then Harry said we should just enjoy this week and then go back to our real lives and..."

"And you really need some sleep," said Gabe, sitting on the bed next to her. "I'm sorry, I really am. Harry seemed truly happy with you."

"Did she?" Emily asked hopefully.

"Happier than I've seen her for a long time. I mean, at first, I was sort of dubious and I did think you were faking it. But then it all seemed so right, so natural that I thought you were the perfect pair."

"If only you could persuade Harry of that." Emily rubbed at her face with her hands. "I don't want this."

Gabe stood up. "I can leave, sorry, I was just checking on you."

"No, no," said Emily hurriedly. "Not you here. I meant that I don't want to be broken up. I think Harry is wrong. And I think if I put the argument to her in the right way then she'll know that she's wrong. I think..." She paused for a second, then shrugged. "I think we might be made for each other."

Gabe sat down again, eyebrows raised. "Really?"

Emily grinned. "What's it called when you want to talk to someone all the time even when they're not there? When you reach out to hold their hand and get sad when you come up empty? When you open your eyes and theirs is the only face you want to see?"

"Stalking," Gabe said promptly, then caught Emily's eye. "Or love, I suppose."

"It feels different than I thought," Emily said. After all, she'd had a lot of practice at imagining. "It feels heavy in my stomach and light in my heart, it feels scary and terrifying."

"Like you have this whole new responsibility, a new thing to take care of," Gabe agreed.

"But also like all the other important things have sort of faded in comparison."

"Right. I could climb Everest now as long as I knew that Sab was waiting at home," Gabe said.

"Yeah, kind of like that. And I know that there are complications, and I know that this isn't going to be a straight up happy ever after, but then, what's love worth if you don't have to fight for it?"

"You want to fight for Harry?" Gabe asked.

Emily nodded. "I do. I very much do. I know that this week is just a vacation, that there's real life on the other side of it, but I would very much like Harry to be involved in my real life."

Gabe scratched his nose. "She's not going to be easy to persuade. Once she's made up her mind about something, Harry can be very stubborn."

"So what should I do?" Emily asked. "My version of romance involves declaring love on stage at the Oscars, or holding a boom box out in someone's back yard, or renting a billboard on her way to work. I don't think any of those things would work with Harry."

"No," Gabe said. "I don't think they would." He pursed his lips in thought. "Listen, Harry's logical more than anything. I think you need to appeal to her sense of logic. If you want to persuade her that this can work then you have to show her how it can work."

"Right," Emily said. "Right, that makes sense." She caught Gabe looking at his watch. "And you need to get back to your wife."

Gabe grinned. "That I do." He stood up again. "I'm rooting for you, Emily. I think you and Harry are good together. Most of all, I like seeing Harry happy."

"I'm going to try and make her happy," Emily said, smiling inside as she said the words. She wanted this. She really did. "And congratulations again, Gabe. You and Sab are the perfect couple."

"No couple's perfect," he said. "But Sab makes me want to try."

Emily laughed because she understood. Harry made her feel the same way, like she wanted to be better than she'd ever been before just to deserve her.

THE HOTEL BUSINESS center was a bank of computers in a dim room just off the main foyer. Emily dragged a picture into a word document and watched on as the document promptly rearranged its formatting and pushed the text into columns. She frowned, removed the picture and tried again. The same thing happened.

"Goddamn stupid computers," she mumbled to herself.

"Problem?"

She looked up to see James standing in the doorway. "No, well, yes, sort of."

He smiled at her and came over to the computer. "Ah, I see what you're doing. Here, give me a second. This is the picture that you want to add, right?"

Emily nodded and watched as he magically inserted the photo. "Like magic," she said when he was done.

"No, just long, long experience of making presentations," he said.

"You?" she asked surprised. "I wouldn't have thought that running a hotel involved all that many presentations."

"You'd be surprised," he answered, blue eyes glittering a little. "It's no secret that the place has had financial problems, and especially at the beginning when the family were trying hard to save the house there were a lot of presentations. Banks, investors, that sort of thing."

Emily wasn't sure what to do with that information, so she just smiled. "It sounds like hard work."

"It was hard work," agreed James. Then he smiled back at her. "But it gave me a wealth of experience that I'm now able to pass along to you."

She laughed. "And I'm very grateful." She looked at her document, it looked professional enough. It was ordered and logical and exactly what she thought she needed. "Is there a printer?"

"Right over there in the corner," James said. "Hit the print icon and I'll grab the papers for you."

She did as she was told James collected the document as it came hot off the printer. "Here you go," he said, looking down at it as he handed it over.

Emily blushed. "Um, yeah, it's a...um..."

"Presentation to persuade someone to be your girlfriend," he finished for her. "The title sort of gives it away, I think."

"Um, yeah." Why We Should Stay A Couple, the headline was in bold and a bigger font. "It's, um, a project for..." She trailed off.

James grinned and shook his head. "None of my business," he said. "We do strange things for love."

"We do, don't we?" Emily said, looking down at the presentation in her hands. She hoped this was enough, hoped that she was doing the right thing. It wasn't exactly romantic, but it was logical and sensible.

"Good luck," said James, making for the door.

"Thanks," said Emily, distracted. Then she looked up. "Oh, and good luck with the hotel, with the financial problems and all, I'm sure it'll work out."

James stared at her for a second then smiled again. "It might," he said. "It just might."

CHAPTER THIRTY THREE

Harry stood back and surveyed the effect. It was by no means perfect. For a start, the fake Christmas tree was missing several branches toward the top. But then again, she was lucky that the hotel had had one at all, and that they'd been willing to let her use it.

"What do you think?" she asked Sara.

Sara looked up at it and nodded. "Looks pretty stable," she said.

"Hold on a second." Harry stepped back, flicked one switch and then another. She heard Sara gasp.

The Christmas tree was lit with dull yellow bulbs, making it look like candles were burning on the branches. But above, hung in strands from the ceiling, twinkling white fairy lights stood in place of the stars. Even the ground around the tree was strewn with balls of cotton wool that looked like snow.

All in all, Harry was pretty pleased with the achievement, though she didn't completely understand what it was all about.

"So, tell me just one more time why I needed to put up a Christmas tree at the end of August," she asked Sara.

Sara clicked the lights back on. "Because of the book."

"The Christmas Bride," said Harry dutifully.

"Right," Sara said. "It's Emily's favorite and she reads it every single summer at the beach."

"She reads a Christmas book at the beach."

Sara sighed and nodded. "I know, I know, we all give her shit about it because if we didn't she might feel like she wasn't included. I mean, Sab and Sav and I are so mean to each other sometimes, we have to include Emily in the pattern, don't we?"

"I guess," said Harry. Personally, her brother and sister were quite nice to her, though she was distinctly younger than both and had the feeling that a lot of the time they just indulged her.

Sara tilted her head, looking at Harry, then obviously came to some kind of decision. "It was the book she read after her parents died."

Harry frowned at this. "Then maybe not a reminder she wants to have."

"No, not at all. The Christmas Bride was the book she could disappear into, the one that could take her away from real life for a little relief, if you see what I mean. It's why it's so important to her and it's why she re-reads it all the time. Enough times that the pages fall out of the important section."

Harry nodded, she could understand that, she supposed.

"And this is the most important section of all," Sara said. "The couple hate each other, despise each other. But they have to get along because they're looking after this little girl whose parents have died. I think the woman is her aunt or something and the guy... maybe a neighbor? Anyway, the point is that they hate each other and they're pretending not to."

"Right," Harry said following this slowly. "And?"

"And so they go Christmas tree shopping, but the hatred is turning into something else, and they're arguing about buying a tree when the man has the idea to go out and cut one down instead. It's cold and beautiful and they're out in the woods and, long story short, they end up kissing for the first time next to the tree under the stars."

"Got it," said Harry. She sighed. "Actually, I think it's a little ridiculous, but I understand the comfort in the story. And I understand that it's important to Emily and I want to make her happy."

"So you should after dumping her so unceremoniously."

"I deserve that," Harry said, looking up at the tree.

"Yep. But now you've seen the light and you're going to do the right thing."

"As long as Emily will forgive me," Harry said. She could feel a heaviness on her shoulders, could feel the threat of this not all working out now that she'd given herself over to the idea that it might.

"I think she will," Sara said. "And I think the two of you together might just be something special."

"What makes you say that?" Harry asked.

Sara laughed. "You've spent all morning with me, Harry, and you haven't stuttered or spilled anything or fallen or anything like that."

"You've been friend-zoned."

She laughed again. "Not that I mind that. But I think what really happened was that you were so busy thinking about Emily that you forgot to be nervous around me. Because Emily is good for you. And you're good for her too."

"I have to trust in all of this," Harry said, still looking up at the tree. "I have to believe in the romance, that it's going to carry us through. I have to believe that we can overcome whatever needs to be overcome, the distance, our work, everything else."

"It's a lot to ask of someone," Sara agreed.

"But it's really not, is it?" said Harry, finally looking at her. "It's really nothing at all. It's just a little faith, a little belief, and I can do that. I can do that because I honestly think that she's my person."

Sara smiled at her. "You don't need to be telling me this, you need to be telling her."

"Agreed," Harry said with a sniff. "So, are you going to take care of this last part?"

"I certainly will." She looked at her watch. "I'm guessing that everyone's still nursing their hangovers and staying out of trouble. It shouldn't be too much trouble to find Em. I'll text you when we're on our way, alright?"

Harry nodded and Sara left.

Alone with the tree, Harry had sudden doubts. What if this wasn't right at all? Not her and Emily, not that. But this, the tree and everything. Maybe she was going to ruin it. Maybe Emily didn't want reminders of the book. Sara had been persuasive though, and it wasn't like she could change things now, could she?

Elsie got up from the corner she'd been napping in, stretched, and came over to lay her head on Harry's knee.

"It's hard believing," Harry told her. "You're lucky you don't have to. Your life is so simple."

Elsie looked up at her and sighed, giving Harry a waft of dog biscuits from her breath.

"Alright, alright," Harry laughed. "I'm sorry for assuming that your life is easy. I'm sure it's terribly hard work."

Elsie gave a short woof and then Harry's phone was buzzing in her pocket. It couldn't be. Not already. But it was. Emily and Sara were on their way.

"It's meant to be," she whispered to herself.

She wished that she could talk to Gabe or her dad, someone to reassure her, someone to tell her that everything was going to be alright. No, strike that. She really wished she could talk to Emily about this, which was silly because she couldn't talk to Emily about Emily, could she?

Except maybe that was exactly what she needed to do.

Her hands were starting to shake. She stood up and went over to the door then changed her mind and went back to the tree, standing beside it like she was about to get her photo taken.

No, no, that wasn't right. She took a step back.

But the door was already opening.

Shit, she'd forgotten the lights.

She rushed over to the switches, hitting them just in time as the door fully opened and Emily walked in.

Her hand flew to her mouth and Sara had to push her gently until she was fully in the room.

"Oh, Harry," Emily said, seeing her for what felt like the first time.

Every nerve in Harry settled. Every doubt she'd had flew out of the window. This was right. She held out her hand and Emily took it. Together they walked toward the tree, Emily pulling Harry along.

Which was when everything started to go wrong.

Sara whistled for Elsie as she'd been told to do. But Elsie was so overjoyed to see Emily that she didn't obey, which meant that Sara sloped into the room to catch the dog by her collar in order to lead her out.

At about the same time, Harry caught sight of something and realized just why she'd been so busy staring at the tree this whole time. Something had bothered her about it, something had seemed off, and just in that moment she finally realized what it was.

For a millisecond she wondered just how this was possible, and then in another millisecond remembered that both she and Sara had left the small conference room to grab a sandwich for lunch and walk Elsie.

All of which was just enough time for the inevitable to happen.

Elsie turned toward Sara, tail wagging and bumping against the tree, the tree shivered a little and there was a groan of metal. Harry knew exactly what had happened now and couldn't believe that she'd been stupid enough to think that the truth about the sabotage hadn't mattered now that the wedding was over.

Because this had never been about the wedding at all. It had been about something else entirely.

She turned and grabbed Emily by her upper arms, finding a strength that she didn't know she had and physically lifting her out of harm's way, placing her back on the ground out of reach of the toppling structure.

Elsie sensed something and made a break for the door.

Harry called Sara's name, but Sara was too busy paying

attention to the dog.

And the tall, heavy Christmas tree slowly, slowly tilted and then, as though in slow motion, began to fall.

Harry heard Emily scream, saw Sara look around, and then it was all too late as the tree came crashing down on top of Sara's head.

CHAPTER THIRTY FOUR

"This is not how I imagined this afternoon was going to end," Harry admitted, as she handed Emily coffee in a cheap plastic cup.

"At least there's no major damage," Emily said.

"Yeah, but Sara's going to have that scar for a while."

"As long as they let her fly, it's fine." Emily sipped at her coffee and pulled a face.

"Sorry, the NHS isn't known for its culinary skills," Harry said.

"I'm just glad that Sara's in safe hands." Emily lowered her coffee cup and sighed. What, with the rush to the hospital and all, it felt like this day had been twice as long as normal. But at least Harry was talking to her. At least Harry... Her breath caught in her chest.

"Harry?"

"Mmm?"

"What you did, it was..."

"Awful? Terrible? At the very least ill-advised?" offered Harry.

Emily shook her head. "No, it was the sweetest and most romantic thing that anyone has ever done for me," she said. She could still feel that sparkle inside that she'd felt when she'd first opened the door. Her voice grew thick. "Harry, I really don't know what to say. How did you know?"

"Sara helped," Harry said. She reached out and took Emily's hand. "She said, um, she said you read this book all the time and that this was what happened in the book and so I wanted to make it true for you. Because I might have been an idiot."

"You're not the only one." Emily pulled a file out of her bag. James had found her a manila folder, so everything looked very professional. "This is for you," she said.

But before Harry could open it, a chatter of noise came down the corridor and then they were swamped. Sara's parents plus Savannah and Sabrina, and, of course Gabe, all descended on them.

"What happened?" Sabrina asked, eyes full of horror.

"Where is she?" asked Sav.

"Is she hurt?" asked Mrs. Laretto.

Emily cleared her throat and stood up, holding up both hands until everyone was quiet. "Sara's with the doctor now, she's getting a couple of stitches, that's all. She's going to be absolutely fine, but there's some question about whether or not she'll be allowed to fly tomorrow."

"Oh god," Sabrina said. "We can't spend our honeymoon with my sister."

"She'll stay with me if there's a problem," Harry put in. Emily gave her a look. "What? It's my fault."

"What's your fault?" asked Mrs. Laretto looking very suspicious.

"What happened anyway?" Sav asked.

Emily sighed and scowled at Harry, she'd been hoping to get away with not explaining anything other than that Sara had been in an accident. "Sara got hit on the head by a falling tree."

"Jesus, Joseph, and Mary," said Mrs. Laretto, crossing herself.

"A plastic Christmas tree," Harry hurriedly added. "Not an actual tree."

Mrs. Laretto narrowed her eyes. "And how exactly did my daughter get hit by a falling Christmas tree in August?"

"It's the end of August," Harry said, looking down at the floor.

"Well," Emily started. But she was rescued by the appearance of a nurse.

"Are you all here for Sara Laretto?"

There was a scramble of voices and pleas to see her and Harry took Emily's hand again and pulled her out of the hospital corridor. They'd both already seen Sara and knew she was fine. "Let's leave her to the family."

"Let's make our escape," Emily said, directing them out of the revolving doors and into the fresh evening air. She saw a taxi waiting, it must have brought the Larettos and was still waiting for a fare back, so she hailed it, gave him the address and she and Harry piled into the back.

"Just how did it happen?" she asked, once they were settled.

"Sabotage," Harry said darkly.

"Sabo—"

"I know who's behind all of this," Harry said. "What I don't know is what I should do about it. Should I call the police?"

"Sara got hurt," Emily reminded her.

Harry nodded. "Alright then, I suppose we'll take care of it when we get back to the hotel."

The taxi bumped along a country road and there was so much that they hadn't said. Emily wanted to know who was behind the sabotage, she wanted to know how Harry had worked it out. She wanted to know exactly what Harry meant by recreating The Christmas Bride. She wanted to know what all this meant, if they could still be together.

But she said nothing, content just holding Harry's hand in a taxi that was creaking its way through the twilight and back to the hotel.

"IT WAS SIMPLE once I realized the mistake we made," Harry said.

They were arm in arm walking through the orange woods with Elsie bounding along in front of them.

"We made a mistake?" Emily asked, still in awe that she was holding onto Harry, still unable to believe that anything had changed but so glad that it had.

Harry nodded. "We assumed something, and you know what they say about assumptions?"

"They make an ass out of you and me," Emily filled in promptly.

"Right," said Harry. "So, we pretty much decided from the start that someone was trying to sabotage the wedding, which was our first big mistaken assumption."

"Because it wasn't about the wedding," Emily said. "If someone sabotaged that Christmas tree then it couldn't be."

"Indeed. And because we assumed that we then went on to draw up a list of suspects based on who would want to stop the wedding. A suspect list that hovered somewhere between short and non-existent, which is unsurprising because no one really wanted to stop the actual marriage."

"Savannah definitely didn't," Emily said. "She and I talked. She's... special. She's Sav. But she's not mean and she wouldn't hurt her sister like that."

Harry nodded. "I had my doubts about her, I can't say that she's my favorite person in the world. When that cake nearly fell, I was sure that Sav was the saboteur, that she'd gotten caught too close to things and had to save the cake in order to not get caught. But in the end, you're right, it wasn't her."

"Sav will grow on you," Emily said confidently.

Harry looked down at her and then smiled. "Perhaps she will."

Which was all the information Emily needed to know that Harry was in this for the long term now, that some miracle had happened and she'd changed her mind. Her heart skipped a beat and she squeezed Harry's arm tight.

"We were looking in entirely the wrong direction. We shouldn't have been looking at the wedding, which means we shouldn't have been looking at the wedding guests."

"But there was no one else..." Emily started. Then she stopped. "Those Americans. The ones that wanted to buy the hotel."

"Close," Harry said. "You're getting warmer. They're definitely involved, but only tangentially."

Emily groaned. "Miss Marple makes this look easy."

Harry laughed. "Alright, how about I give you a clue? The person who did it was someone that we dismissed very early on. And we dismissed them for the exact reason that they actually did it. Someone very closely involved with the hotel."

Emily frowned for a second as she thought this over. "Wait, we said that James couldn't have done it, that he wouldn't do anything in front of those inspector people to ruin the sale of the hotel."

"Right," Harry said. "But what if that was his aim all along?"

Emily paused for a moment. "Why?"

"Because the hotel is actually a house, or was a house, one that belongs to James's family. A sort of... birthright, if you will. And now his parents are thinking about selling it and he doesn't want that to happen. He wants a chance to prove that he can make the business a successful one."

"So he tries to dissuade the American inspectors from buying," Emily said as it all began to make sense.

"There are things that he can't change, like the building itself or the way the hotel is run, things he'd have no control over. But he can change the hotel's reputation, making it seem like a lawsuit in the making."

"Especially to litigation-happy Americans," Emily said. She took a deep breath and blew it out. "Are you sure about this?"

Harry shook her head. "No, I'm not. I've got no evidence. But I realized last night, when the cake was sliding and then James appeared to smooth things over. He had easy access to every accident, no one would question him."

"So what happens now?" Emily asked quietly.

"I think we find the hotel manager and have a quiet word with them and see what he or she says."

"Okay," Emily said. She hung onto Harry's arm as Harry whistled for Elsie and then they turned around and walked back to the hotel.

IN THE END, it didn't take much convincing for the manager to see their point of view, given that the manager in question was James's father. James admitted to all he'd done, and the Larettos were informed and given the option of pressing charges, which they declined, promises of apologies were made and James was fired. Then it was all out of Harry and Emily's hands.

An hour or so later, just as the sun was starting to set, they walked out of the manager's office and Emily heard Harry breathe a sigh of relief. She smiled to herself.

"So, Harry Lorde, what do we do now that our case is solved?"

Harry's eyes crinkled a little at the corners as she looked down at Emily's face and Emily found herself wondering if it was possible to be breathless every time someone looked at you.

"I think it's about time you and I sat down and had a talk, don't you?" Harry said.

CHAPTER
THIRTY FIVE

T he hotel was quiet, most guests either still hungover or packing for their trips home. Emily and Harry were able to pick up sandwiches from the buffet and a couple of bottles of water before planning to head somewhere else. Harry's room was Harry's first thought, but then perhaps that was too much.

She watched Emily out of the side of her eye as she chose just the perfect bottle of water and wished that she had more to give. Emily loved romance and Emily deserved romance. Too bad that Harry's first and only attempt at being a romantic had ended up with Emily's best friend at the hospital.

Her stomach squeezed a little. Was this real life getting in the way? Perhaps but... but the problem wasn't insurmountable. Just disappointing. She wanted to give Emily what she wished for, that was all.

Harry was just tucking a water bottle under her arm when Gabe came rushing in, cheeks red and hair uncharacteristically a mess.

"I've been looking everywhere for you," he said to Harry.

"What is it? Where's Sara? Is she alright?" Emily said.

Gabe grinned. "Perfectly fine and dandy and ready to fly tomorrow no problems. The girls have taken her up to her room and are sitting with her. I, on the other hand, have been having some very interesting conversations."

"You have?" Harry asked. "With whom?"

"You can use whom in a sentence," Emily said. "Be still my heart."

Harry pulled a face at her.

"With just about everyone," Gabe said. "Including Sara and the hotel manager and I think I've just about put together all the pieces and…" He blushed even darker red. "And I don't know how to thank you. The two of you were secretly body-guarding our wedding this whole time."

He held out a piece of paper folded in half.

"It's not much, but consider this a thank you from Sab and I. We're lucky to have friends like you."

Harry took the paper and was about to open it when Gabe stopped her.

"Oh, and you two should definitely go check out the conference room. You know, the one where you almost got my sister-in-law killed."

"It was an accident," Harry said. "And why would we want to do that?"

"Apart from anything else, Elsie is there," grinned Gabe, already taking a step back. "I'd better get back to my wife. Go on, go find your dog."

Harry rolled her eyes and grumbled. "I hate when he does things like that. All mysterious and knowing." She crammed the paper into her shirt pocket and sighed. "I suppose we'd better go and get Elsie. Then…" She thought for a second. "Then we can go have a picnic outside and talk things over?"

"A moonlight picnic," Emily smiled. "Sounds romantic."

Which was better than not-romantic even if it wasn't exactly what Harry had planned.

Together they made their way to the conference room.

"You know, I can't quite believe what James did," Emily said.

Harry shrugged. "He wanted a chance, I kind of get that. He felt like the hotel was being sold under his feet before he'd even had a chance to save it. And he thought that this house, his house, could be saved. When the truth of the matter is that the world doesn't have a place for houses like this anymore."

"Which is sad," Emily put in.

"It is. But James went the wrong way about doing things."

"He didn't seem like a bad guy. He was smart and funny."

"He's not a bad guy, I don't think," said Harry. "Just a bit misguided. And he is smart and funny. He's young, he'll find his place in the world, I'm sure." She opened up the door to the conference room and gasped.

"What?" Emily asked.

Harry stood back and let Emily see.

The tree was up again, the star-lights were twinkling, the cotton wool snow was pristine. Harry's heart hammered in her chest and she couldn't help but grin. Sara must have told Gabe what she was up to and Gabe had taken care of everything, just like he always did.

As irritating and interfering as he could be, Gabe was her best friend for a reason and he always came through for her.

There was a stirring in the snow and Elsie's tail slapped the floor. "Good girl," Harry said. Then she looked over at Emily, whose eyes were shining in the fairy lights and suddenly she relaxed. All nerves were gone. She held out her hand. "Come on, there's something I've been dying to do."

Emily let herself be led into the winter wonderland and Harry marched her right under the tree and then pulled her in very, very close. She said nothing before tilting Emily's chin up with one finger and softly, sweetly kissing her lips.

There was a sigh of contentment and Harry opened her eyes before pulling back with a grin.

"You're giving me a fairy tale," Emily said quietly.

"Because you're worth it," said Harry. She looked down at the ground. "I'm just sorry that it took me so long to realize."

"No, Harry, don't be sorry."

"But I am," Harry said sincerely. "I've never really done this before and I got confused about what I was supposed to want and what was supposed to happen and in the end, I think I just over-complicated things. This has nothing to do with real life or Savannah or any of those other things. It has to do with two things: you and me."

Emily laid a hand on her arm, her eyes dark and soft.

"I've spent my whole adult life being an idiot in front of attractive women," Harry continued. "And then along come you, the most attractive of them all, and all of a sudden everything slips into place. I was just waiting for you, I think. And I'm no expert, I don't know what love is or how it's supposed to feel. But I do know that being with you is like being at home. It's like everything makes more sense, everything fits better, everything is comfortable and familiar."

Emily said nothing, her lips curving into a sweet smile.

"I think what I'm trying to say, Emily Jackson, is that I love you," Harry said seriously. "I love you and I know life won't be perfect but I'd still rather spend it with you than with anyone else. And maybe that's love, I think that's love, but I'd like to know what you think."

Emily pulled back a little. "Where's that folder that I gave you?"

Harry swallowed. This wasn't the response she'd been expecting. "Um, here," she said, pulling off her backpack and unzipping it.

"Right," said Emily. "Take a seat." She sat down on the cotton wool covered floor and Harry, after pausing for only a second, followed suit. "Now, if you'd like to open your file."

Harry did as she was told.

"Alright," said Emily. "We're going to start from the given that I love you and want to spend time with you."

"You—"

"That's a given," Emily said again sternly. Harry closed her mouth. "Now, if you'll look at page one, I've costed out the price of flights when booked in advance, so we'll have to have our act together when it comes to planning. I've got seven weeks of vacation remaining, and you're a freelancer which gives us a certain amount of flexibility when it comes to time frame."

Harry was running her eyes over the papers in front of her and grinning and then chuckling to herself as Emily went on.

"And as you can see from phase two of the plan, I've included information both about how my veterinary credentials could potentially transfer over to the UK, and how you as a freelance writer could be eligible for a US visa, so both possibilities are open to us there, assuming we want to move forward after phase one, frequent visits and Zoom calls, is completed."

"I see," Harry said, pretending to be serious but her lips twitching. "And do you have contracts already prepared to sign or do we need to schedule another meeting?"

Emily took the folder out of her hands. "Harry, I wanted you to see that this could work if we're both willing to put the effort in. I know it's not ideal, and I know real life has to intrude sometimes. But I don't think that's a reason to stop this."

Harry nodded slowly.

"The truth of the matter is, Harry, that I'm no expert in this either. Sure, I've read all the romance novels and had other relationships, but this is... different. For the first time I feel like I'm really myself with someone, that there's no pretending, that everything is perfectly comfortable."

She took a deep breath.

"The bells and the whistles, the chasing people down at the airport and huge declarations of love, are all very well. But this, this is... it's better. It's smaller, more intimate, but somehow it means all the more for that. It's hard to explain."

"It's not," Harry said, taking both Emily's hands in hers. "It's actually not hard to explain at all."

"You're the wordsmith," Emily said. "You try then."

"It's perfectly simple," said Harry. "This is right."

Sensing a moment happening, and not approving of not being a part of it, Elsie got to her feet and pitter-pattered over to where they were sitting, sinking to the ground with a sigh and resting her head on their clasped hands.

Emily laughed. "I think we might have a seal of approval."

"She's a dog, not a seal," Harry said.

"And you're an idiot," said Emily, leaning forward and ruffling Harry's hair.

"I'm your idiot," Harry said. "If you'll have me, that is."

"Oh Harry." Emily shuffled over so that she was as close as she could possibly be to Harry. "I don't ever want anyone else. I think it's always been you. All the practicing, all the dates, all the longing and fantasizing, I was just waiting for you all along and didn't realize."

Harry put her arms around Emily, pulling her in and holding her close, Elsie's tail thumping against her leg. "And we're not supposed to be kissing while angels sing, or making a blood oath, or anything like that?" she asked anxiously.

Emily nestled her head against Harry's chest. "No," she said. "No, I don't think so. In fact, I think this is just perfect, don't you?"

And Harry couldn't help but agree. As Emily snuggled closer, the paper that was in Harry's pocket crinkled and Harry reached to pull it out and unfold it. When she saw what it was, she started laughing so hard that Emily had to take it from her hand and look for herself to see what it was.

The receipt for a first class ticket to the States in Harry's name stared back up at them.

"Good to know that Gabe had faith in us," Emily said.

"But better to know that we have faith in us," Harry said, pulling her back in close. "It'll be the first flight of many."

"Think of all the air miles."

But Harry was far too busy thinking of something far, far removed from air miles as she bent to kiss Emily.

EPILOGUE

J FK was simultaneously the best and the worst place that Harry had ever been. For the last three years she'd been over the moon every time she arrived and ready to wither and cry every time she left. Which made it strange to be standing in the arrivals hall waiting for someone else to come.

She checked her watch and tapped her foot. The stupid plane was delayed and if it didn't arrive soon she was going to have to leave or risk missing the wedding altogether.

Wedding.

The word made her shiver a little with anticipation. It made her nervous and ecstatic at the exact same time. It made her heart give a little squeeze and her mouth get dry. It made...

"Harry!"

Finally.

She waved big and tried not to be shocked at just how small her father looked in the crowds of travelers. She scooped him into a hug as soon as he came through the barrier. "Dad. Thank you for coming."

He pulled back with a sniff. "Think I'd miss it, did you?"

She shrugged. "It's a long way to come, dad." As both her brother and her sister had told her. Both with families of their own and neither in a financial situation that let them jet off to New York.

"I might not get out much, love, but when I do, it's go large or go home." He gave her a steely look. "That DVR thing had better record Eastenders though, or you're going to be in trouble."

"It will," she said, taking his suitcase with one hand and his arm with the other. "How's Elsie?"

"Just fine, nothing for you to worry about. Mrs. Khan next door is looking after her and you know how she dotes on her. You'll be lucky to get Else back at this rate."

Harry pulled a face. "I'm not looking forward to putting her in a crate," she said. There was no getting around the fact that Elsie was going to have to fly and Harry hated the thought of what was going to happen.

"Old Else will be fine," her father said. "Trust me."

Which was unlike him, because usually he was even more protective over Elsie than she was. But Harry didn't have time to think about it much since her phone started ringing.

"Harry Lorde."

"Harry, it's Sara, listen, don't freak out."

"Way to make me freak out."

There was a sigh on the other end of the phone. "The flowers haven't arrived," Sara said. "But I've fixed it, don't worry."

"Fixed it how?" Harry asked suspiciously.

"There's a florist at the end of the block," Sara said. "They might not be the perfect flowers but they are beautiful, I give you my word."

Harry took a deep breath and forced herself to smile. Things were going to go wrong, that was the nature of weddings. "Perfect," she said. "Thank you. Um, and... Emily?"

"Is unsuspecting and totally fine," said Sara. "I'm taking care of things."

Which was exactly why when Harry and Emily had decided that marriage was the way to go, or the only way that Harry was likely to get a US visa, Harry had immediately taken Sara into her confidence.

"Thanks," she said to Sara before hanging up. "Come on dad, Gabe's waiting at the hotel, we're on a tight schedule here."

✻ ✻ ✻

"Stop making such a fuss," Emily said, batting away Sav's hand.

"She has to make a fuss, that's what she's designed to do," Sab said grumpily from her armchair. Her feet were propped up on a stool and her enormous stomach almost covered her face.

"Be quiet, whale," Sav said, adding just a touch more blush to Emily's face.

"Whale yourself," said Sabrina. "One day this will be you."

"Chance would be a fine thing," Sav mumbled, stepping back to look at Emily in the mirror before giving a nod of approval.

"Oh, that's right, you're too busy juggling two potential baby daddies," snapped Sab.

Sav rolled her eyes and grinned at Emily in the mirror. "I'm poly. Having multiple partners is part of the deal. And when and if the time comes that we all want children, we'll figure it out together."

Emily grinned right back at her because for once, Sav seemed... calm. Happy, certainly, but also at peace with something. She had to admit that Sav turning up last Thanksgiving with both Mark and Leo had been somewhat of a surprise. But Sav turning up with both Mark and Leo at Christmas and then Easter and now for the wedding was even more of a surprise.

It seemed like the Laretto wild child was finally settling down, in her own way, of course.

"Eugh, I'm the only one left," Sara said, perching on the edge of Emily's bed. "I'll be an old spinster and you'll all be off chasing grandchildren."

"Yes, but your boobs will still be perky," pointed out Sav, attacking Emily's hair with a brush.

"Your time will come," Emily said. "Take it from me, you need to stop looking and love will appear, that's how it works."

"It worked for you, look at you, getting married," Sara said, nudging her.

"Well, it's not quite how I imagined it," Emily said. "I mean, a courthouse wedding isn't the most romantic thing in the world. But I'd marry Harry anywhere."

"As long as she gets a Green Card," added Sav.

Emily stuck her tongue out. "Not the point. Well, kind of the point. It is about time we lived together properly. But I love her and she loves me and we'd be doing this eventually anyway."

"Nothing wrong with getting married for the visa," Sabrina said, taking another cookie from the plate by her side.

"If you don't stop snacking you'll be the size of two whales," Sara said, confiscating the plate from her sister's side. "And if you don't let Emily put her dress on first, then she's going to ruin whatever you're doing to her hair," she added to Sav.

Sav grunted but stood back and Emily stood up to get the dress bag that was hanging on the closet door.

It took a good two minutes to realize that the dress wasn't fitting. It had fit six months ago, which was when Emily had broken down and just had to buy it. The woman in the bridal store had assured her she looked perfect in it, and, in truth, Emily had been consoling herself a little about a courthouse wedding by buying a real wedding dress.

But now, it just... wasn't right.

"Maybe if we pull it down a bit," Sab said doubtfully.

"Maybe if we put a safety pin here," added Sav.

"Maybe, maybe," Sara said, shaking her head. Then she yelled: "Mom!"

Mrs. Laretto came running down the corridor. "It's not the baby, is it?" she cried.

"No," said Sab. "Which is a good thing since there's another month and a half to go."

"It's the dress," said Sara.

Mrs. Laretto stood in the doorway, looking at Emily and the once perfect dress and then she smiled. "I'll take care of it, dear," she said quite calmly. "Let me just get my sewing box."

But Emily couldn't help but worry that the day wasn't going quite as well as it should be.

* * *

"Alright, Gabe?" asked Harry's dad as they walked into the hotel suite.

"Oh, don't ask him," Harry said. "He's as jumpy as a dog in a butcher's doorway."

"Am not," Gabe said.

"You've lost about a stone and you jump a mile in the air every time your phone rings," Harry said. "I'm not entirely sure you and fatherhood are a match made in heaven."

Gabe took a deep breath as though he was going to argue this point, then sighed it out and shook his head. "It's a lot of responsibility," he said.

"And one that you'll handle just fine," said Harry's dad, pulling out a silver flask and handing it to Gabe. "You know, it has its good sides as well. It's not all about being terrified all the time." He seemed to consider this. "Well, it's mostly about being terrified all the time, but you sort of get used to it."

"Not sure that's helping, dad," Harry said. She unzipped her suit bag.

"Fine, then I'll go and get myself a shower. I've heard we're in a hurry," said her dad grumpily, and disappeared off into the bathroom.

"I'm sorry, Harry," Gabe said. "Sorry I'm being such a sad-sack, this is your day."

"You're just worried," Harry said, grinning at him. "But you shouldn't be. Not really. You know that Sab is going to handle this as smoothly and perfectly as she does everything else, you have nothing to worry about."

"But I do worry," Gabe said. "I worry that I'll be terrible at this, I worry that something will happen to the baby." He gulped. "I worry that something will happen to Sab."

Harry sat down on the edge of the bed. "Gabe, I can't tell you that everything is going to be alright. I don't know that. But I do know that life is about taking risks, it's about pushing for the thing you want, because if you don't, well, you get left behind, don't you?"

Gabe nodded. "Right. Yeah. I know. I'm just... I'm nervous is all." He looked over at her. "Speaking of, aren't you? Nervous, that is?"

Emily blew out a breath. "Are you kidding me? Of course I am. But I'm in such a hurry to get everything arranged that I don't have a lot of time to think about it."

"Has Emily uncovered your secret yet?"

"I hope not," Harry said, busily starting to strip off her jeans and t-shirt. "Do you think we could fly Elsie in the cabin if we went first class?"

"No," Gabe said. "Although maybe you could if you chose a private airline."

"You mean like rent an entire plane?" asked Harry as she buttoned up her shirt. "I'm pretty sure we can't afford that."

"You're about to get married and all you're worried about is flying with Elsie," Gabe said, standing up. "Here, let me." He took her tie and laid it around her neck, his fingers working quickly to tie it.

"Hey," Harry said. "You learned how to tie a tie."

"Precisely for this moment," Gabe grinned. "And stop worrying about Else, she'll be fine."

"That's not all I'm worried about," Harry said, having caught a glimpse of the time. "Shouldn't our car be here by now?"

"Finish getting ready, I'll deal with it," said Gabe quickly as he pulled out his mobile.

Harry pulled on her jacket and was busy tying her shoes when Gabe came back into the bedroom. "Um, I'm not sure how to tell you this but the car was canceled."

"What?" Harry said.

"Calm down, it's going to be fine," said Gabe. "Just let's get out of here, get your dad, I'm sure we can get a cab."

Harry rolled her eyes but went chasing after her father anyway. Could this day get any more stressful?

❊   ❊   ❊

Emily slid into the back seat of the town car, Sara getting in behind her and making sure that her white dress wasn't getting caught in the door. With a sigh of relief, Emily sat back in the seat. "To the courthouse," she said.

"Yes, ma'am," the driver agreed, before pulling away from the curb.

"I think this is the traditional time for me to ask you whether you're sure et cetera, et cetera," Sara said. "But given the fact that you and Harry are still so disgustingly in love that it's nauseating, I'm going to skip that part."

"How about we skip to the part where I tell you I wouldn't want to be sitting here with anyone else right now?" Emily said.

"Not even Sav?"

Emily rolled her eyes. "No, not even Sav. She seems happy, like she's finally figured things out and I'm happy for her. She was never a traditionalist, and I'm glad that she's found out what she needs in life. Just like you will one day."

Sara squeezed her hand. "No regrets?"

"About Sav? Not at all. It took me a minute to see it, but Harry is what I need in my life. She might not always be the most romantic of people, and she's definitely not a crier or a hugger or a public declaration of love kind of person. But she makes me a better person. She makes me want to be a better person. In the end, none of the other stuff matters. The only thing that matters is that Harry is the other half of my heart."

Sara looked out of the window and Emily wondered if she was hiding something, not for the first time in the last few weeks. Even as a kid, Sara could never look someone in the eye and lie. But as Emily followed her gaze she noticed that the car was going in distinctly the wrong direction.

"Hey," she called out to the driver. "We're supposed to be headed to the courthouse down town, where are you going?"

The driver's eyes met hers in the rear view mirror and promptly dropped again. He cleared his throat. "Um, where instructed, ma'am."

"Well I instruct you to take me to the courthouse, right now. Turn this car around or I swear I'll start to scream."

The driver's hands clutched at the wheel.

"I'm calling the police," Emily said, fear starting to brew. "This is kidnapping." She pulled out her phone but Sara's arm shot out to stop her dialing.

"Um, here's the thing," Sara said. "We might not be going to the courthouse and I'm going to need you to trust in the process here for a minute, okay?"

Emily frowned. "What the hell?"

"Just, um, just go with it," Sara said, eyes wide. "Please? For me? I swear this is a good thing, but it's not really my thing to say out loud. Not yet."

Emily bit her lip. She hated not knowing what was going on. "I'm still getting married?"

"Yes."

"And this is planned?"

"Yes."

Emily hesitated. Sara was her best friend, she'd looked after her for as long as she could remember. "Alright," she said with a sigh. "Okay, let's keep going."

✳ ✳ ✳

Harry stood on the steps, checking her watch over and over.

"It's not time yet," Gabe said. "And Sab said that Sara and Emily got in the car just fine. They'll be here, don't worry."

"What if she hates it?" Harry said, looking back through the doors of the little chapel. The aisle was decorated with white roses and their friends and families were starting to fill the seats.

"Who could hate this?" asked Gabe with a laugh. "She's going to love it and you know she will. She wanted a fairy tale wedding, Harry, and that's exactly what you've given her."

"Well, I had help," Harry said. Planning an entire wedding without Emily finding out about it had been a nightmare. But the second Emily had proposed that they tie the knot, forgoing the down on one knee business and framing it as a logical idea that would enable them to live together, Harry had known that this was the wedding Emily deserved.

"Excuse me?"

Harry turned around and her mouth opened and then closed again.

"Are you the bride?" asked the woman, a tall red-head dressed in a simple gown covered by an open black cleric's robe. She had high cheekbones and bright green eyes and Harry's mouth was too dry to speak properly.

"Um, er, maybe, yes, I think," stumbled Harry, unable to tear her eyes away from the woman.

"Ignore her," Gabe jumped in. "Yes, she's the bride. One of them."

The woman smiled. "Great, I'm afraid that there's been a problem. The celebrant you booked, Mr. Davidson? I'm afraid he's been taken ill."

Harry's eyes flashed to Gabe. "Sabotage," she said. "It has to be."

"No," Gabe said patiently. "It's real life. Interfering, as it has a tendency to do."

"But what am I supposed to do?" Harry wailed. "First the flowers, then the car, now this."

The red-head cleared her throat. "Um, if it's alright with you, I'm here to take Mr. Davidson's place?"

"Oh, um, well..." Harry stuttered.

"What she means is thank you very much that would be perfect," Gabe said.

The woman smiled. "In that case, I'll see you inside the chapel."

"Nobody is sabotaging your wedding, Harry," said Gabe. He checked the time. "Other than you, unless you come in right now. You don't want to spoil things, do you?"

Harry took one last anxious look at the street. "Okay," she said. "Alright, let's go in."

Gabe took her arm and they walked into the vestibule where Harry's dad was chatting to one of Emily's cousins.

"Let's go, dad," said Harry.

Her father grinned. "Actually, I'm going to stay out here for a minute. There's something I think I need to do. I'll be in my place on time, don't you worry."

Harry opened her mouth to argue but then shook her head. It wasn't worth it. Real life was always going to get in the way of things, whether she liked it or not, the only thing she could control was her own reactions.

She squeezed Gabe's arm with her own, and then together they made the long walk down the aisle.

❀ ❀ ❀

Emily practically crawled out of the back of the town car, her mouth agape, her eyes filling with tears as she looked up at the little chapel.

"What... what is this?" she choked.

"I've been instructed to give you this," said Sara, pulling a small white envelope out of her pocket.

Emily took it and tore it open.

> *Don't be angry. This is the wedding you deserve. You are my heart and I will strive every day to be the wife that the universe owes you. I love you with every fiber of my being, and know that this ceremony is only the very beginning of our adventure.*
>
> *—Harry*

It was all Emily could do not to sob. She blinked as hard as she could, driving the tears back until Sara dragged her up the stairs. But before they could open the door, it opened itself and a figure stepped out, closing the door behind him.

"Mind giving us a minute?" Harry's dad asked Sara.

"Um, no," Sara said, looking from him to Emily and back again. "No, I guess not. I'll go in and warn the organ player that you're on your way." She left.

Harry's dad coughed. "Um, well, I know we don't know each other very well," he said.

Emily smiled. They'd met a handful of times and she'd always liked him, he made her laugh and had welcomed her into his little family immediately. "Well enough, Len," she said.

He blushed. "Well, in that case it makes what I want to say a bit easier," he said. He looked down at the ground. "I realize I'm a pale imitation of what came before. I'm no vet." He chuckled a bit. "Probably get bit by all the dogs and I'm allergic to cats."

Emily laughed. "It's not that bad."

"Yeah, well, like I was saying, I know I'm not the man that you wish could be here today. But I am a man that's delighted to have another daughter, married into the family or not. And, um, well, I was wondering if perhaps you'd do me the honor of letting me walk you down the aisle."

The lump in Emily's throat grew so big she was afraid for a second it was going to choke her. She swallowed once, twice, and blinked frantically again. "I think I'd like that very much," she said quietly.

Len grinned at her. "Well, in that case, shall we go inside and get you married?" He held out his arm.

For a long moment Emily looked up at the chapel imagining what waited inside, imagining what waited in the future, feeling herself fill up with happiness that she hadn't known she was capable of feeling. Then she took Harry's dad's arm.

"Yes," she said simply.

❊ ❊ ❊

Emily's head lay on Harry's shoulder and Harry swayed gently to the music wondering if she'd ever been as happy in her life. Seeing Emily walk down the aisle on her father's arm had made Harry's heart practically explode with love.

And now they were married. For better or worse, they could finally start their lives together. No more commuting, no more waiting for holiday time, no more anything other than moving the rest of Harry's things over to the States.

Harry felt a burst of anxiety at the thought of getting Elsie on a plane, but forced herself to push it to one side.

"Happy?" Emily asked, raising her head so she could look at Harry.

"Do you even have to ask?" Harry said with a grin.

Around them their friends and family were laughing and drinking and having a wonderful time. But to Harry it was like she and Emily were in a bubble of their own.

"I can't believe you did that," Emily said for about the hundredth time. "You kept all that from me, you arranged all that."

"With Sara's help," Harry reminded her. But she grinned anyway. "It was a pretty romantic surprise, right?"

Emily stood up on tiptoes to kiss her. "It was the most romantic surprise that anyone has ever had," she said solemnly. She dropped back to her feet so that they could keep moving slowly to the music. "You know you're not the only one that can keep secrets," she said.

"I'm not?" Harry asked, quirking one eyebrow up.

Emily pulled back and took Harry's hand. "You're definitely not," she said. "In fact, there's one for you waiting at our table. And if you don't open it now you're going to lose your chance for the next eight hours or so because I think the speeches are about to begin."

Harry smiled and let her wife pull her back to the top table where, sure enough, she found a long white envelope waiting beside her dessert plate. "What's this?"

"Open it and find out," said Emily, sitting down and taking a gulp of water.

Obedient, Harry opened the envelope and pulled out two tickets. "Wait, cruise tickets?" she said.

"I know, I know, we said we were going to wait on our honeymoon, but this seems too good to be true," beamed Emily.

"Liverpool to New York?" Harry said, looking more closely at the tickets. "It's not exactly the Caribbean, is it?"

"It's not," Emily said seriously. She took the envelope and pulled out the rest of its contents, a shiny, folded brochure. "But there is a dog park, and even little lamp-posts on the top deck where Elsie can pee like a pro, and—"

Harry interrupted her with a squeal of delight, finally understanding what Emily had given her. "And Elsie doesn't have to fly!"

"Well, you did seem worried about it, even if your wife, who is a vet, by the way, assured you it would be perfectly fine." Emily grinned. "So I thought of a better, more logical solution."

Gabe stood up and clinked his fork against his glass. "Attention!"

Harry looked at her wife and smiled. "I can't think of a better gift. I can't think of anyone else that would have thought of that gift. It's the most lovely thing anyone has ever done for me."

"Not quite as lovely as arranging an entirely secret fairy tale wedding," Emily said.

"Oh yes it is," whispered Harry, pulling her closer. "In fact, I don't know how to repay you."

"Nor I you," Emily whispered back. "So isn't it fortunate that we have the entire rest of our lives to figure out a repayment plan?"

Harry's lips brushed against Emily's for the briefest of moments.

"Ladies," Gabe said. "It's speech time."

Harry realized that all eyes were on her and Emily and for a moment she was about to pull back. Then she thought better of it, pulling Emily closer and crushing her into a kiss that made everyone whoop and cheer.

The speeches went well, the cake cutting was perfect, the party continued long into the night.

It was three o'clock in the morning when Harry, with her jacket hanging from one finger swung over her shoulder, and Emily, with her high heels in one hand and sneakers under her white dress, finally walked the four blocks home.

But it was a lot later before the lights were turned out.

THANKS FOR READING!

If you liked this book, why not leave a review? Reviews are so important to independent authors, they help new readers discover us, and give us valuable feedback. Every review is very much appreciated.

And if you want to stay up to date with the latest Sienna Waters news and new releases, then check me out at:

www.siennawaters.com

Keep reading for a sneak peek of my next book!

BOOKS FROM SIENNA WATERS

The Oakview Series:

Coffee For Two

Saving the World

Rescue My Heart

Dance With Me

Learn to Love

Away from Home

Picture Me Perfect

The Monday's Child Series:

Fair of Face

Full of Grace

Full of Woe

The Hawkin Island Series:

More than Me

Standalone Books:

The Opposite of You

French Press

The Wrong Date

Everything We Never Wanted

Fair Trade

One For The Road

The Real Story

A Big Straight Wedding

A Perfect Mess

Love By Numbers

Ready, Set, Bake

Tea Leaves & Tourniquets

The Best Time

A Quiet Life

Watching Henry

Count On You

The Life Coach

Or turn the page to get a sneak preview of Play It Again, Ma'am

PLAY IT AGAIN, MA'AM

Chapter One

"Y ou can't marry a singer in a band." Amelia put her glass down on the bar with a sense of finality.

"Why not?" asked Cass. "I mean, she's not talking about getting with Adele or Taylor Swift or anything."

"Both of which are solo artists, not singers with bands," said Amelia.

Jules tried very hard to ignore their sniping, wiping glasses behind the bar and keeping her eyes trained on Alea, whose sultry voice was curling around the cozy pub and sending shivers down her spine. Well, it was that or the fact that Alea's dark hair was curling around her shoulders and her eyes were soulfully closed in a way that Jules thought was probably very similar to how she looked under other circumstances. Bed kind of circumstances.

"My point stands," Amelia said. "You can't just go around marrying singers in bands."

"It's not singers in bands," Jules said, finally giving in to her sister's poking. "It's a singer in a band. And it's Alea, not just any singer. And apart from anything else, why not?"

"Well…" Amelia said more carefully now. "Well… we don't

even know if she's... you know."

"Gay," Jules said. "It's the twenty first century, and this is Whitebridge, not Afghanistan, you can say it." To prove her point, she called on the old man at the end of the bar. "Hey, Dave, what do you call it when two women are in love?"

He paused over his pint for a minute and then hesitantly said: "Queer?"

"Close enough," said Jules. "And she is. Well, she's bi, so close enough for me. Or pan, I forget which."

"Which is the peril of sinking ten pints with someone whilst trying to get to know them," observed Amelia.

"Listen, why don't you mind your own beeswax for once and let nature take its course," Jules said, pulling out a pint glass and tilting it under the beer tap.

"Just because mum said you'd be married by the time you're thirty doesn't mean you have to go around chasing pub singers."

"Yeah," agreed Cass. "Your mum was full of shit."

"Oy," both Jules and Amelia said at the same time.

"Oh, right," Cass said, blushing slightly. "Is full of shit, sorry."

"She's not dead, just gone," Amelia reminded her. Cass was Amelia's best friend and had been since playschool and therefore was treated like a member of the family. Even if that meant occasionally being insulted, because after all, wasn't that what families did to each other?

"And she wasn't always full of shit," said Jules. "What about when she predicted the score of the Arsenal game? Or when she said that we'd find Mini-mia dead?"

"The match was on DVR," Amelia said. "And frankly, the chances of finding a three year old hamster alive after it's been out of its cage for a long weekend are slim to none."

Jules grunted and moved down the bar to serve Dave his next pint. She knew that Amelia had never bought into their mother's clairvoyance, and in public, Jules tried not to either. But then in the dark of the night when she was alone she had a hard time not believing. Or maybe she just wanted to believe, that was what Amelia said.

Which was a fair point. She'd been eleven when mum had gone walkabout. Old enough to remember the important stuff, old enough to be hurt and sad, but not really old enough to understand why. Amelia, on the other hand, had been fourteen, and more than old enough to not only understand, but also to act out and start spraying graffiti and smoking and a ton of other disgusting habits.

Granddad Jim had fixed all that of course, as well as letting them live under his roof and signing all their school papers and keeping the social off their backs, but then he'd always been less than forgiving of his daughter's dubious fortune-telling gifts.

Dubious enough that when he moved into the oddly fancy old people's home on the edge of town he'd left his terraced house to Amelia and Jules. And to Cass by default since she and Amelia were joined at the hip.

Jules put Dave's money into the till and went back down the bar. Alea was still singing, a more upbeat song now, something Jules recognized but couldn't name. She tried to keep her eyes off Alea's hips when she worked. The distraction was enough that she'd broken more than one glass already.

"Is Josh around?" Amelia asked.

"He'll be in later," said Jules. Josh was the landlord but just at the moment he was far too engrossed in this season of Dancing with the Stars to worry about something as banal as running a pub. "Why?"

"Want to ask him if it's alright to put up some posters," Cass said airily.

Jules looked from her sister to Cass and back again. Something was brewing. Yet another of their get rich quick schemes, she suspected, as she saw how Amelia's eyes danced and how Cass was practically bouncing in her seat. "What kind of posters?"

Amelia sniffed. "For our new business."

Jules thought about this for a second. No packages had arrived. The little living room at home wasn't crammed with tupperware or protein drinks or weird smelling candles or anything. Nope, she didn't have a clue. With a sigh, she had to ask. "What kind of business?"

Cass grinned at Amelia and then they both said together: "Spray tanning."

"Spray… tanning," Jules repeated slowly. She squinted at them, saw Amelia's stunningly white hand on the bar next to Cass's dark black one and frowned. They weren't exactly poster children for spray tans.

"It's a big thing now," Amelia said. "Just you ask Josh, all those Dancing with the Stars people get spray tans. Everyone's doing it, and it's easy to get into."

"We just have to go on a day's course," added Cass. "And the equipment's cheap as chips."

"We're renting to buy," said Amelia.

Jules sighed. "Is this like the meal in a bar project that left us eating grape flavored protein bars for six months?" she asked. "Or more like the aura reading thing that got Cass punched and meant I had to double lock the front door for months?"

"Neither," Amelia said. "This is a solid business. We've got a business plan and everything."

Jules shook her head. "Spray tanning," she said.

"What of it?" asked Cass.

"It's just…"

"Is it because I'm black?" Cass said. "You can say it. This is Whitebridge and the twenty first century, you can say I'm black. Hey Dave." Dave looked up from the other end of the bar. "What do you call someone that looks like me?"

"Bit of a looker," he said with a leer.

Jules laughed and Cass growled but looked secretly pleased.

"Nothing to do with being black or white," Jules said. "And everything to do with me not wanting the living room being turned into a tanning parlor."

"Which it won't be," Amelia said hurriedly. "The beauty of spray tanning is that it's movable, we go where the demand is, we'll—"

"Be needing the car during the week," finished Jules. She sighed again, then shrugged. "I suppose you've already rented the equipment and all."

"There's work enough for three," Amelia said.

"I've got a job," said Jules. "One that I'm very happy with."

"Well, you can just help out during your days off then," Cass said as though the matter was settled.

Jules rolled her eyes but didn't argue because Alea had stopped singing and was thanking the small audience in the pub while her guitarist walked around with a hat. There was the desultory clink of change.

Jules straightened up and flattened her blonde hair with her hands to try and make herself look a bit more presentable.

"Heartbreaker," Cass whispered.

"Charmer," said Amelia.

Jules grinned. They were both a pain in the arse. But they were her pains, and it was nice to have a little encouragement.

"Drink?" she asked Alea coolly as she walked over.

"Wouldn't mind a half," said Alea, her green eyes crinkling a little at the corner when she smiled her thanks. "I've got to drive home, Mick's lost his license again."

"Drink driving?" asked Jules, horrified that anyone at the pub would have served someone they knew was going to drive.

"No, literally lost it," said Alea. "And we get stopped more nights than not when we're driving around the countryside. Not worth risking the van for something as stupid as a lost license, not when we're so close to the tour."

Ah. The tour. Jules had been very carefully not asking about the tour for at least two months now. "Right," was all she said. She put the glass in front of Alea and wondered what it would be like to trace her fingers over the dark tattoos that covered her upper arms.

Not that this was just a physical attraction. Not at all. They had things to talk about. Well, they would, once Jules could talk properly without having four drinks first. And without just imagining what it would be like to wake up next to Alea.

Alea who smelled of incense and sweat and the metal of a microphone.

Jules's heart beat harder.

"I'll be in tomorrow," Alea said, rapidly draining her glass. "You'll be working?"

Jules nodded, looking at the tiny mustache of beer foam on Alea's top lip.

"See you then, then."

She took off, leaving Cass and Amelia bursting with giggles.

"Cat got your tongue?" Amelia asked.

"Nah, Alea's got her tongue," said Cass.

But Jules ignored them because she knew the truth.

She knew that her mum's predictions weren't always on the up and up. But she also knew that this one was, that it had to be, that it had been the last thing her mum had said to her and therefore it had to mean something.

And if her mum was right, if she was getting married before she was thirty, then time was getting awfully short. She was twenty nine and a half, and Alea was the only eligible woman in town. So the conclusion was inescapable. Less than six months from now, she and Alea would be getting married.

CHAPTER TWO

Dan, the aptly named 'Man With a Van' that Billie had hired to move her things back from London, had turned out to have a surprising addiction to eighties pop ballads. Well, that was what she got for hiring someone based on a flyer on a noticeboard in a laundrette, she supposed. Given his long hair, tattoos and leather jacket she'd been expecting Metallica over Celine Dion, but there you go.

"This is a good one," he said, as the chorus to Glory of Love kicked in for the second time. "Best known for featuring in the Karate Kid II soundtrack, of course, and Cetera's first hit after leaving Chicago."

Billie sighed and murmured something that might have been agreement.

She'd spent a lot of the journey pretending to be asleep, which given that she had so much on her mind, wasn't exactly difficult to do. Dan had spent most of the journey humming along to songs she hadn't heard for years and hadn't liked when she had heard them.

Still, he wasn't charging her much, and given the state of her finances, it was probably for the best. And it wasn't like his van was full. He could easily have taken another load and doubled his money if he'd wanted to.

Pretending to be asleep had also had the advantage of closing her eyes, which meant that she hadn't had to see the landmarks growing slowly more familiar over time.

"Now this, this is a classic," said Dan, as All by Myself came on. He clicked the volume up a notch. "Eric Carmen, obviously, but what most people don't know is that it's based on a piano sonata."

"Concerto," Billie said before she could stop herself. "The Adagio Sostenuto from Rachmaninoff's second."

Dan side-eyed her. "Funny, you knowing that."

She hadn't known it. But she had recognized the chords almost immediately and her with her big mouth hadn't been able to resist showing off. "We should, um, probably listen in silence?" she tried.

"Yeah, yeah," Dan nodded wisely. "Appreciate the genius and all."

She sighed. Coming home wasn't meant to be like this. Not that she'd exactly had a plan for her great return, but if she had she was fairly sure it would have involved at least a limo. And probably some sort of security, a bodyguard or two. Possibly even dark glasses and fending off the press.

But it definitely wouldn't have involved sitting in the passenger seat of a grubby van with split vinyl on the seats and listening to Bonnie Tyler. Or Eric Carmen for that matter.

"Almost there then," Dan said because he was apparently incapable of going for more than thirty seconds without speaking.

"Mmm," said Billie.

Not that she could help but notice. The flowers on the roundabout by the supermarket had changed, and there was a new housing development popping up in what had once been a cornfield that the sixth formers had used for... illicit activities. Billie hadn't been invited to those, but she had a fair idea of what had gone on and hadn't been interested.

Well, it would have been nice to have been asked. But at the time she'd been busy anyway. She'd always been busy. Busy every minute of every day so that this sudden, new emptiness was novel at first. It had turned depressing in the end, of course, but the novelty of having nothing to do had been distracting for a few weeks.

"Just up here, is it?" asked Dan, swinging the van around a corner.

Billie saw the postbox at the end of the street and her stomach sank. "Yes."

"And then it was number forty one, wasn't it, love?"

For God's sake, he had a GPS. Billie said nothing and Dan peered over her at the numbers of the houses until he finally turned on his indicator and turned into a driveway. Then he came to a slow stop and whistled.

"Alright for some, innit?" he said as he looked at the neat little cottage with its neat little garden and neat little front door.

"It's not mine," Billie said as she climbed out of the van.

Not strictly true, but also not strictly untrue. With her parents in Portugal now the place was hers for the foreseeable future. An arrangement that had just happened to be the perfect safety net since Billie's life had fallen apart.

"You'd be doing us a favor, darling," her mother had said.

"Just tell me by the end of the week or I'll have the electric switched off," her father had said.

"Yes," Billie had said, because she had no other choice at that point.

The lease on her London flat was almost up and she had nowhere else to go and nothing else to do and this had been the easiest of solutions. Except it wasn't exactly a solution. Then her mother had chipped in and said that Mrs. Lawton had retired at last, her arthritis too bad to play the piano for school assembly anymore. So that had worked out as well.

In a way.

Teaching music for three mornings a week at a primary school wasn't going to make her rich. Actually, it wouldn't even pay the electric bill, which her father had warned her was going to be astronomical if she insisted on leaving lights on all over the place like she had when she was a teenager.

Billie had snorted at this because she was well over thirty and not a teenager at all. But then she did leave the lights on all night to keep her company.

"You going to let us in then, love?" Dan asked, his voice muffled as he ruffled around in the back of the van.

Billie pulled the keys out of her pocket. There wasn't any point in putting this off any longer. She walked to the door and unlocked it, letting the smell of old house out, before setting foot inside.

She had, at one point, thought that this place might be a museum. She'd been young and arrogant and fresh off a school trip to the Bronte house, and she'd imagined that one day people would come here and see the table she'd eaten at, the piano she'd first learned at, the bed she'd slept in.

And it sort of was a museum in a way. Nothing had changed, not really. The place still smelled like it had, still looked like it had, still felt like it had. But it had always felt like sort of a prison, a holding cell that she had to wait in until the rest of her life could begin, so that lack of change wasn't exactly a good thing.

"You get yourself settled," said Dan, struggling in with a box that Billie knew contained scores. "I'll get these things in for you."

She might be arrogant and cold, but she wasn't rude, so she asked if he'd like something.

"A cuppa wouldn't go amiss," he said as he went back out to the van.

She went into the kitchen and put the kettle on, pulling out a mug from the cupboard and everything else she'd need without having to search. This had been her house for eighteen years, after all.

"Milk and two sugars," Dan shouted through as he came in with another box.

Billie did it all automatically. The fridge had a picture of her on it, her long dark hair cascading down her back, her dark eyes focused on the music on the stand in front of her, her body not shown off to its best advantage in school uniform.

She's always been what her mother called 'a big girl' when

what she'd meant was it was impossible to find bras and school shirts that fit properly. Her cleavage had been an asset when she was auditioning. Hardly a feminist thought, but a true one.

The kettle clicked off and she waited for the water to stop bubbling before she poured it over the tea bag.

Dan was depositing yet another box as she walked into the living room. The bay window looked out over the garden, what her mother had called 'the music corner' was lit by the afternoon sun. The music corner had spread like some kind of weed by the time Billie was eight and actually took up most of the room. Enough that her father, grumbling, had taken to watching the cricket in his study rather than on the larger living room screen.

"Thanks, love," said Dan. "Just put it down, I'll get the last couple of things and be right with you."

Billie reached for a coaster before remembering that her mother wasn't there and that she didn't care enough about a coffee table to put one down.

Coming back to Whitebridge had been the best of a not very large set of bad options. One that she was already starting to regret. People would recognize her, she knew that. Obviously they would, she'd grown up here, started her career here.

Career. Ha. A big word for something that didn't exist anymore.

"Where shall I put this then?" asked Dan, coming in with what Billie knew was the very last thing in the van.

She knew that because at first she'd been going to leave it behind. She'd only picked it up and shoved it behind her seat at the very last moment.

"On top of that dresser over there," she said, because that's where it had always lived.

The familiar black case that would open up to show the familiar dark sapphire velvet and burnished wood, the slender shape of the violin nestled inside its cushioning.

Not that she would open it up. Though that wasn't the whole truth. The truth was more that she couldn't open it up. That even touching the silver metal catch made her feel nauseous, that the thought of opening the lid might even make her pass out.

Because every time she looked at the damn thing the only thing that she could think of was Cora. The only thing she could think of was that last night, and then Cora was gone and everything was broken and it would never, ever be fixed again.

"Good cuppa this," Dan said, not at all appreciating the emotion of the moment. "If this music thing don't work out for you, you could make a pretty penny with cuppas like this."

Billie wondered if she could physically throw him out just so that she could be left with her own misery. But he was already slurping away and turning toward the open piano and asking if he could have a go.

Get Your Copy of Play It Again, Ma'am Now, Only From Amazon!

Printed in Great Britain
by Amazon

36860467R00136